Old Loves Die Hard

A Mac Faraday Mystery

By

Lauren Carr

Old Loves Die Hard

For information call: 304-285-8205
or Email: writerlaurencarr@comcast.net

ISBN-10: 1460935136
ISBN-13: 978-1460935132

Printed in the United States of America

To my son Tristan,

You are the center of my universe.

PROLOGUE

Georgetown, District of Columbia—Three Years Ago

Does heavy rain affect the murder rate the same way a full moon does?

Squinting through the rain flowing down his windshield like a waterfall, Lieutenant Mac Faraday pondered this question while easing his sedan around the emergency vehicles surrounding an SUV in the downtown parking lot.

Mac hoped the patrolman in the yellow rain parka flagging him down wouldn't comment on his car's grinding brakes. Payday was Friday. Then, he could replace the brake pads. With his luck, the pads would wear down to the rotors first.

"What've we got?" Mac blinked against the raindrops splashing onto his face and into his blue eyes while calling out the window.

"Looks like a robbery gone bad, Lieutenant," the officer reported. "One shot behind the ear through the driver's side window. Wallet and watch are missing."

"M.E. here yet?"

"Not yet," the officer said. "Everyone is taking their sweet time hoping the rain will stop."

"Either that or they know something we don't and are gathering the animals."

Before Mac could wind up his window, the officer cleared his throat. "Uh, Lieutenant?"

"Yes?"

"You should get your brakes checked. They're grinding."

"I'll do that," the detective replied. "Thanks for telling me."

After parking between two patrol cars, Mac climbed out of his car and pulled the collar of his raincoat tight around his neck a moment too late. His auburn hair clung to his scalp while cold heavy raindrops formed a watery path down the sides of his head and the back of his neck to send a shiver down his spine.

The forensics team parted when Mac jogged up to where they were searching the inside of a dark blue SUV that looked black under the storm clouds. The only one who didn't move out of his way was the lifeless body slumped over the center console. The shattered glass from the window resembled a sequined baby blanket where it covered his black trench coat.

Except for the stream of blood that flowed from the hole behind his left ear, Mac guessed that in life, he had been a good-looking fellow. His black hair had been neatly trimmed. Judging from his buffed fingernails, he had been meticulous about his grooming.

The parking lot belonged to a six-story red brick office building. In a previous life, it had been an eighty-year-old tenement. After forcing the neighborhood unfortunates out, a group of entrepreneurs renovated the building to house judges and lawyers in posh office suites.

Mac asked, "Anybody know who he is?"

"Dylan Booth." From behind his back, Mac heard one of the uniformed officers who had been the first on the scene answer. "He worked for Judge Randolph Daniels on the top floor. He was an intern."

"He was going to graduate from law school this spring," another voice came from behind the officer. Drenched to the bones by the storm, a gray-haired man with a worn wrinkled face stepped up to the detective. He wore a light jacket over his security guard's uniform.

Searching for reasons someone would want to kill the law student, Mac asked, "Would I be correct in assuming he wasn't working on any criminal cases?"

"Nah," the guard responded. "He did mostly research and stuff for Judge Daniels, and he worked hard." Noting that it was Saturday, he went on, "He came in bright and early this morning. Left about two o'clock. He signed out at one-fifty-eight. He said he was going to finish up at home."

From where he stood, the guard glanced into the back of the vehicle. "Did you all find a box?"

"Box?" Mac glanced over his shoulder at the forensics officers to see that they were also puzzled by the question.

"A document box." The guard held out his hands a couple of feet apart. "You know. The kind you carry file folders in. When he left he was carrying one. I could tell by the way he was carrying it that it was heavy. He must have had it full."

The uniformed officers and forensics team responded in unison with shakes of their heads to the inquiry about the box.

"Do you have any idea what he had in it?" Mac asked.

It was the guard's turn to shake his head. "I assumed case files, being that he worked for the judge and all. What about his computer case?"

"No laptop or case," an officer within hearing distance reported.

Mac summarized, "Looks like we have a missing laptop, watch, wallet, and mystery box. Very interesting."

He turned to the officers inside the SUV. "Did the killer leave anything behind?"

"He missed his cell phone." Like a prize, a young officer held up the phone encased in a plastic bag.

Mac examined the instrument, which contained so many features that he had trouble determining which button to push in order to find the call log. Seeing his problem, one of the forensics officers took it and pressed a couple of the buttons until he found the log.

"What's the last call he made?" asked Mac.

The officer read off the number. "He made the call this afternoon at one-fifty-two. Didn't the guard say he signed out at one-fifty-eight?"

Mac noted, "Then he made this last call right before he left."

"And he was shot shortly after two."

While the number was being read off, Mac had dialed it into his cell phone. "Let's see who the last person he spoke to happens to be."

He pressed the phone to his ear. After four rings, a voice mail system picked up: "You have reached the office of Assistant U. S. Attorney Stephen Maguire..."

CHAPTER ONE

Spencer Manor, Spencer, Maryland—Present Day

"Are you ready for a break?" Mac Faraday heard Archie call out before she came into view. The multi-colored leaves of the trees off Spencer Manor's deck concealed her approach.

A half-dozen lake houses growing in size and grandeur rested along Spencer Court, which ran the length of Spencer Point. The court ended at the stone pillars marking the entrance to Mac Faraday's multi-million dollar estate on Deep Creek Lake.

Six months earlier, Mac had inherited the stone and cedar home from Robin Spencer. The world-famous mystery writer's sudden death from a brain aneurism had revealed the secret that forty-seven years earlier, as a teenager, she had given birth to a baby who had been put up for adoption. Her baby boy grew up to become a homicide detective named Mac Faraday.

Marking his place with his forefinger before closing the book he was reading, Mac welcomed the opportunity for a cocktail before dinner. When he saw Archie jog up the steps leading down to her cottage tucked in the corner of the rose garden, he realized that he had been waiting for her all afternoon.

9

Archie Monday was in faded jeans and a rose-colored cashmere sweater that fit her slender figure like a glove. With her short blond hair and bare feet with nails painted in rose-colored polish, she looked like a sensuous fairy dispatched to spread red, yellow, and gold pixie dust on the leaves surrounding the manor.

Mac had felt like the luckiest man in the world when he had discovered that his inheritance included a beautiful woman living in the stone cottage at the end of his back deck.

Archie had been Robin Spencer's editor, researcher, and personal assistant for over ten years. When the author passed away, she had left Archie the guest cottage to live in for as long as she wanted. The cottage and a generous allowance from a trust fund afforded Archie the freedom to take on freelance editorial assignments at her choosing. With a decade of being the right-hand lady to one of the world's most successful novelists on her resume, she had her pick of only the juiciest assignments.

This week, she was editing and proofing the last installment of a popular thriller trilogy. The second book in the series, which had been released the month before, ended in a cliffhanger. Now the public was clamoring for the conclusion. With the author and her agent breathing down the editor's neck to meet the publisher's deadline, and hackers lurking on the Internet to find out who had the final manuscript in order to leak the ending, Archie had been locked up in her cottage, glued to her laptop, eighteen hours a day.

"I need air and an exquisite glass of wine." She dropped down into the chaise across from him.

"I have just the thing for you." Trying not to look like he had been waiting for her, Mac casually strolled inside to the kitchen where he had been chilling a bottle of wine that matched her order and had a serving tray with glasses and shrimp cocktails waiting. "Do you think you're going to meet your deadline?"

"I always meet my deadlines," she called back. "That's why everyone loves me."

Her face lit up when he came out carrying the tray loaded with everything she wanted for her break, only for her expression to change to horror when Gnarly, the hundred-pound German shepherd that was another part of Mac's inheritance, tore around the corner of the house and raced for the open door.

The dog cut so close to Mac's legs while darting inside that it was only due to some fancy footwork that he kept from dropping everything onto the deck.

"What was that all about?" Recalling that she had seen a large bone sticking out of Gnarly's mouth, she asked, "Where did he get that bone?"

Too preoccupied with not spilling the pinot grigio to notice anything other than a furry blur that almost clipped his legs, Mac set the tray on the table. "I'm afraid to find out."

"Where has he been all day?"

"I don't know," he replied. "It's impossible to contain that dog. He's smart. He's determined and innovative. I have actually seen him studying me to determine how best to get around me." He pulled the cork out of the bottle and poured her a taste of the wine. "It's downright creepy."

She went over to the door and looked for where Gnarly had gone inside. She saw him burying something under the cushion on the love seat in the living room. "Mac, we don't want the neighbors to get mad at us again."

"I'm trying to keep him entertained. I walk him twice a day." Offering a glass of the white wine, he went over to her.

"Why did he look so guilty when he went running into the house to hide?"

"If we're lucky, we'll never find out." They clinked their glasses together in a toast just as Spencer's chief of police, David O'Callaghan, turned the corner to come around from the front of the manor.

After giving birth to her son, Mac's teenaged mother had been sent off to college to end her relationship with Patrick O'Callaghan. By the time she had returned to Spencer, Mac's birth father had married and had a son.

David followed in his late father's footsteps to become the chief of police. Mac had learned from his mother's journal that over the years, Robin had come to love David like a son, to the point of providing a trust fund to care for his elderly mother, the woman who happened to marry the love of her life.

"Well, if it isn't Spencer's finest," Mac called out.

Without a word, Archie fetched a third wine glass.

David's attention wasn't on Mac and his greeting so much as it was on Gnarly, who was bellying out onto the deck to hide behind Mac's legs. "There you are, you canine thief."

"What did he do?" Mac wanted to know.

"I got a call from the market in town."

"What town?" The closet market Mac knew of was across the bridge in McHenry, which was over three miles away.

"McHenry," David answered. "Forty-five minutes ago, someone walked into the market, went to the pet department, selected a large rawhide bone valued at eight dollars, and walked out the front door without paying for it."

Aware of the wet snout pressed against his ankle, Mac pointed out, "McHenry isn't your jurisdiction."

"But our perp lives in my jurisdiction," David argued. "Three and a half feet tall. One hundred pounds. Black, brown, and bronze hair. Brown eyes, and of German descent. We have three eyewitnesses who swear they'll be able to pick Gnarly out of a line-up."

Archie was doubtful. "He walked in, took a bone, and walked back out with it."

"How?" Mac asked.

David answered, "Automatic doors."

Mac pointed out, "But the pet department is all the way in the back."

"Yeah. They said he actually nosed through the inventory to pick just the one he wanted."

"Why didn't anyone stop him?"

"By the time the manager and clerks got over their stunned disbelief, Gnarly was long gone." David pointed his finger at the shepherd hiding his face against the back of Mac's legs. "You need to do something about your klepto dog."

Before Mac could respond Gnarly jumped to his feet, went on point, and barked to signal the arrival of a visitor. As if on cue, the doorbell sounded.

"We have visitors," Archie said.

"Probably the FBI to pick up Gnarly for robbing the Bank of America," David said.

Grateful for the interruption, Mac went inside. From the back deck, he had to cross the dining room, up three steps and across the living area to the front foyer. Months after his windfall, he still had to get used to the vastness of his inheritance. The granite floors, antiques passed down through generations, authentic paintings including a Monet, leather furniture, stone fireplaces in each room, they were all his.

He was still in awe of the painting above the fireplace mantle of Mickey Forsythe, Robin Spencer's chief detective. The image was that of a man, dressed in stylishly casual clothes, sitting in a wing-backed leather chair. Gray touched the temples of his auburn hair. His facial features included chiseled cheekbones and a strong jaw. His blue eyes seemed to jump out of the painting. Mickey's German shepherd sat at attention by his side.

Mac wasn't the only one who had noticed the similarities between Robin Spencer's fictional detective and her long-lost son. Like Mac, Mickey was a homicide detective when he came into a multi-million dollar inheritance. Retired from police work, he spent his time solving murder mysteries with Diablo, his faithful canine companion.

Sometimes the painting over the fireplace would make the hair on the back of Mac's neck stand up. So much so that he had considered sending it up to the Spencer Inn on the top of Spencer Mountain to hang in the lobby across from Robin's portrait.

Mac sensed that Gnarly followed him more in need of his protection from the authorities than to protect his master from any potential danger that might be waiting on the other side of the door. As they passed the love seat in the living room, Gnarly, who had taken ownership of the chair, jumped up and peered over the back of it to the foyer.

Through the beveled cut glass in the door, Mac could make out a woman smoothing her hair and straightening her clothes in anticipation of his greeting her.

A forced grin filled her face as soon as her eyes met his. "Mac!" she sang out as if no time had passed since their last meeting in divorce court when the judge had ended their twenty-year marriage with the single pound of a gavel. The year before that, she had thrown him out of their home.

Feeling as stunned as the market manager when Gnarly walked in and walked out with his stolen goodie, Mac uttered her name in two disjointed squawks. "Chris—tine?" After staring at her long enough to determine that her presence on his doorstep wasn't a nightmare from his imagination, he asked, "What are you doing here?"

"I decided to come out for a visit." When she craned her neck to see beyond him into the manor, he caught a whiff of the alcohol on her breath. She was wrapped in her decade-old blue trench coat. Under that, Mac saw she wore blue jeans over white athletic shoes.

She had to be curious about what he had inherited on the day their divorce had become final. Out of spite, he wanted to tell her to ask their two children, both college students who had inherited large trust funds from their grandmother for their education. Since the home she had won in their divorce was over three hours away, she had to have driven quite a way to see what would have been hers if she had only stayed married to him for just a little while longer.

Mac gave in to his manners. "Do you want to come in?"

As if she feared he would change his mind, she hurried across the threshold into the foyer. "You look good. You're tanner than usual. Have you been using a tanning booth or some of those lotions?"

14

Showing her into the living room, Mac replied that he had spent a lot of time outside.

"Golf?"

"Tennis. I play twice a week." He wondered if he should return her compliment by saying how good she looked. Catching his reflection in the mirror in the corner curio containing glass artifacts Robin had purchased during a trip to China, he had to admit that he did look good. The regular tennis games with Garrett County's prosecuting attorney Ben Fleming kept him trim and fit even if he did lose the majority of their matches.

She wasn't paying much attention to him. Her blue eyes, rimmed in red and framed with dark swollen circles, gazed up at the beams in the two-story foyer and living room. Her mouth hung in awe at the discovery of each new treasure that she had missed out on.

"What are you doing here, Christine?" He decided to skip the vacant compliment about her looking good to go straight for the heart.

Her eyes filled with tears and spilled down her cheeks. "I screwed up."

"I know," Mac said. "You didn't need to drive all the way out here to Spencer to tell me that."

Wailing, she buried her face in her hands.

Behind her, Gnarly watched while sitting up in the love seat with his front paws resting on top of the back. When her cry rose to a loud shriek, he buried his face in his paws.

"Mac, what's going on?" Archie rushed in from the back deck with David close behind her.

The two women met each other's gaze.

Christine asked first, "Is this Archie?"

As if she didn't know the answer, Archie looked at Mac.

"Yes." Standing up straight, Mac crossed over to stand next to her. "This is R.C. Monday. She lives in the guest cottage." He went on to introduce David. "David O'Callaghan is our chief of police. He's a good friend of mine. He came to ask for my help in solving a robbery that happened in town today."

"*Our* children told me a lot about you," she told them. "I'm Christine. I'm sure Mac told you a lot about me."

"Not really," Archie replied quickly.

As if to remind Mac that he had forgotten someone during his introductions, Gnarly let out a loud whine.

Startled by the noise behind her, Christine whirled around. Spying the German shepherd filling the love seat and almost at eye level with her, she announced, "That's a dog."

"That's Gnarly," Mac said.

Eying Gnarly with a mixture of fear and curiosity, Christine stayed rooted in the middle of the living room without moving toward him. Gnarly was equally ambivalent about her.

"Did you drive out here alone?" Mac wondered how she had managed to drive in her inebriated condition without being pulled over by the police.

"Yes," she mumbled.

"Where's Stephen?"

At the mention of the name of the man for whom she had divorced him, she burst into hysterical cries again. "I'm so sorry, Mac. Please forgive me. Please let me have another chance. After all we had been through together—" Suddenly, she was on her knees with both arms wrapped around his legs while sobbing into his thighs.

David snatched his keys from his pocket. Announcing that he had reports to finish at the police station, he hurried past them.

"But what about the robbery at the market?" Mac called out.

"I'll pay off the manager." David was out the door and gone.

Mac didn't know whether to ask Archie for help or not. She answered for him. "I have a tight deadline." She galloped out to the deck to head down to her cottage.

When Christine began choking on her sobs, Gnarly dug his stolen bone out from under the cushion and leapt over the back of the love seat to follow after Archie.

"Get up, Christine." Mac pulled her up to her feet by her armpits and dragged her over to the sofa.

Her tears had glued strands of her golden blond hair to her wet cheeks. Mac recalled a time, as recently as the day that he had come home to find his belongings packed up in the garage, when she would never have left home without each hair being in place.

"Stephen left you, didn't he?"

"We did have a good marriage," she choked out. "If I hadn't made that one mistake—" Clasping her arms around his neck she tried to kiss him.

While diving backwards to dodge her lips, he released her hold on his neck. "You threw me out of my own home." He folded her hands in her lap.

"You were always such a good gentle man." Each word came out slowly and deliberately in her effort to appear in control.

"Funny," Mac said, "that's not what your lawyer told the judge."

"Stephen told him to say that." Her tears fell anew. "If he hadn't seduced me—he made me all these promises and told me how you didn't treat me right and how I deserved so much better than our little house in the suburbs with its little lawn and...He said that I deserved so much more and that he could give it all to me because I deserved more." Batting her tears out of her eyes, she waved her hands and glanced at the elegance surrounding her in the manor. "Like this."

"Maguire certainly thought what we had was good enough to take away from me and move into," Mac noted. "What about your job?"

"You want to rub my nose in it, don't you?" she spat out. "Tristan told you." She guessed which of their two children had spilled the beans about her losing her job due to her alcoholic state.

"You got laid off," Mac stated.

She corrected him. "Fired."

"You'd been with Robertson and Sons for over fifteen years," Mac said. "You were head of the paralegal team. What happened?"

"It was political."

"What did they say?"

"The complaint was absenteeism." She rushed on, "I had leave saved up. And then they started complaining because I'd have a few drinks at lunch. Like I'm the only one to have two-martini lunches."

Mac asked her, "How much have you had to drink today?"

She glanced over his shoulder at the bottle of wine on the back deck. "You first."

"That was my first drink of the day and I didn't drive over the mountains after drinking it." He asked her again, "How many glasses of wine did you have before you decided to come out here looking for me?"

"Everyone needs some liquid courage before begging for mercy." She reached for his hands. "Forgive me."

"I forgive you." Mac pulled his hands away. "I can do that. I've moved on. If you need my forgiveness in order to move on with your life after all that's happened, then I can give it to you."

She tried to make her smile as becoming as possible in her condition. "What about us?"

"There is no us, Christine."

"You can't abandon me like this, Mac," she cried. "I've lost everything. I've got nothing. When Stephen left..." she broke into heavy sobs. "Oh, Mac..." She collapsed into his lap.

* * * *

Seeing that Christine was unfit to drive, Mac grabbed her suitcase from the back seat of her five-year-old Mercedes and

18

drove her in his car to the Spencer Inn, another part of his inheritance, so that she could sleep it off.

The resort rested at the top of Spencer Mountain. The front of the stone and cedar main lodge offered a view of the lake below and the mountains off in the distance. While resting between boating, golf, skiing, mountain biking, hiking, or any of the other host of activities, guests could enjoy the view in cane rocking chairs on the wrap-around porch. Between activities, they could partake of refreshments in the outdoor café on the multi-level deck among the flora of an elaborate living maze or, if the weather was too chilly, the lounge inside. For more formal eating, the Inn's five-star restaurant offered dining experiences that had been favorably recorded in gourmet magazines for decades.

Mac was still trying to wrap his head around owning a resort that he couldn't have afforded to visit a year ago.

Even with all the twists and turns driving up to the top of the mountain from Spencer Point, Christine had managed to fall asleep in the passenger seat of his Dodge Viper. When the valet opened the door to help her out, she almost fell onto the red carpet leading up the steps to the main entrance. With a bellhop in tow carrying her suitcase, Mac led Christine across the lobby to the front desk.

Seeing the inn filled with guests—some resting in front of the fireplace, others reading in front of the waterfall fountain on the other side of the lobby, and a large group going into the lounge for cocktails—Mac worried that no rooms would be available.

When the desk clerk asked if he wanted to check Christine into his private penthouse suite, he replied, "I have a private suite?"

Mac's reaction amused the clerk. "On the top floor. We never book it. It's available only for you and your private guests."

Mac turned around. The guests that littered the lobby now resembled money in a coin jar. They were paying guests. Paying to stay at *his* resort. The resort *he* owned. It hit Mac as it had been hitting him time and again: This all belonged to him.

A wail snapped him out of his daze.

Realizing that Christine was no longer at his side, Mac whirled around.

Her shoulder bag held up to strike, Christine had run across the lobby toward the lounge. Even with the target's back to him, Mac recognized his broad shoulders, dark hair, each strand in place, and sophisticated demeanor. With the grace of a ninja, he raised his arm to block her blow while grabbing her bag with the other to prevent a second strike.

"What are you doing here?" Stephen Maguire demanded to know. His tone suggested that he found the Spencer Inn permitting such low class through its doors offensive.

"Who is she?" Christine shoved him out of her way to get to the woman by his side.

Younger than other women that Mac had seen in Stephen Maguire's company, Christine's rival was as slender as his ex-wife had been in her youth. Her silky copper-colored hair and porcelain skin only further enraged Christine.

"Who she is, is irrelevant." Stephen Maguire made no move to protect his companion when Christine charged. The girl's eyes widened like those of a deer about to be struck by a speeding vehicle. Crying out for help, she dove to hide behind him.

Mac grabbed his ex-wife while trying to disarm her. "They're not worth it."

Christine danced around her ex-husband to get at the other woman. "Who do you think you are?"

"What's up with you, bitch?" the girl replied.

The commotion had drawn Jeff Ingle, a willowy man in a gray suit that matched his slicked-back hair, from his corner office down a hallway that led back to the business offices. The Inn's manager jumped in to reinforce the blockade to protect the girl. "Madam, if you don't quiet down, I'm going to have to ask you to leave."

"If you know what's good for you, then I suggest you leave—now!" Christine raged. "I'm going to kill you!"

"You're crazy." She turned to Stephen. "Who is she?"

"Some drunken lunatic," Christine's former lover replied.

"Lunatic?" Christine shouted.

"Stop it, please!" Mac reached out to grab her arm, which she jerked away so hard that he had to duck to avoid being slapped.

"Who drove me to lunacy? You! Like you have every other woman that's crossed your path."

Leading his companion away by the arm, Stephen Maguire left the conversation and the lobby. When Mac and Jeff Ingle forcibly kept Christine from following, her rage reached hysterical heights.

"Don't you walk away from me, Stephen. You won't get away with this. I'm not going to let you get away with this. Do you hear me? I'm going to kill you! I'm going to kill you, Stephen Maguire! I'm going to kill you dead!"

"Shut up!" Mac cut off her madness with a slap across her face.

Startled by the assault, Christine yelped and grabbed her cheek.

"Mac?" Jeff noticed the guests staring dumbfounded at the scene.

"What is wrong with you?" Any sympathy that Mac had had for his ex-wife earlier was now gone.

Jeff Ingle gestured to the desk clerk. "Make sure a bottle of champagne and fruit tray is delivered to Mr. Maguire's room with a note of apology."

"Why are you apologizing to him?" Christine demanded to know.

"You attacked him," Mac said. "He's a guest at my inn and you attacked him."

"You do know who that was, don't you?" Jeff asked both of them. "That was one of the Maguires. Tycoon Broderick Maguire. Supreme Court Justice Everett Maguire. The social register."

"I am very familiar with all the power and influence of the D.C. Maguires." Mac recounted in a mocking tone, "One call and I can have you wiped out and licking the curb." He shot a glare at Christine. "Heard the threat and experienced it."

Wiping his sweaty brow with the handkerchief that he carried and used often, Jeff said, "Let's hope Mr. Maguire doesn't decide to take down the Spencer Inn by telling his friends about this incident and suggesting they start going to the Wisp for the season instead." Grabbing Christine's suitcase, the manager ushered them into an elevator to take them up to the top floor.

As part of the hotel security, the elevator wouldn't take them up to the penthouse floor until Mac held his personal Inn key card to the eye beam for it to read the security code.

The elevator would only take registered guests and hotel employees to floors containing guest rooms and suites. Guests expecting visitors not staying at the Inn had to notify the front desk, who would issue the visitor a temporary key card.

There was no shortage of other facilities at the Inn that visitors not staying overnight could enjoy, like the conference facility, award-winning spa, and restaurant and lounge on the first three floors of the Inn. The elevator would allow guests without key cards access to those areas.

As the elevator took them up, Mac ordered Christine, "Stay in the suite. Order whatever you want from room service for dinner and get some sleep. I'll come by for breakfast in the morning and we'll talk about how to fix things."

"Stephen Maguire ruined everything in my life." She blinked the tears out of her eyes.

When the doors opened, they stepped down the corridor that ran the length of the top floor to the service elevator and stairwell at the other end.

Jeff warned Christine about using the stairwell. "Don't go in without your key card. Once you go into the stairwell, none of the doors to any of the floors will open without your key card except the doors to the main areas down on the first, second, or third floor. We've had more than one guest go into the stairwell in their bathrobe or less and have to traipse through the lobby to the front desk to get let back into their room."

With pride, Jeff said that every penthouse suite, except Mac's, had been reserved for that weekend. "It's the height of the autumn foliage and the Inn has the most beautiful views of the colors across the mountains and around the lake. This will be our biggest weekend until ski season starts in about six weeks." He gestured at the door across from Mac's suite. "This weekend, we have an ambassador from eastern Europe staying here. He says he has never seen the autumn foliage before."

Mac recalled before the dissolving of their marriage, when Christine would have gushed over the elegance of the two-bedroom suite that afforded a view of the lake and wooded trails leading down to the water's edge. There was a time she would have thrown off her clothes and jumped into the hot tub out on the balcony before curling up with glee in front of the fireplace.

Instead, she miserably gazed out the picture windows at the multi-colored landscape without seeing it while mumbling thanks to Jeff when he handed her the key card.

After the manager left, Mac got her attention. "I'm going now. Like I said, enjoy the suite. Order dinner, stay here, and stay away from Stephen Maguire. I'll be back tomorrow at nine o'clock. We'll have breakfast and discuss how we can get you back on your feet again then."

"It's not supposed to be like this." She stomped her feet. "My life has gone to hell."

"Then get out of hell," he said. "You're a big girl and you've made some dumb mistakes. We all make mistakes. Do what a grownup does. Fix it. You crawled into bed with a snake and got bit. Learn from it and make it right."

Christine returned to gazing out the window. "You're right, Mac," she said in a strangely quiet tone. "That's what I have to do."

CHAPTER TWO

Mac knew in his heart that his Saturday night had to be better than Christine's. He was positive that his Sunday morning would be less traumatic due to the absence of a hangover. Still, this knowledge didn't console him any when he returned to the Spencer Manor to find a note taped to Archie's cottage door:

> My dearest Mac,
>
> Gone out to visit an old friend. See you tomorrow.
>
> > Love,
> > Archie

It was a defining moment.

It was when Archie wasn't there that Mac came to realize how much he had come to depend on her company.

In the five months since he had moved to Spencer, they had spent every Saturday night together, as well as most other evenings and days. Many evenings, they would go to the Spencer Inn for a dinner prepared especially for them by the chef, who delighted in treating Archie to new exotic recipes from faraway lands.

Having been Robin Spencer's travel companion around the globe, Archie was fearless when it came to trying strange and unusual foods. Her adventurous taste buds delighted the Inn's chef.

Other times, Archie would work her own culinary magic in the manor's gourmet kitchen, and had taught Mac a few simple tricks in an effort to teach him to cook.

After dinner, they would either sit together on the deck to watch the sun set, or in the hot tub on cool evenings, or watch a movie together in the home theater. Afterwards, they would say good night with a hug and a kiss, at which point Archie would return to her cottage while Mac escorted Gnarly up to the master suite.

Tonight, Archie wasn't there.

Mac was spending Saturday night in the manor alone, unless he counted Gnarly. Missing her companionship also, the dog opted for drowning his sorrows in a bag of popcorn.

The man and his dog stayed up late into the night watching a horror movie in the home theatre. The feature about a war between werewolves and vampires was already on when Mac had arrived home to find Gnarly with an open bag of popcorn, which he had stolen off the kitchen counter. Mac rooted for the vampires while Gnarly howled his allegiance to the werewolves.

The triumph of the vampires over the werewolves was a hollow victory without Archie sitting next to him covering her eyes during the gory parts, or better yet, burying her whole face against his chest while he held her, at which point the scent of her perfume would excite his senses.

Funny how you don't notice how much someone's scent excites you until it's replaced by dog breath.

The next morning, Mac woke up on the sofa when Gnarly alternated between licking his nose and pawing at his hand. The two of them had been up so late that Gnarly missed his six o'clock morning patrol of the Point.

Rubbing the sleep from his eyes, Mac dragged himself up the stairs with one hand on the banister while Gnarly guided him with the other until they made their way to the deck's doors, where the dog suddenly jumped on the doors with both front paws pounding. His urgent barking seemed to bounce inside of Mac's head like a ping pong ball.

"What's your problem?" he demanded to know. But Gnarly wasn't sticking around to answer. As soon as the door was open, he shot out like a bullet, across the deck, down the steps, and around the corner of the house. His barking sounded like a battle charge.

The bright morning sunlight momentarily blinded Mac, while at the same time the chilling autumn breeze that swept in off the lake sent a shock through his body that woke up any part of him that hadn't been awakened by Gnarly's barking.

Archie was his first vision of the day.

As always, she was barefoot with her toes dressed up in bright red polish that matched her floor-length silky bathrobe.

"Rough night?" she asked him.

"What's his problem?" Mac asked.

"It's not his fault. Otis keeps provoking him."

"Who's Otis?" Mac looked around off the deck in search of another dog. Gnarly's barking could now be heard at the front of the house.

"That big fat squirrel," she answered. "You can't miss him. He's the biggest squirrel on the Point. Otis keeps coming up onto the deck and shaking his fat butt with his bushy tail at Gnarly. He's begging for a fight."

Though he could see that she was serious in her version of the war between the dog and squirrel, Mac couldn't help being amused. It sounded like an animated movie. To him, it was simple. Gnarly was territorial and couldn't stop barking at everything that moved on the Point.

"This squirrel actually has a name?" he asked.

"Everyone has to have a name."

Usually, she would come in and they would share a cup of coffee. If he was lucky, she would prepare breakfast.

This morning, she made no such movement. Instead, she gazed at him with emerald eyes that didn't look angry, but sad.

Mac wondered, as he often did with women, if he had done something to offend her. Maybe he hurt her feelings when he laughed about Gnarly and Otis.

"I'm surprised Gnarly's barking didn't wake Christine up," she said.

"Why would it? What makes—"

Christine's car. It's still in the driveway. Archie must have seen it when she came home.

He asked, "Do you think Christine spent the night here?"

"Yeah."

"No, no." Taking her hand, he led her inside. "Want some coffee?"

In his haste to get breakfast, Gnarly plowed into her, causing her to fall against Mac when the three of them squeezed through the open doorway. While he fed Gnarly, she prepared the coffeemaker and pressed the button to grind the beans and brew a pot of coffee for the two of them.

After Mac told her about the scene that Christine had caused in the lobby of the Spencer Inn, she asked, "Why did you take her up to the Inn instead of letting her stay here? It isn't like you don't have enough room." She collected the cream and sugar for their coffee.

"Would you have wanted her to stay here?" After Gnarly attacked the food in his bowl, Mac took two mugs from the cupboard. He paused to watch her reaction.

"Spencer Manor is your home. You can let whoever you want to stay here." Those beautiful emerald saucers seemed to bore into him.

"I asked if you wanted her to stay here."

Each one dared the other to say what was on his or her mind.

The only sounds in the kitchen were the churning of the coffeemaker and Gnarly devouring his breakfast. When he was finished, the German shepherd sat between the two of them and licked his chops while looking from one of them to the other as if to ask what was going to happen next.

"I'm going to step out on a limb here," Mac announced.

"You first." Leaning back against the counter, she looked as if she was bracing for him to punch her.

Crossing his arms across his chest, he leaned against the kitchen table. "If the situation was reversed, and it was your ex-husband—"

"I don't have an ex-husband."

"Imagine you did," he said. "If you had an ex and he came here, I wouldn't feel comfortable with him spending the night under the same roof as you—even if nothing happened between the two of you." He plunged on. "The cottage is yours. Even if it legally belongs to me, Robin said that you can live there as long as you want. That makes it your home. Since it's your home, you can invite whoever you want to spend the night with you, but..."

"But..."

He hated that but.

Haven't I said enough? I told you that I don't want you having other men around. What more do I have to say?

"You were upset because you thought Christine had spent the night with me," he came back at her. "Why were you upset about that?"

There. Let's put it back on you.

Seeming to have seen the invisible ball tossed into Archie's court, Gnarly turned his gaze from Mac to her.

"Because I was jealous."

Mac waited for her to go on, but she didn't. "Of what?"

Now her hands were on her hips. "Christine kicked you out of your home. She and her lover conspired to wipe you out. They stripped you of everything and then she had the gall to come here to ask you to take her back. When I came home last night and saw her car here, I thought—" She clenched her jaw shut.

"You thought I had taken her back," he finished for her.

"Meanwhile..." Seeming to change her mind about what she was about to say, she turned her attention to the coffee. She took the pot from the burner and filled both of the mugs.

28

Mac stepped up behind her and wrapped his arms about her waist. "Meanwhile, you've been here for me," he whispered into her ear.

Saying nothing, she nodded her head.

He kissed her ear. "I'm sorry I'm not good at saying how much people mean to me. But you do mean a lot to me. I missed you last night."

Suddenly, her arms were around his neck and her mouth on his.

He welcomed the return of her scent and her taste as he held her against him. It was as if she didn't want to lose the chance to have him now that he offered the opportunity.

With no clear memory of the last time that he had felt wanted by any woman, Mac had forgotten the joy of the touch of feminine hands on him. He gasped with shock and pleasure when he felt her fingertips and nails on his back when she pulled him to her.

The bongs of the grandfather clock in the foyer chiming the eight o'clock hour brought Mac to his senses with a jolt.

"No," he gasped out while pulling away from her. Apologetically, he unwrapped her arms from around his waist.

"No?" she whimpered.

"I have to go." He kissed her fingertips. "I'm meeting Christine for breakfast at nine o'clock."

"Are you serious?"

Not wanting to let her go, he clung to both of her hands in his while begging for her to understand. "I have to talk to her. I couldn't last night because she was so inebriated. She's been asking the kids for money from their trust funds, which since I'm the trustee I won't let them give her, which makes her mad at them. Tristan refuses to talk to her anymore because she's drunk all the time. I'm going to talk to her about going into rehab and I have to do it at breakfast before she starts drinking again."

He pressed her fingers to his lips. He wished that this had been another time, another day when neither of them had any responsibilities calling them away. He wanted to spend the whole day alone with her and no one else, to get to know her in ways that he had only been imagining for a long time.

"Later?" he whispered to her.

The sadness in her eyes was replaced with an invitation. "Hurry back."

"Oh, I will." He brought his lips to hers. "I'll be back by lunchtime. I'll have Antonio prepare a special lunch for us and bring it home. Cheese and fruit—"

"Strawberries dipped in chocolate?" Her eyes lit up.

The grin on her face melted his heart. "Strawberries dipped in chocolate it is."

"And we'll eat them in the Jacuzzi together." Like a child excited by the prospect of a dream come true, she clapped her hands.

"Together." He kissed her one last time before going upstairs to prepare to meet his ex-wife.

* * * *

It took every fiber of Mac's being to force thoughts about his and Archie's plans for later out of his mind and replace them with the matter awaiting him at the top of the mountain.

It wasn't as if he hadn't had visions—in reality they'd been fantasies—of this moment. He'd rehearsed them in his mind more than once ever since discovering Christine's affair with Stephen Maguire.

Every vision contained a common thread. Christine would realize that while her lover had looks, position, prestige, and wealth, it was her devoted husband who'd always been there for her. Upon making this realization, she would beg for him to take her back and Mac would take much relish in saying, "No, no, no, and hell no. You made your bed, baby, now lie in it."

Then he would leave her on her knees, tearing at her clothes, and beating on the ground with her fists in anguish.

Old Loves Die Hard

Now that the opportunity had presented itself for him to live out his fantasy, Mac didn't have the heart to bring it to life. Christine's pitiful condition had sucked the joy out of his vengeance. She had already made her bed and not only lain in it, she had made a full-fledged nest out of it.

Mac couldn't leave the mother of his children there.

His private table was waiting for him in the corner of the Inn's restaurant. As soon as Mac walked through the cut glass doors, Antonio, the host on duty, whipped a fresh pot of coffee from the burner and took it to the table to fill his cup.

"Will Archie be joining you this morning, Mr. Forsythe?" With a snap of his fingers, Antonio signaled for a server to fetch a basket of hot croissants for Mac's table.

"It's Faraday," Mac replied. "No, another friend is visiting from out of town. But I do have a special lunch order that I'd like for the kitchen to prepare for her."

"If it's for Archie, then it won't be anything less than special." Antonio announced before hurrying to the kitchen to put in Mac's order for their romantic lunch.

While Mac watched for Christine, or Stephen Maguire's entrance into the restaurant to flaunt his blue blood among the common folks, the servers continued waiting on other customers. Seeing their nervous glances in his direction, he noted that he still hadn't gotten used to being the boss. His employees' anxiousness made him uncomfortable.

During his career as a homicide detective he had encountered many powerful people who delighted in crushing those who worked for them. Mac wanted so much to not become one of "those bosses".

When Antonio asked if he wanted to go ahead and order, Mac checked the time on his watch. It was twenty minutes after nine o'clock. Assuming Christine had overslept, he used his master key card to take the elevator up to the penthouse.

"Christine!" Mac called out while pounding on the door when she didn't answer after his second knock. "Wake up. It's time for breakfast."

"What the hell is going on?" The door across the corridor, which had a Do Not Disturb sign hanging on it, flew open.

Mac's apology for the disturbance was cut short by the shock of seeing the short, squat, bald-headed man standing naked before him. As bald as the top of his head was, his face was covered in a thick gray beard that went down his barrel chest and stomach and the rest of his exposed body.

"Don't you know that people are trying to sleep?" the naked man asked in a European accent so thick that Mac could only decipher his demand by piecing together what words he understood and the context of the situation.

Mac found his voice. "I think my—" He stopped when he caught himself starting to call Christine his wife. "My friend was supposed to meet me for breakfast. I guess she slept in."

"Why don't you try calling her instead of standing here pounding on the door like some heathen?" the naked man suggested. "All this noise and interruptions. If it isn't the maid with towels, it's someone playing horror movies, and now we have—"

"Omar!" A woman came into view from the sitting room behind the bald man. "Who are you talking to out there?"

Mac saw that the tall red-headed woman was as naked as her companion, though notably more attractive.

"Some heathen trying to wake up the people in the suite across the hall," he called back to her. Based on how he had left the door wide open, he didn't seem to care if Mac saw her unclothed.

"Well, if I were you I'd hurry up. The clock is ticking and my twenty-four hours is up in two."

With the eagerness of a boy being told that this would be his last chance to kiss his date good-night, he slammed the door shut.

Using his key card, Mac let himself into Christine's room.

At first, the silence in the suite made Mac think that Christine had sobered up and, realizing how foolish she had behaved the day before, left to return home. Then, he realized that her car was still at Spencer Manor.

The suite was too quiet.

It was possible for Christine to have left through the lobby to take a cab to the manor to get her car while he was waiting for her in the restaurant. Mac hoped that, if that was the case, she wouldn't run into Archie. If so, he was glad he wouldn't be there to witness the scene.

The empty room service tray was a clue that Christine had taken his advice to have dinner sent up. Not seeing any dishes, a quick check told him that she'd had the presence of mind to put her dirty dishes in the kitchenette's dishwasher and run it. During his check inside the dishwasher, Mac noticed two plates and two wine glasses.

It was a dinner for two.

"No, Christine," he murmured. "You didn't."

He noticed the first blood splatter on the wall as he rounded the corner into the sitting area.

That splatter was followed by another, then another, then a smear and a pool of blood.

In the middle of the sitting room, Mac first saw the leather shoes covered in blood. As he stepped into the room, he saw the rest of the body lying behind the coffee table, which had been overturned in the mêlée.

Christine, what have you done?

The blood that saturated the carpeting soaked into the knees of his pants when he knelt to press his fingertips against the neck that had been sliced open.

"Oh, Christine, no." Mac tasted his tears in his mouth.

Anger welled up inside him when he looked at the once handsome face of the man who twelve months before had been his enemy.

"Why did you come up here?" Mac yelled at the dead man. "She said she was going to kill you. You heard her. She swore. Why didn't you stay away, you bastard?"

Emotion overrode decades of police training that had become second nature to him. If he had been one of the detectives who had worked under him before he retired, Mac would have raked him over the coals for not leaving the suite immediately and containing the crime scene.

With the back of his hand, Mac slapped the dead man's body, getting more blood on his sleeve and hand. The body didn't move in response to his slap. Rigor mortis had already set in.

She killed him last night.

With the sound of his heartbeat racing in his ears, Mac climbed up to his feet to go in search of clues to his ex-wife's whereabouts.

At the door to the master bedroom, his detective training kicked back in. Stephen Maguire had been stabbed several times.

Where's the murder weapon?

Mac guessed that she had put it in the dishwasher when she washed the rest of the dishes to get rid of the evidence.

Using a paper towel from the kitchenette in order to not disturb evidence on the door handle, he went into the master bedroom.

He was surprised to find her blood-soaked clothes scattered on the floor around the bed. Her suitcase rested on the luggage stand.

"Christine," he called out. "What happened?"

With no other place to search for her in the suite, Mac threw open the bathroom door.

The room shone like it had never been touched by human hands, or live ones.

He found her naked in the bottom of the shower tub. Her damp blond hair was plastered to her head and neck.

Mac pressed his fingers against her neck to check for a pulse. There was none.

Like Stephen Maguire, her body was still.

Suddenly, all the wounds from the past were gone. Once again, she was his wife, the girl he had felt honored to have gone out with him. The girl he had protected and taken care of. The girl he had loved.

Holding her cold body, he rocked her in his arms while searching for any sign of life, and finding none.

While wiping her hair from her face, his fingers found a deep bloody gash at the back of her head at the base of her neck. He looked up at the towel rack in the shower above.

"So that's what happened," he said to her dead body.

He spied chunks of skin under her fingernails and deep red scratches on her arms and neck.

Sobbing, he asked her, "Christine, what are we going to tell the children?"

CHAPTER THREE

"Mac, are you okay?" Jeff Ingles asked a third time while shaking a tumbler filled with bourbon on the rocks in an effort to get his attention. With two dead bodies in the owner's private suite at the Spencer Inn, Jeff felt like downing it himself. After receiving Mac's call about the tragedy on the penthouse floor, Jeff directed him to his office on the ground floor to await the police.

Sitting motionless on the manager's sofa, Mac replayed the whole scene over and over in his mind.

"Mac!" The sharpness of Jeff's voice snapped him out of his thoughts. The call sounded foreign coming from the soft-spoken manager's lips.

After following Jeff's eyes to the glass he held out to him, Mac understood the offer. "I shouldn't."

"If you don't, I will," Jeff said.

Mac didn't feel up to a discussion about drinking habits. He took a sip of the bourbon and found that Jeff wasn't steering him wrong. It did help to calm his nerves.

"I called Ed," Jeff reported. "He's on his way."

"When I was a cop, the suspects who lawyered up the fastest were always moved to the top of my list."

Jeff pulled around a chair from the conference table to sit across from him. "Mac, do you know how long the Spencer

Inn has had its five-star rating?" Before Mac could respond that he didn't know, Jeff answered, "Seventy-five years. That's longer than either you or I have been alive. Now we have two dead bodies, one being a direct descendant—"

Later, Mac wouldn't recall rising up off the sofa. All he could remember was the roar of his own voice in his head. "I just found my children's mother dead. Do you know who has to call them to give them that news? Me. That's who. I have to tell them that their mother is dead and you want to talk to me about how to spin this tragedy to keep from losing some lousy stars to the Wisp?"

The terror in Jeff's face matched the silence in the room.

They were both grateful when the office door opened. As they had expected, it was Police Chief David O'Callaghan and his deputy chief, Arthur Bogart, who carried a canvas bag under his arm.

Deputy Chief Art Bogart, called Bogie, was a mountain of a man. His thick mustache and hair were touched with gray. The lines on his strong face told of a man who had lived a life as hard as his body. The late Patrick O'Callaghan's closest friend and colleague, Bogie was like a second father to David.

"Is everyone okay in here?" David's tone reeked of his authority. It sounded more like an order for any disagreements to be settled now.

"No." Mac fell back onto the sofa.

Jeff told him, "I'm sorry, Mac. I was out of line."

"Yes, you were," Mac said. "But I do know that Robin Spencer hired you to run this place because you're the best at what you do." In spite of his best efforts, he heard his breath shudder. "Do what you have to do to protect the Spencer Inn's reputation."

Jeff reached out to touch Mac's hand. "I won't do anything without clearing it through you first." He grabbed his smart phone and notepad from his desk. Before following David's silent order for him to leave them alone, he stopped to clasp Mac on the shoulder. "In case I haven't already told you, I'm sorry for you and your family's loss."

Mac grasped his hand and replied in choked words, "Thank you."

The manager hurried from the office.

Mac waited for the door to shut before asking if David had been up to the penthouse to survey the scene.

"Yes." The police chief turned around the chair that Jeff had vacated and straddled its back. "It's a mess." He gestured at Mac and his clothes. "I see that you've touched the crime scene."

"I did more than touch it," Mac muttered. "I jumped in with both feet and contaminated it like some rookie."

"It happens," the police chief said. "We'll sort it out."

Try as he might, Mac couldn't adjust his thinking from that of the family of a murder victim to that of cop.

"Mac, are you okay?"

He was aware of David's touch on his hand. Instead of becoming detached from the scene, he had instead gone back to relive it in his mind. "I was checking to see if either of them was alive, but they weren't. Rigor had already set in."

Look at him.

Aware that he'd been avoiding David's eyes, a sign of guilt that he would have quickly spotted when he was a cop, Mac forced himself to look into his eyes. The pity he saw in their blue depths was unbearable. He hated pity.

"I didn't do this." Unable to stand the sight of his sympathy, Mac looked over at Bogie who was at the table in front of the window unpacking the canvas bag, which contained an evidence kit. Bogie had put on a pair of gloves.

David said, "Bogie will have to take your statement." When Mac started to object, he reminded him, "I was at the manor when Christine showed up yesterday. Having seen the two of you together, if I take your statement, someone could later construe it as a conflict of interest that made us eliminate you as a suspect." He took Mac's hand which was covered in Stephen Maguire's blood. "About your clothes—"

"Archie is bringing a change of clothes for me."

38

David asked in a gentle tone, "Did you call your kids yet?"

"No."

"I suggest you do that as soon as Bogie is through. The media has already gotten wind of this and they're coming out here in swarms."

"I'm ready, Chief." Bogie stepped over to them with an open evidence bag in his hand. "Let's start with the shirt."

Mac stood up and unbuttoned his shirt. Glancing down at it, he realized that it was a new shirt that his daughter Jessica had sent to him from a shopping trip to New York.

A third-year student at William and Mary, she enjoyed shopping trips with her friends and sending stylish fashion to her father, who despised shopping as much as she loved it. His distaste for shopping showed in his casual blue jeans, faded t-shirts, and worn dockers.

As he unbuttoned it, Mac recalled that he had put it on that morning because Archie had commented about how it brought out the blue in his eyes the first time he wore it. He had put it on for her.

While watching David fold his shirt, Mac recalled the touch of Archie's hands on his bare back less than two hours earlier and his anticipation of being with her—all while the woman who'd borne his children was lying dead.

Mac's stomach churned. His ears filled with a roaring sound.

"Mac, are you okay?"

Jerked from his thoughts, Mac was aware of David's hand on his shoulder, while Bogie had his other shoulder in a firm grasp.

"You're going to be sick," David yelled through the roar that filled his head.

Through a hazy fog he saw David pointing to Jeff's private bathroom.

Mac sprinted to the small room where he fell to his knees and emptied his coffee, toast, and bourbon into the toilet. A cold sweat bathed his shoulders and back. He could feel it dripping down his bare chest while he knelt in front of the toilet.

By the time his stomach stopped churning, he became aware of David stepping around behind him to take the hand towel off the rack and run it under the faucet in the sink.

"I feel like such a rookie," Mac spoke into the toilet bowl. "Twenty years in homicide. Hundreds of cases. Never once did I ever contaminate a crime scene or toss my cookies." He flinched when he felt the cold towel on his bare shoulders. David pressed it against the back of his neck.

"Were any of those murder victims your wife?"

"Ex-wife." Mac glanced up at him. "She was murdered, Dave. Someone killed her."

"She has skin under her fingernails." David ran his fingers from Mac's shoulder and down his side. "And I see you have scratches on your back."

*　*　*　*

David wanted to get upstairs to talk to the M.E. before she left with the bodies. He needed a preliminary report to know where to start in his investigation. With the murders happening at the Spencer Inn in Mac Faraday's penthouse suite, everyone was going to be demanding answers.

He was coming out of Jeff Ingle's office after Bogie had started interviewing Mac when he practically collided with Archie, who was trying to go inside with his change of clothes.

"Is he okay?" she wanted to know when David took the clothes and sent them inside without letting her see Mac.

"As well as you'd expect him to be," was all David said while ushering her down the corridor and away from the office. "What did he tell you?"

"Nothing," she said. "Only that Christine and Stephen Maguire, the guy she divorced him for, were dead and that he had been in the crime scene and needed fresh clothes. How did it happen?"

"You know that I can't talk about it, Archie." As they neared the lobby, he was aware of more people, many resembling the media, milling around. "Where were you last night?"

"Do I need an alibi?" she asked him.

"You and Mac have become pretty tight in the last few months." He was pleased when he saw her cheeks turn pink. "We both saw Christine yesterday asking Mac to take her back. If he had—"

"He didn't."

"Now that she's gone—"

"I have an alibi," Archie said.

"Mac?"

"What's the time of death?"

"I'm going upstairs to find that out." David glanced at his watch.

Archie said, "I went to visit a friend of Robin's. She's a literature professor at Frostburg. She has issues and last night she called upset. I went to cheer her up. We had a couple of drinks in a lounge near the university campus. I'm sure people saw me there. I got home around midnight. I can give you her phone number."

"What about Mac? Did you see him when you got in around midnight?" He held his breath while waiting for her response.

"No, I went straight to my place. I didn't see him until this morning around seven-thirty." She added, "But he was with Gnarly last night."

"I wonder if he'll give me a statement." Frustrated by her failure to volunteer for being the source of the scratches on Mac's back, he asked, "Did Gnarly put scratches on his back?" When her face turned a deeper shade of pink, he sighed with relief. "It was you."

"I did that this morning before he came to see Christine. I was excited." His chuckle only added to her embarrassment. "Don't tell me that you've never had a woman scratch your back."

"Not an hour before I became a murder suspect."

"Mac didn't do this," she insisted.

"I know." The corner of David's lips curled. "While your scratches were impressive, they weren't anywhere nearly deep enough. Whoever Christine scratched before she died, she drew blood."

*   *   *   *

The police presence on the top floor had caused the guests in the other suites to clear out. Any ruffled feathers were soothed with Jeff offering guests a free day of pampering at the Spenser Inn resort's award-winning spa. Each guest's displeasure dissipated. Some were so anxious to take advantage of the offer that they rushed off to the spa in bathrobes and towels as soon as the police released them after giving their statements.

Two police officers stood guard at the suite's door to keep unwanted visitors out. They parted to allow their chief to cross the threshold.

When David had first arrived at the hotel, the horror of what had happened hit him like a slap in the face upon entering the sitting area. Furniture was overturned. The victim that Mac had identified as Stephen Maguire rested on his side in the middle of a blood-stained carpet. Blood splatters and drops covered the walls, furniture, and floor like brown polka-dots.

The bathroom was another story. The counters and surfaces shone like they had never been used.

Mac had left Christine's body in the tub where he had found it. Her blood-soaked clothes were scattered around the bedroom where she appeared to have discarded them after killing her lover.

When David returned, he found the lead crime scene investigator packing up her equipment in the dining area. Cindy's tiny build made her look too young to drive, let alone lead a forensics investigation.

"Is it too early for you to have anything for me?" the police chief asked.

"That's the cleanest bathroom I've ever seen in my life," Cindy reported. "It was scrubbed down with bleach. No fingerprints, except for those that we are assuming right now belong to Mr. Faraday. Don't count on getting any other prints or DNA. Everything was soaked and washed down with bleach. Then the shower was left on to wash everything else down the drain."

David scratched the side of his head. "He didn't say anything about the shower being on when—"

"It'd been shut off," she interrupted to explain. "Each of these suites is outfitted with timers on the showers, sinks, and appliances that automatically shut off the water for the whole unit if it runs too long. It's a safeguard device to prevent water damage from overflow or leaks if the plumbing breaks or a guest passes out drunk after turning on the shower. When I got here, the shower handle was turned to the on position, but the water control valve for the unit was still shut off."

"I should have noticed that," David admitted.

Pleased with herself, she shot him a grin. "That's why I'm forensics and you're the chief."

"How about Mrs. Faraday? Did she slip and hit her head in the shower after killing Mr. Maguire?"

Cindy shook her head. "We need to open her up first. She has a serious bruise and laceration on the back of her head and neck. I heard that she was intoxicated. You may not be far off."

"Her husband—ex-husband—says she was an alcoholic," David said. "The manager stated that she was seriously intoxicated when Mr. Faraday checked her in. Plus, she'd gotten into an altercation with the victim around five-thirty yesterday afternoon. Based on what you've collected, what do you think happened here?"

"Time of death on him is approximately ten-thirty last night." Cindy pointed at the dishwasher with her hand encased in an evidence glove. "We have dinner plates and glasses for a dinner for two." She gestured at the table under her evidence kit. "They have dinner. She's drunk and volatile. They get into a fight." She led David into the sitting room. "This is where things go really bad. She attacks him with a knife, probably from their dinner—I found steak knives in the dishwasher—and kills him. She needs to get rid of the evidence, she returns to the kitchen."

Cindy pointed at the drops of blood leading into the kitchenette. "She puts the murder weapon in the dishwasher along with the dinner dishes. I guess she thought that as long as she was cleaning the murder weapon that she might as well."

Leading the way into the bedroom, she continued her breakdown of the murder. "Now she comes to the bedroom and realizes that she has Stephen Maguire's blood and tissue all over her and her clothes. She strips off her clothes and goes into the bathroom to wash away the evidence. After cleaning the bathroom, she climbs into the bathtub to take a shower, slips and hits her head and dies."

David glanced around the bathroom. "There's a problem with your theory."

"The skin under her fingernails," Cindy said. "The stabbing victim has no scratches. She could have had another altercation with someone else. Maybe the ex?"

"Not him." David picked up the trash can and peered inside. Not only was it empty, but it was clean. "Have you checked the trash can in the kitchen?" He checked the cabinet under the sink. That, too, was bare.

"Yes," Cindy answered. "It was empty. All of the trash was taken out."

"By whom? You said this room was scrubbed down with bleach. Who did that?"

"Christine Faraday."

"If she had left to take out the trash she would have needed her key card to get back into the room; in which case, security would have record of it," David explained. "According to them, Christine Faraday never left this suite."

Perplexed, the investigator shrugged her shoulders while shaking her head.

"According to you, Christine Faraday died while cleaning the bathroom with bleach immediately after the murder." He held out the empty trash can to her. "How did she get rid of the bottle of bleach she had used to scrub down the bathroom without leaving the room?"

"That's for you to figure out," Cindy replied. "That's why they made you police chief."

CHAPTER FOUR

Isn't it ironic?

Mac and Christine had always expected that he would die first. After all, he was the one out there dodging bullets while tracking down killers. She was home with the kids or working in a law office as a paralegal.

Now, he was trying to put her affairs in order.

While Mac remained in Spencer to keep tabs on the murder investigation as best he could, his daughter Jessica drove up from Williamsburg to stay at her mother's home to make the funeral arrangements.

Immediately came the calls from Jessica about Mac's former in-law's strong-arm attempts to take over the funeral.

Christine's older sibling, Sabrina, enjoyed the role of family matriarch. Since her marriage to the president of an accounting firm, who had provided well for her expensive tastes, Sabrina, with her orange hair and jewels dripping from her queenly figure, viewed the role of dictating what was best for her family very seriously.

Claiming to know exactly how Christine would want her funeral to be handled, Sabrina had swept in and ordered Jessica to sit back and deal with the grief of losing her mother while letting her handle all the details.

"When I told her no thank you," Jessica reported in her latest call to her father, "she got all huffy and stormed out of the house. When I went outside a little bit ago, our garbage cans had been run over. I don't want to be pointing fingers, but I think she did it."

In the background, through the phone, Mac could hear Jessica going through the kitchen cabinets while preparing breakfast after her daily five-mile run, something she did like clockwork. Mac's daughter was a creature of habit and discipline. Before discovering his birthright, Mac had sometimes wondered if she had inherited her strong sense of discipline from someone on his side of the family.

A life-sized portrait of Robin Spencer hung in Mac's study. It had been painted over forty years earlier. Dressed in the strapless gown her wealthy parents had designed for her coming out party, Robin was ravishing with her long dark hair swept up. Her skin was like porcelain against her dark features and sapphire eyes. She looked like Elizabeth Taylor in her early movies.

When he had first laid his eyes on the portrait, Mac had been struck by the resemblance between his birth mother and his daughter Jessica.

Robin's portrait had answered his question about who his beautiful daughter took after.

"You knew this was coming," Mac told her. "This happens every time anyone plans anything in that family. Sabrina has to be in charge and it has to be the social event of the season or nothing else. When it doesn't go exactly the way she wants it, she throws a tantrum. I don't remember one event that involved your aunts that didn't end in a family feud with someone getting slapped and vases getting broken. That's why I always volunteered to work those nights."

With a meeting scheduled at the Spencer Inn later, Mac mentally prepared for the day with more coffee. At his feet, he could hear Gnarly chomping away on his breakfast. He wondered if it was possible to teach a dog to chew with his lips shut.

Do dogs even have lips? If not, what does he flap so loudly when he eats?

"I want this to be over," Jessica sighed with a sob.

Hearing the pain in her voice, Mac's heart ached.

Unknowingly, she added to his pain with "I wish you were here."

"David said that he expects the medical examiner to release your mother's body today. I'll arrange to have it sent to the funeral home in Georgetown as soon as possible." He asked, "How's Tristan holding up? I called last night and he was working at the museum."

"I think he's in denial."

A forensics psychology major, Jessica had diagnosed Tristan as being in denial about everything ever since she first heard the word used by a psychologist on television.

Tristan took after his father with his auburn hair, high cheek bones, and slim muscular build. He had also inherited his father's blue eyes. What he didn't inherit was Mac's love for murder mysteries. Tristan loved animals and nature, in particular, dinosaurs. A sophomore at George Washington University, he was a devoted college student and practically lived at the Natural History Museum.

Mac was grateful that neither of his children had made great changes in their lifestyles since inheriting ten million dollars each in trusts from the grandmother they had never met. Neither of them took to wild parties and extravagant shopping sprees. Jessica did upgrade her wardrobe and bought a Corvette. He also suspected that she'd traded up her hair stylist.

Unlike any other teenager who had inherited millions of dollars, Tristan resisted the urge to buy a hot car, like his father, who had purchased a Dodge Viper sports car within days of receiving his inheritance. Practical to a fault, Tristan pointed out that since he lived in the city, it took longer to drive to campus and find a place to park and walk to his classes than it did to take public transportation. Instead, he splurged on the latest and greatest computer equipment with state-of-the-art scientific research capabilities that only Archie could understand and appreciate.

According to Jessica, Tristan barely missed a beat between his classes and job since his mother's murder. She had talked to him. He had also received a lecture from his Aunt Sabrina about respecting his mother by emoting his grief in a more public manner.

Mac could imagine the motive behind his son's withdrawal into his schoolwork. He recalled receiving the same lecture when his adopted father passed away after a long illness. While Mac grieved the loss, he had also felt relief that his father's suffering was over. Even though Tristan's circumstances were different, Mac suspected that he wasn't in denial as much as he may have been in hiding. It's bad enough losing a loved one without getting flack for handling it wrong.

Tristan wasn't the only one in the family receiving grief from Mac's ex-in-laws.

After discovering the crushed garbage cans, Jessica had called Mac to announce that she was ready to give in to her aunt's demands. "I guess we can let Aunt Sabrina have the reception at her house afterwards. That might placate her."

"This isn't about Aunt Sabrina. Don't let her bully you into doing anything that you think is wrong or that you don't think your mother would have wanted."

Mac felt a grin come to his lips when Archie, carrying a basket filled with croissants, came in from the deck. He could smell the freshly-baked goods as soon as she stepped through the door.

"By the way," Jessica added as he was about to hang up. "I think someone broke into Mom's house."

"Was anything taken?" Mac wasn't surprised. It wasn't uncommon for homes to be broken into after news of the occupants' deaths. Knowing no one was home, the houses were considered easy pickings for thieves.

"Nothing of value," she reported. "I can just tell that your study—I mean Stephen's—had been gone through. The safe was open, but all of Mom's papers are there. I don't know about Stephen's. I assumed he took what was his when he moved out. I didn't even bother calling the police. Do you think I should?"

Mac told her to report the break-in to the police, in case it might be connected in some way to the Stephen Maguire's murder. He was about to hang up and dive into the croissant that Archie had placed in front of him with a helping of strawberry jam, when his daughter went on to the next subject.

"Roxanne wants to know what you want to do about the lake house," Jessica announced.

Mac moaned.

"I told her to talk to you. Did you know that Mom never changed her will?"

Mac told her that his lawyer, Ed Willingham, had already given him that news the day before.

"Aunt Roxanne is having a cow. Something about Mom never signing over the lake house to her. Thought I'd let you know." She finished the phone call with a "have a nice day."

Hanging up the phone, Mac buried his face in his hands and groaned.

"I finished editing the book. Sent it in at three-thirty this morning and made lots and lots of money." Archie rubbed both of his shoulders. "How's your day shaping up?"

"Tell me you don't have any sisters." He realized as he said it that she never talked about her family or childhood. It was always his family that they discussed.

"Only child." She held up her hand in a scout's honor salute.

"Then I'll marry you." He wrapped his arms around her waist and pulled her to him. From where he was sitting at the breakfast counter and she stood, it brought his head to rest on her shoulder.

She returned the hug. "Funerals are always stressful. Death is stressful, especially when it's someone you love."

"Yeah, but the dead person doesn't have to deal with anything. They get to sit back and enjoy it."

She said, "Your mother once said to me, 'Have you ever noticed that it's after you're dead that suddenly everyone is concerned about what you want?'"

"Believe me, these chicks aren't concerned about what Christine wants." When his cell phone rang, he checked the caller ID. It read, "Roxanne Burton." He decided not to answer it.

"Why didn't you answer that?"

"It was Christine's sister. One of Stephen Maguire's colleagues at the U.S. Attorney's Office. He was the head of the criminal division. She's his counterpart in the family court division. She introduced Christine to Maguire." He shot Archie a sarcastic grin. "I never thanked her for that."

He dabbed the butter and jam onto one of her croissants. "Christine was the baby of three girls. Their daddy did a stint for like eight years as ambassador to Brazil. They lived in a big house with servants and body guards and went to swanky parties and dated men in uniforms."

"They became spoiled," she said.

"They were actually called Daddy's Little Princesses," he told her. "It was pointed out to Christine—and me—that she married beneath her station in life. Sabrina, the oldest, married the president of a big accounting firm. Roxanne modeled her way through school and has the ear of every influential legal eagle in D.C. Now she's standing in line to beat my chops about Christine's will."

"You told me yesterday that they found out that she'd never changed it after the divorce."

"Or the beneficiary on her life insurance," he said. "Jessica remembers her mother saying at one point that she was going to make Roxanne the executor and leave everything to the kids, but she never did it."

"Teaches you to never put things off."

"It should be a no brainer," Mac said. "I've already talked to Ed. Okay, I'm the executor. I'll do what she wanted. Split everything between the two kids, fifty-fifty. The house is going to be sold because neither of them wants it. They decide between themselves who wants what." He sighed. "Then Ed took a look at her accounts."

Archie asked, "What's the problem?"

"Christine was head over heels in debt." When Archie cocked an eyebrow at him, he explained, "When I left Christine, she was more than fixed. Her father had died the year before she kicked me out. Each of the sisters had received over a hundred thousand dollars. You might say that inheritance was the beginning of the end for us. Money was always an issue. I never made enough for her. Her father spoiled her rotten. Then, when Big Daddy died—"

She screwed up her face. "Did they really call him Big Daddy?"

"And he was only five feet eight inches tall."

"Unbelievable."

Mac continued, "I wanted to put the money into a trust fund for our retirement and the kids' college. She wanted to spend it on stuff in order to bring us up to par with her sisters. According to Ed's findings, that's exactly what she did after getting rid of me. It's all gone and the bank is about to foreclose on her house. The only thing she had left was her share of the lake house. If Roxanne buys out her share, which when we were married she made no secret about wanting to do, then that might pay off some of her debts."

Mac tapped his finger on the breakfast bar. "This is her sisters' fault. It wasn't 'keep up with the Joneses' in our house. It was keep up with the sisters. Designer clothes. Spas. Parties all the time. I was a drag because I wanted to live within our means. Maguire seduced her into running around with the sisters. She threw me out so that she could do what she wanted with *her* money and it looks like she died with nothing but bills to her name."

"You mentioned a lake house?" Archie asked.

"Right here in Spencer," Mac said. "It's on the mountain and has a lake view. I'd only been there a couple of times. Right about the time she kicked me out, it was appraised at half a million dollars. I'm surprised Christine's name is still on the deed. I know she intended to sell her third to Roxanne."

He glanced at his watch. "I need to go. I'm meeting the chief of security at the Inn for breakfast to see if he can give me any details about where David is in his investigation." He frowned. "David won't tell me anything."

"That's because you haven't been cleared as a suspect," Archie said. "I only just got cleared since Bogie was able to reach my alibi at Frostburg." A naughty grin crept to her lips. "If you and I had been sleeping together then we could have alibied each other and had a good time doing it."

"I'll remember that the next time I plan a murder." Standing up, he kissed her quickly on the lips. When they parted, he held her close, not wanting to let her go. "I promise that when this is over, we're moving forward in what we talked about before all this happened...unless all this made you change your mind about me."

She whispered to him, "I'm not going anywhere."

The dongs of the doorbell made them jump back from their embrace as if they had been caught with their hands in the sexual cookie jar.

"More flowers?" Since Christine's death, he had been receiving tons of flowers and sympathy gifts from many people he didn't know who had been friends of his late mother.

As if he were voicing their displeasure, Gnarly charged for the door.

The two people waiting on his doorstep were yet another piece of Mac's Georgetown past. As he often thought when he saw the two of them together, Natasha Holmstead and Judge Garrison Sutherland made an odd couple.

After years of seeing the two of them out about town together, Mac was still unsure if they were indeed a "couple" in the romantic sense of the word. He never saw them kissing, holding hands, or other body language that betrayed two people as being romantically linked.

They never appeared to be guilty about being seen together, which led Mac to suspect that they were simply very good friends. Considering that she was married to Stephen Maguire and, to Mac's knowledge, had never divorced him, to be romantically linked with Judge Sutherland gave them much reason to be apprehensive...if they were indeed a couple.

Mac was never sure, which bothered him. He hated not being able to pin someone down.

Natasha Holmstead was the personification of brains over beauty. Not that she was ugly. She was as skinny as a stick. Bee stings were bigger than her breasts and she had no butt to speak of. If she would ever do something with her cinnamon-colored hair, which she wore in a chin-length bob style with the part in the middle and combed straight down the sides, she would be considered attractive.

From all the beauties that Mac knew Stephen Maguire had bedded throughout the years, the only reason that he could conclude for him marrying Natasha was the millions of dollars per year she made defending the richest criminals in the world. He certainly didn't marry her for her winning personality.

Mac knew Garrison Sutherland from back when he had held Stephen Maguire's position in the U.S. Attorney's Office. As mediocre a prosecutor as Maguire had been, Sutherland was sharp and fair. He carried his passion to the bench.

While Natasha stood tall and thin, Judge Sutherland was short and stocky with black hair and wire-rimmed glasses. She was aggressive, he was soft spoken. As abrasive as she was, he was compromising.

"Hello, Mac," the judge greeted him in a somber tone, while holding out his hand to him. "Natasha and I came to personally offer our condolences on your loss."

Stunned by the visit from the couple who lived over three hours away, Mac accepted their condolence, while holding Gnarly back by his collar. Gnarly liked to check out every visitor by giving them a nasal pat-down. Mac invited them in to the living room.

Natasha and Garrison reacted with surprise at seeing that their host had company.

"I hope we're not interrupting anything," the judge said, while easing Gnarly's snout away from his pants' pockets.

After assuring them that they weren't, Mac introduced them. "This is Archie Monday." Not sure what to call her, he stumbled over the words, "She's my friend." He realized, even as he said it, that his tone sounded guilty.

He didn't like the knowing glances that Garrison and Natasha exchanged upon hearing the introduction.

After he had finished checking out the judge, Gnarly moved on to examine Natasha, who gave his snout a quick swat. She might as well have called him out for a duel. The German shepherd backed up and sat with his eyes on her. He dared her to make her next shot.

Judge Sutherland waited until after they had taken seats on the sofa across from Mac and Archie to explain the reason for their visit. "I don't know if you're aware, but Natasha has suffered a loss as well. You see, she and Stephen Maguire were still married."

Archie said, "I'm sorry to hear that."

"Thank you for your kindness." Natasha blinked away non-existent tears while wiping one away from her cheek.

Having seen the defense attorney in action in the court-room, Mac was very familiar with her techniques. She was like any predator. She laid low and observed her prey before devouring it, with no regrets for doing so.

Garrison went on in his methodical tone, as if he were explaining the intricate steps of a murder plan to a jury. "For a variety of reasons, which we won't bore you with, Mac, Natasha and Stephen had made a decision to remain married while living separate lives. They were still each other's bene-ficiaries. As a matter of fact, Stephen had left Natasha sole heir to his estate, which leads to the reason for our visit."

Natasha jumped in. "I'd like to know when I can pick up Stephen's stuff."

Mac asked, "What stuff?"

"The stuff he left at Christine's house," Natasha said. "He left it all there while he was looking for another place to live. Since he left everything to me, then it's mine, and I want to make arrangements to pick it up. Also, I want any personal effects that he had left in his room at your hotel. The police have taken it into evidence, but surely they don't need it. Everyone knows what happened. Christine flipped out and gave Stephen what he had coming for a long time. The police don't need to keep his personal effects to prove that."

Garrison said, "We tried to talk to the police chief about it, but he's been stonewalling us. We were told that you two are pretty good buddies. Maybe you can use your influence—"

"You and Maguire haven't been living together for years," Mac replied. "According to my information, he's lived with at least three other women since leaving you."

"But we did remain friends," she said.

"Friendly enough for him to leave you everything," Mac said. "Sounds to me like a motive for wanting him dead."

When Natasha made a move, threatening to jump across the room to physically force Mac to give her what she wanted, she became aware of Gnarly between them.

The dog's unblinking eyes were on her.

Easing back into her seat, Natasha said, "Since there's no shortage of rich criminals looking to get away with murder, I'm very wealthy in my own right. Compared to my own financial portfolio, his estate isn't worth the energy it would've taken to kill him."

"Money isn't the only reason to kill someone," Mac said. "Why are you so anxious to get your hands on his stuff now? What did Maguire have that you wanted badly enough to exert your energy killing him?"

"I resent that." She shot a glare at Mac and another one at the dog that refused to stop staring at her.

"Natasha, please," came a plea from her companion, who patted her hand. "It isn't like you don't know how this works. Ask Mac to tell you what Stephen had with him, and then if it's there, ask him nicely if he can help you get it back. If it isn't pertinent to the case, then maybe the police chief will let you take it without the pissing contest."

For her own curiosity, Archie asked, "What is it?"

Natasha gritted her teeth and looked over to Garrison who waved his hand in a gesture for her to go on. Finally, she told them, "A watch. A gold pocket watch. It had belonged to my father. When I married Stephen, Dad gave it to him."

"Why didn't you take it when you separated?" Mac wanted to know.

The attorney's face flushed. "I didn't know he took it with him until after he had moved out. I asked him to give it back, but Stephen argued that it was a gift, which, yes, it was, but my father never would have given it to him if he'd known what a prick he was. Since we never officially got divorced—"

"Why didn't you divorce him?" Archie asked.

"It's complicated."

Natasha rolled her eyes in a way that reminded Mac of when his daughter had been an adolescent in middle school. After years of being on the receiving end of the teenaged eye roll, such gestures now instantly got under his skin.

The defense attorney said, "It's of purely sentimental value to me. Since Stephen's dead now—Christine probably didn't even know he ever had it."

"A watch? A pocket watch?" Mac scoffed. "You're here making all this stink over a watch, which since you're his heir you're going to get eventually anyway?"

"It belonged to my father." Natasha moved to the edge of her seat.

Like an army general seeing the enemy make an advanced move, Gnarly inched forward. All he needed was the word.

"I don't believe you," Mac said. "Someone broke into Christine's home and went through her stuff. Why shouldn't I think it was you?"

Garrison grasped her arm as if to hold her back. "Offer him something to work with, Natasha."

She asked Mac, "If I tell you what I know about who else would have wanted Stephen dead, will you help me get what is rightfully mine?"

"Tell me what you know, then I might be persuaded to help you."

When Mac turned to follow her eyes to that of her companion in search of his opinion, he noticed the judge staring at him. After years of knowing and working with Judge Garrison Sutherland, he recognized the expression on his face. It was one of study. The man had seen something that captured his interest.

Seeing that the judge's thoughts were elsewhere, Natasha said, "I really shouldn't do anything to help catch whoever did society a public service by killing that slime bucket."

"Think of it this way," Mac said. "For once, you'll be helping to catch a murderer instead of getting him off."

Somehow, that persuaded her. "Stephen was extremely ambitious."

"Now tell me something I don't know."

"Boris Hunter, the U.S. Attorney, has been burning up the phone lines to get on the short list to be appointed U.S. Attorney General to replace Reed ever since the grapevine started murmurings about him announcing his retirement before the holidays. I suppose you didn't hear that his cancer resurfaced?"

"No, I didn't."

"Meanwhile, this whole summer, Stephen and Roxanne Burton have been neck and neck to replace George Vance." Natasha shot Mac an aside, "Did you know Hunter's deputy, George Vance, got appointed judge?"

"Vance deserves it," Mac said. "He's a good guy."

"Well, according to my sources," Natasha said, "Hunter decided on Stephen Maguire. It wasn't official and he hadn't announced it yet. I guess now that Stephen is dead, he'll be falling back to number two."

"Christine's sister, Roxanne," Mac noted.

The judge jumped back into the conversation with the question, "If Boris Hunter gets appointed attorney general and Vance is judge of the criminal court, then who'll take Hunter's place?"

Mac's and Archie's faces were blank. Even Gnarly's expression was questioning.

Natasha said, "Not Vance. He's got what he's always wanted. He's not going to step down from judgeship to take Hunter's old job."

Archie looked over at Mac. "Stephen Maguire?"

Tapping his hand on imaginary steps on the coffee table, Garrison told them, "Stephen Maguire was looking to go from criminal prosecutor straight into the seat of U.S. Attorney."

Mac pointed out, "That's a really big jump for a prosecutor who didn't have a very good conviction record."

"But Stephen figured out a way to do it," Natasha said. "He was investigating wrongdoing in the U.S. Attorney's Office. Once he got his evidence, he was going to go public with it. He'd smuggled out some case files. Hunter sent Hamilton Sanders, Maguire's assistant, here to get them back. He's probably at the police station right now."

"Evidence of what wrongdoing?" Mac wanted to know.

"That I don't know," she said, "I only know that he was planning to make a big media splash by exposing or insinuating unethical, or maybe downright illegal, dealings in the prosecutor's office to get his name and face out there. Then he planned to ride that media wave to get appointed U.S. Attorney for D.C."

"But if he found something dirty and went public with it, wouldn't that ruin Hunter's chances of getting appointed attorney general?" Archie asked.

"Yeah!" Natasha said. "But Stephen didn't care about that."

"The way Maguire saw it, he could win either way, whether Hunter got the appointment or not," explained Garrison.

Mac said, "If Maguire was onto something and the man who had put him on the fast track got wind of it—"

"Which he did," Natasha smirked.

"You sold him out and warned Hunter," Mac said.

"Stephen did nothing to earn my loyalty." She pointed out, "It wasn't a week later that someone slipped arsenic into his champagne at a retirement party for Judge Anderson at the Chase Club."

Archie wanted to know, "How do we know you weren't the one who slipped it to him? Were you at that party?"

"Yes, I was there, but I had no reason to want him dead." She glanced at Gnarly as if to tell him that she wanted him dead.

"What were you doing Saturday night?" Mac asked her. "Were you here at Deep Creek Lake?"

"I won't dignify that question with an answer," she replied forcefully. "For one thing, you're not even a cop anymore. You have no right to treat me like a murder suspect."

"You came to me," Mac reminded her. "I doubt if you drove all the way out here from Washington only to give me your condolences."

"Half of the attorney's office was at that party," she scoffed, "people who I just told you Maguire had been investigating."

"Where were you while your husband was being killed?" Archie demanded to know.

"She was with me," Garrison answered in a bored tone. He asked Natasha, "Why do you have to make everything so hard?" He went on to tell them, "Yes, we've been in the area since the Thursday before the murder. Purely coincidence. Natasha and I are staying at the Carmel Cove Inn, a favorite little bed and breakfast we like to visit in the autumn. We checked in Thursday afternoon. We were already here in Deep Creek Lake when we got the call from the police." He responded to Natasha's glare by telling her, "A simple check of your cell record would have told the police that we were already here."

"Can you give us names of witnesses to confirm you were at the Carmel Cove Inn?" Mac asked.

Garrison said, "The owner saw us when we came back from dinner and went up to our room at around ten o'clock Saturday night."

"Okay, we answered your stupid and insulting questions and it's apparent that you don't intend to willingly turn over my husband's things, so I guess we'll be going on our way." Natasha stood up.

When Gnarly mirrored her move, she uttered a growl from deep in her throat.

"Just one more thing," Mac asked before she had time to follow Judge Sutherland into the foyer. "Do you have any idea what business Stephen may have had here in Spencer?"

Tearing her attention from the dog escorting her out, she turned back to him. "Business?"

"He paid for his suite with a federal government credit card," Mac explained. "That tells me it was a business trip."

"That doesn't mean he was here on business," Natasha laughed. "Stephen never paid for anything with his own money unless he had to. That's one of the reasons I kicked him out. Most likely his visit was enjoyment."

"He was seen out here with a woman," Garrison said.

"And Christine tried to punch her lights out. She also announced to everyone within hearing distance that she was going to kill him dead hours before he got his," Natasha reminded them. "I did hear about Stephen having a new woman. I never saw her. Personally, I didn't care to see her. I couldn't care less about what he was up to."

"Unless he pawned your father's watch," Mac said.

*   *   *   *

Until Mac was officially cleared of suspicion, David wouldn't let him in on any details in his murder investigation. Unable to stand not knowing what the police had uncovered, Mac met his only source into the goings on: Hector Langford, the Spencer Inn's chief of security.

A lean, gray-haired Australian, Hector had been with the Inn for over twenty-five years, which was longer than Jeff Ingle had worked there. Hector knew the resort inside and out. When they'd first met, he took great delight in informing Mac that Robin Spencer had often asked for his help in planning her murders for her books.

With it being mid-week, the Inn's restaurant was quiet for their nine o'clock meeting. Mac wondered if the murders could be the reason for the solitude. Jeff had been predicting guest registrations would plummet as a result of the press about the owner's ex-wife and her lover getting slaughtered in his private suite. So far though, there'd been no cancellations.

After placing their breakfast order, Mac asked Hector, "What can you tell me?"

"The maid did it."

"Which maid?" Mac turned to scrutinize a woman in the cleaning staff uniform washing the windows.

Every Spencer Inn employee wore a uniform. Office and desk clerks were distinguished by their black suits with white shirts. The restaurant staff wore white long-sleeved shirts over black slacks with a black apron that hung down to their knees. A similar uniform with black smock or apron was reserved for the cleaning staff.

No matter what type of uniform the employee wore, it displayed the resort's insignia, which consisted of the Spencer family crest, stenciled on the blazer's breast pocket or on the top portion of the apron.

"The maid did it?" Mac asked Hector to elaborate on what sounded like something out of a B-movie. It sounded as bad as saying that the butler did it.

Both men sat back and fell silent while the server returned to the table with the bread basket and fresh coffee.

"The name she gave was Nita," Hector told him in a low voice.

"The name she gave?" Mac repeated. "Don't you know? If she's an employee—"

"That's the problem," the security chief said. "No one knows her except for a few service people who never saw her until a few days before the murders and never since. The chief of housekeeping has no idea who this Nita is. It's very embarrassing. I'm surprised Jeff said nothing to you."

When their food arrived, they fell silent while the server placed their plates in front of them. Mac had ordered French toast and sausage while Hector had ordered a fruit and yogurt plate.

"Tell me about this Nita." Mac poured the syrup over his French toast.

"According to everyone who spoke to her, she barely knew English, if any," Hector reported. "We got her on the security video. Unfortunately, we don't have a good enough picture to show anyone. The service staff gave us a description though."

"Why would she kill them?" Mac took a bite from his French toast. He chewed while waiting for the security chief to answer his question.

Hector stared at his plate.

Mac asked, "Does anyone have any idea who she is?"

"All we know is that she had long thick black hair and wore black glasses. She was seen wearing a cleaning uniform mixing in with the help."

"What about the key card that all the employees get?" Mac pointed at the identification card that Hector kept in his breast pocket.

For security, all employees had identification cards that contained encrypted codes which allowed them access into areas where they needed to work. Key cards wouldn't grant access for areas where the employee had no reason to enter. For example, a bartender's key card wouldn't allow him into the accounting office. Since access cards were needed to get into several areas of the resort, most employees wore them attached to lanyard cords around their necks. Other employees would clip them onto their belts.

There were very few security key cards that granted access into all areas of the Spencer Inn resort. Mac possessed one. As the Inn's manager, Jeff Ingle also had one, as did Hector Langford and his deputy chief.

The security chief told Mac, "The employees I interviewed said she wore a lanyard cord around her neck and they saw what looked like a security pass in her breast pocket. But when I pressed them, they realized they never saw her use it."

"It was for show."

"She could've used any card or had her picture taped to a white blank one." Hector laughed. "It's one of the oldest tricks in the book. A guy hangs out in front of an apartment building that has a security lock. When someone else goes in, the guy follows him inside. Happens all the time."

"But who..."

Hector took a sip of his coffee before saying, "The police found a black wig and black glasses and the smock from the Spencer Inn cleaning uniform in Christine's suitcase. Nita was first seen here at the Inn on Thursday. That's the same day Stephen Maguire checked in. No one has seen her since the murders." His tone softened. "I'm sorry to say this, Mac, but I think she was stalking Maguire. I'm pretty certain the police agree."

"What does David O'Callaghan say?"

"He's not talking to anyone." His displeasure about not being on the inside of David O'Callaghan's investigation was evident.

Jeff Ingle appeared at Mac's elbow. "How are you and your family holding up?"

"We'll be okay." Mac thought, *What's the alternative?*

Jeff slid into the seat next to him. "I just wanted to let you know that I'm worried about something."

"You're always worried about something." Mac finished off the last of his French toast. "That's what I pay you for."

Seeming to miss the humor behind Mac's comment, the manager plunged on. "Stephen Maguire was killed three days ago. The media has covered it. I've seen it on the news. They say the Maguire family has refused comment and to date, no one from the Maguire family has contacted me. You'd think Ed would have at least gotten a call from their lawyer."

"Isn't no call from them a good thing?" Mac asked. "Do you want them to call to accuse us of wrongdoing?"

Jeff mopped his brow with the napkin from the place setting he was sitting at. "No, I don't want the Maguire family demanding to know what we did wrong. But no call at all from them? No family representative telling the media that they intend to get to the bottom of this? That doesn't happen."

"I haven't released any statements about Christine's death," Mac pointed out.

"You aren't Broderick Maguire." Jeff leaned in to whisper, "It makes me wonder if they aren't saying anything because they're preparing to slap us with a humungous multi-million dollar wrongful death lawsuit."

"We didn't do anything wrong." Hector pounded the table top with his fist. "Whoever killed those people are the ones who did something wrong."

"But the hole in our security is what allowed it to happen," Jeff said.

"Now you sound like you're talking for their side," the security chief objected.

Mac was grateful for the vibration on his hip signaling the call on his phone. It gave him an excuse to end the conversation. "Quiet, men." He checked the text on his phone.

Jeff looked as if he feared that his wish to hear something from the Maguire family had been answered. "What is it?"

Mac smiled. "Spencer's police chief is now ready to talk."

CHAPTER FIVE

The Spencer police department resembled a mountain sports club. The offices were housed in a three-story log building on the lake with a boat launch and dock. The cruisers were all-wheel drive SUVs in order to make their way up and down the mountain, both on and off the road. The department also had four speed boats and a fleet of jet skis for patrolling the lake.

A fire was roaring in the stone fireplace in the reception area when Mac arrived for his meeting with David.

The desk clerk, Tonya, had lived on the lake her whole life. Many suspected the long hours she put in at the station were an excuse to not go home, to which two of her three grown children had returned with their offspring after a short time spent in the outside world.

Tonya greeted Mac with her usual toothy grin and asked about life at the manor, Archie, and Gnarly. Sometimes, Mac felt like she was simply going through the paces while making small talk until they arrived upon the topic of Gnarly and his latest escapades. She had three dogs of her own that she clearly loved more than her kids. The dogs were more self-sufficient and independent.

On this visit, Tonya was unable to resist asking for the low-down on Gnarly's bone theft. "When are you going to bring Gnarly in for his mug shots?" she asked with a laugh.

"Depending on what progress David is making on his investigation, maybe Gnarly and I can both get fingerprinted and photographed at the same time," Mac replied. "Do you think they'll let us share a cell?"

When he stepped to the back of the reception area to go upstairs to David's corner office, she stopped him. "The chief wants you to meet him in the conference room."

Mac cringed. He winced a second time when she asked if he would mind turning in the semi-automatic he wore concealed under his shirt. In all the times that he had visited David at the station, he had never been asked to check his weapon.

While he wasn't completely up to speed on how the Spencer police did things, Mac was familiar enough with procedure to know that interrogations took place in the conference room where they could be recorded. He half-wished that he didn't know as much as he did about the workings behind the scenes of a murder investigation.

Tonya escorted him to the room he had suspected he would be interrogated in. It had a two-way mirror, and a hidden camera built into the intercom.

"Would you like a soda?" she asked before leaving to return to the front desk. The mention of the soft drink made him realize how thirsty he was. At the same time, he was too offended to appreciate her offer.

This meeting wasn't going to be a friendly little sit-down. It couldn't be.

The media was all over Deep Creek Lake covering the murders in the penthouse belonging to Robin Spencer's son. The story was too juicy not to cover. Even though his statement had been taken and evidence collected, journalists were still asking, "Has Mac Faraday been questioned yet? Is he a suspect?"

If David didn't formally question the media's prime suspect, then when the real killer was found, the defense attorney would quickly lay the groundwork for an acquittal with insinuations of police cover-up. The fact that Mac was the direct descendent of the town's founders was enough. If it became public knowledge that the police chief was his half brother, then the media would have the town council screaming for David's badge. Even with no cover-up, the appearance of an impropriety would be enough grounds to fire him.

David had to question Mac, and he had no choice but to do it by the book.

Still, Mac couldn't help feeling insulted.

His first instinct was to sit at the table with his back to the camera. Reminding himself of why this interview had to take place, he took the chair of honor facing the camera and two-way mirror.

Looking at his reflection, Mac wondered if Ben Fleming, the prosecuting attorney, was waiting in the room next door to observe the interrogation. So far, all he had heard from Ben was a phone call urging Mac to let him know if he needed anything. Mac wondered if the Maguire family had been talking to the county prosecutor instead of Jeff.

Mac wished he was on the other side of the mirror looking in. Now he was going to find out what it felt like to sit on this side of the table. So far, he didn't like it.

"Hey, Mac," David called out when he came in. In one hand he carried a coffee mug. In the other, he had the root beer Mac had requested from Tonya. A bag of donuts hung from the fingertips of the hand grasping the soft drink. "Have you had breakfast yet?"

Having eaten Archie's croissants and the French toast, Mac clutched his stomach. "Sorry. I'm stuffed."

David held a brown accordion folder so thick that it threatened to drop out from where he had it pressed against his ribs with an elbow. After tossing the folder onto the table, David set the root beer in front of Mac before placing a donut from the bag in front of his place. He then went back out into the hallway and called out, "Anybody want some donuts? We have plenty."

Alone with the accordion folder that obviously contained files, Mac's curiosity took hold. He wondered what the collection of files had to do with Christine's and Maguire's murders. He saw that there was a yellow notepad under the brown folder.

"This case has had me running around all over town," David announced when he came back into the interrogation room. "I've been living on fast food."

"Murder cases are like that," Mac said. "You'll get used to it."

"I hope you don't mind if I eat while we do this." The police chief took a bite out of his donut and chewed before washing it down with a gulp of his coffee.

Both grateful and suspicious about his pleasant nature, Mac eyed the thick folder that David had shoved to the side. "What's that?"

"Just some case files."

After taking a big bite from the donut, he wiped his mouth with a paper napkin, opened his leather-bound notepad, and took out his pen. "Unfortunately, the DNA from the skin under Christine's fingernails wasn't viable. There was bleach all over that room and the medical examiner thinks her hands were soaked or wiped down with it. Forensics didn't get any usable DNA."

"Then the DNA you collected from me was useless."

"Of course, you're aware that bleach destroys DNA." David spoke around another bite of his donut. "If that was your skin under her fingernails, we can't prove it."

"You also can't clear me," Mac said. "If I was going to kill Christine and Maguire, the last place I would've done it would be my private suite. Every cable news station around has been at the Inn asking when I'm going to be arrested. They've been hounding Willingham for a statement, which he won't give. Do you think I like being under a microscope? Do you think I enjoy getting calls from my daughter, crying because one of her friends asked her if her daddy flipped out and killed her mother? If you can't use DNA to clear my name, then I'll do it the old-fashioned way."

Even as the words came out of his mouth, Mac regretted allowing his temper to slip. He thought of how many suspects who had spouted similar declarations of innocence that he had ignored.

"My dad didn't raise no dummy." With a chuckle, David referred to his notes. "My officers have questioned everyone at and around the Spencer Inn. No one saw you. Of course, since you're the boss, your employees could be lying."

"I wasn't there."

"Hector voluntarily handed over the security tapes immediately. The originals. Of course, he made copies for the Inn's own investigation. Forensics confirmed that they haven't been edited. You aren't on them anywhere after checking Christine in. Nor did your access card get used."

"Then I'm cleared."

"Were you that quick to clear a suspect when you were a detective?" David asked.

Mac didn't want to admit that he wasn't.

"You have enough money that you could've paid to have it done." Even though David's tone was casual, Mac picked up a serious note to it.

"What would be my motive?" he asked. "Christine did make a bid for part of my inheritance, but the judge laughed her out of court. We were through. I've moved on."

"Calm down," David told him. "We took a look at your financials, with a warrant, of course. There're no suspicious withdrawals or transfers that look like they went to pay for a hit."

The police chief concluded, "I know you didn't do this, but you aren't the only one that's had people breathing down your neck. The town council ordered me to haul you in here in the back of a cruiser for the media to see to prove that we aren't crooked and you don't own Spencer's law enforcement. I wouldn't do it. But I still had to do all I could and look at this from every angle before I could scratch your name off my list."

With a stroke of his pen across the notepad, David put a line through Mac's name.

"I appreciate that," Mac replied. "As long as I'm sitting in your hot seat, can you make it worth my while? Tell me what you do have on Christine's murder."

"T.O.D is ten-thirty," David recounted from his notes in his case file. "You need a key card to go anywhere in the hotel except the general public areas. Security doesn't register when a guest opens the door from inside the room to let someone else in. It only registers when the key card is used. Based on the evidence we've collected and what we know, Christine had stayed in the suite after you left and never went anywhere, or even used the phone in her room. Her cell records indicate that she had called her sister Roxanne Burton shortly after you checked her in, at around five-thirty, to tell her about her spending the night at your penthouse."

"Did you get a statement from Roxanne?"

David leafed through some reports before stopping to tap his pen on the statement Mac was asking about. "Roxanne told us that Christine had been depressed ever since Maguire left her a few weeks ago. Roxanne suggested that she come out here to a lake house they have to clear her head. She came out on Thursday, which happens to be the same day Stephen Maguire checked into the Spencer Inn. Roxanne swears that it was only a coincidence."

Mac was startled. "I never knew Christine was here. I thought she'd come out the same day that she showed up at my house."

"She was in Spencer," David said. "At six-thirty-seven, according to hotel records, Christine ordered two filet mignon dinners and a bottle of red wine from room service, which was delivered at around seven. The server said Christine was alone when he delivered the dinners. Shortly after eight o'clock, her cell records show a series of calls to Stephen Maguire's cell. He was having dinner with a woman, who we have yet to identify, in the restaurant. Their dinner ended between eight-thirty and nine o'clock. Security records indicate that he used his key card to go up to his floor and enter his room around that time. Meanwhile, from eight o'clock on, Christine kept calling his cell every ten to fifteen minutes—for over two hours until Maguire finally called her back at around ten-fifteen. They spoke for four minutes. He used his key card to take the elevator up to the penthouse floor at around ten-thirty, at which time he was killed."

After setting down his pen, David folded his hands on top of the folder. "Did Christine speak Spanish?"

Mac replied, "Hector told me that you suspect she was stalking Stephen Maguire."

"Then you know about the black wig and Spencer Inn cleaning service smock we found in Christine's room." David popped the last bite of his donut in his mouth and washed it down with coffee. "The Inn's security videos have footage of a woman in a black wig who seems to be following Maguire while he was there. Employees who encountered her said she knew very little English."

"I can't believe Christine would kill anyone," Mac argued.

David said, "If she had summered here at the lake throughout the years, she would know what she needed to do in order to mix in with Inn employees so that she could follow him. Maguire did ruin her life. According to her sister, a couple of weeks ago she filed a petition to have Christine declared mentally incompetent."

"I don't want my children to think their mother was a lunatic," Mac insisted. "She was an alcoholic and she had made some very bad decisions but—"

"Someone went to a lot of trouble to make this happen." David sat forward in his seat. "Maybe Christine was stalking Maguire, but someone else was in that room. We found a black wig in her things. It had her hair and epidermal cells in it. She wore it. We also found black hairs from a wig in Stephen Maguire's blood and caught in a class ring he was wearing. Whoever attacked him—stabbed him twenty-seven times—was wearing a black wig. But it wasn't the wig Christine had in her suitcase. The way the blood was splattered in that attack, the wig would've gotten some in it. There was no blood in the wig we found and it hadn't been washed."

Mac said, "That proves Christine didn't kill Maguire."

"She got into a fight with someone besides Maguire," David said. "He had defensive wounds, but no scratches. Also, Christine died of a cervical fracture but she didn't get it in the shower tub."

"She didn't fall and hit her head on the towel rack?"

"Her blood alcohol level was point-two-six, plus she had enough Valium in her to kill an elephant. It's unbelievable that she was even conscious." David marveled. "Her head wound didn't match with the towel rack or anything else in the shower tub, but it does match with the corner of the sink. We believe that she got into a fight with whoever was cleaning up the bathroom after Stephen Maguire's murder—"

"The killer had to be covered in blood after stabbing him twenty-seven times," Mac agreed.

"With all the alcohol and drugs in her system, Christine had to be unconscious. The killer puts on her clothes and kills Maguire in order to get his blood on Christine's clothes to make it look like she'd done it. Christine comes to while the killer is getting rid of the evidence and attacks the killer, getting skin under her fingernails. Christine falls and hits her head. The medical examiner said she died instantly." He added in a soft voice, "So she didn't suffer."

"That's good to know."

"The killer put Christine's body in the tub to make it look like she'd killed Maguire and then had an accident while cleaning up." David folded his hands on top of his notepad. "Tell me about Stephen Maguire."

"If you're any type of detective, you've already found out all about Stephen Maguire," Mac countered.

"I want to know what you know about him."

"He was a bastard," Mac said. "He broke up my family."

"Didn't you two work together?"

"Yes." Mac swallowed in hopes of keeping down the anger that he still felt rising inside his chest when he talked about Stephen Maguire. "He was an assistant U.S. attorney in the District of Columbia. I worked with him on some murder cases. In my personal opinion, the only reason he got as far as he did was because he was a Maguire."

"I'm not up on the social register," confessed David.

"Neither was I until I had the displeasure of working with Stephen Maguire," Mac said. "In the twenty-odd years that I was a homicide detective, I got to know a lot of U.S. attorneys. Some were okay. Others were great. Maguire wasn't either. But because his great-grandfather was Everett Maguire—"

"And that's important because?"

Mac chuckled. "You really aren't into high society goings-on."

"All bastards look the same to me no matter who their daddy is."

"Everett Maguire was a Supreme Court Justice a hundred years ago," Mac explained. "He was a blue-blood from off the Mayflower, or something like that. He had eight children. Half of them went on to become self-made millionaires. The other half married into millions. They all went into high society and became movers and shakers about town. Broderick Maguire went into real estate and by the 1940s owned half of D.C. Now, he's a billionaire. He had seven kids. I think he has like fifty grandkids and a dozen great-grandchildren." He held up his hands as if he was going to count up the Maguire family on his fingers. "And that isn't counting Broderick's brothers and sisters and nieces and nephews. The Maguires own high society in the United States Capitol."

"And Stephen Maguire is—was—one of them?" David asked while referring to a report from his case file.

"What Maguire lacked in legal know-how, he made up for in arrogance and political pull," Mac said. "He never let anyone forget about his family connections. The judge who presided over my divorce had a son who wanted to get into

74

the same fraternity at George Washington University that Maguire and his family had belonged to. She buried me. The kid got in."

David's expression was one of genuine confusion while he sipped his coffee.

Mac finished off his root beer. Seeing his reflection in the mirror, he remembered that they were being watched and was surprised that he had forgotten. He guessed that David had appointed his deputy Bogie to do the honors.

"Has the crime scene been cleared yet?" Mac asked.

Ignoring his question about the crime scene, David said, "I was hoping that you could clear some things up, but instead I'm more confused."

Mac cringed again. He thought of how many times he had started interrogations with a pleasant request that the suspect clear up some confusion. He reminded himself that David had said he was cleared as a suspect.

David removed two reports from his folder. "I'm sure you know that it's SOP to run background and credit checks on murder victims." He turned the report around for Mac to review. "Christine was in hock up to her eyebrows. Did you know that?"

"Ed told that to me yesterday. Apparently, my ex-wife was living large."

"Did Ed tell you about the state of Stephen Maguire's finances?"

"He had no reason to check on Maguire's finances," Mac said.

Turning the second report around, David asked, "How long were Maguire and Christine together?"

"A couple of years."

David held the paper down with his hand over the top. "This is where I get confused. The way Jeff is acting you'd think Maguire was Prince William, complete with the silver spoon still in his mouth. But that's not what I see here." He slid the report across the table to Mac.

The personal and financial report read quite differently from what Mac had expected.

As Mac had expected, the report showed that Stephen Douglas Maguire was a lawyer with the U.S. Attorney's Office in the District of Columbia. He was also a graduate of George Washington University Law School.

Mac was surprised to find that, before law school, Stephen Maguire had in fact received his bachelor's in political science from The Ohio State University. He swore that someone had told him that Maguire had received his bachelor's from Oxford University.

Mac was still scratching his head over that when David gave him the run-down. "Maguire was nowhere near in debt. On the contrary. He'd made some good investments and had substantial money in various accounts. He's made large deposits. He's got a condo in Hilton Head and a boat. He's got a Hummer and BMW, all registered in his name. According to Christine's credit report, the lease for the Beemer is in her name."

"He's got the car; she's got the payment book. Sweet," Mac noted with sarcasm.

"His most recent investment was some commercial property right here on Deep Creek Lake."

Mac felt his blood pressure jump up a notch. "Here?"

"Sully's over on the other side of the lake," David explained. "The perfect establishment for lakeside dining."

Mac knew the property. Sully's had been a lakeside restaurant and lounge. The outdoor patio was adjacent to boat docks that allowed customers to dock their boats and jet skis in order to relax for dinner or a cocktail before going back out onto the water. Mac and Archie had eaten there once before it was foreclosed on and the property put up for sale.

It was located directly across the lake from Spencer Point.

"How would you feel about Stephen Maguire, the man your wife traded you up for, opening a restaurant and watering hole directly across the lake from you?" David asked. "You'd see his place first thing in the morning when you got up and his joint would be the last thing you'd see before going to bed at night."

"I had no idea Maguire was moving out here," Mac argued. "Why would he? He was on the fast track with the prosecutor's office when I left Georgetown."

"Don't worry. I believe you," David said in a calm voice. "It was a surprise to me, too. I knew the bank had sold the property. I didn't know who to." Without exerting any effort to conceal the information from Mac, he studied the reports in his file.

From across the table, Mac read upside down the list of known addresses for Stephen Maguire. He had moved many times over the course of the last several years.

"Maguire was well to do, but his finances don't look like what you'd expect of someone descended from billionaires and millionaires," David said. "He had money. He was worth about one and a half million, but from what I see in their credit reports, that's because they were living off Christine's money while he was socking his away."

"His grandfather was Broderick Maguire," Mac argued.

"Who were his parents?" David asked.

Mac's mind went blank. As he thought back over the years that Stephen Maguire had been in his life, he realized he had never asked, and was never told, who Maguire's parents were. He didn't care. He was only reminded when he felt like decking Maguire that he was a member of D.C.'s unofficial royal family.

David recalled some friends who came from affluent families who weren't allowed free access to their parents' fortunes. "There're many wealthy families that insist their kids earn their own way. They want to teach them the value of a dollar."

He went on to tell of two brothers with whom he had attended school who became drug dealers when their parents insisted they earn their own money.

"Think about it," David said. "Their parents made their fortune before they had these kids. All they saw was Mom and

Dad hobnobbing with the rich and making business deals over cocktails or while playing golf. Then, they're told that they need to learn how to work hard. Thing is, all they knew how to do was use their charm to make big money. Working hard was a foreign concept to them. Now these two guys I knew are spending life in prison for two murders instead of hitting golf balls at the Inn." He suggested, "Maybe that's what happened with Stephen Maguire."

"Are you trying to make me feel sorry for him?" Mac gritted his teeth so hard that his jaw hurt. "From what you're telling me, Stephen Maguire worked hard and earned his own way by living off his mistresses."

"One of the oldest games in the book," David explained. "I believe the name for men like Maguire is gigolo. Then once the money runs out," he tapped his copy of the credit report on Christine, "like it did for your ex-wife, he moves on to a fresher target. Kind of like one of those vampires you were watching with Gnarly the other night."

"After I moved out, they went on cruises," Mac recalled. "They spent last New Year's Eve in Paris." A quick check of the report confirmed that Christine had paid for the trip via a credit card. "I thought at the time that it was Maguire's money they were spending." He glanced down at Christine's credit report. Her rating had fallen like a boulder in two short years. He shoved the report across the table so hard that it flew over the police chief's shoulder. "Bastard!"

David reminded him, "That bastard was staying in your inn the night he was killed."

"I didn't know he was there until Christine attacked him while I was checking her in."

David leaned across the table toward him. "Why did you take her there? The manor has seven bedrooms. Why didn't you let her stay there with you?"

"Because I didn't want her to stay there with me," Mac argued. "You saw her. Christine wanted to reconcile and I didn't. If I had let her spend the night, especially in the frame of mind she was in, it would have given her some glimmer of hope that I'd take her back and I didn't want her to have that hope."

David asked, "And you had no idea that Stephen Maguire was going to be at the Inn at the same time?"

"I know it sounds like a very big coincidence, but that's what it was. Anything other than that, I'm unaware of." Mac thought about how many times suspects had said those exact same words to him and he didn't believe them.

David referred to his notes. "Jeff told me that this isn't the first time Stephen Maguire has stayed at the Inn."

"With Christine?" Mac wondered if his ex-wife had come to the manor intending for him to take her to the Inn in order to make Maguire jealous.

"No," David answered. "Jeff swears he'd never seen her there before. But he could be mistaken. The Inn has thousands upon thousands of guests a year. However, he's positive that Maguire has never been at the Inn with Christine." He tapped a page of his notes with the tip of his pen. "Jeff told me that Maguire came to the Inn regularly. Always during ski season. Always with different women. He always booked a deluxe suite with a view of the lake."

"It's not ski season yet." Mac leaned across the table to decipher the upside-down words in the police chief's notes.

"What's different about this visit is that Maguire booked a basic suite at the last minute during the height of the leaf peeper season. He was willing to take whatever he could get." David added, "He also came alone."

Mac recalled, "There was a woman with him the afternoon before the murders. Maybe she's local and he met her here. Any ID on the woman?"

"Not yet," David said. "My officers are showing her picture from the security cameras around the Inn to see if anyone knows her. No evidence in the room suggests that he had someone staying with him. Forensics did find vaginal fluid on his sheets and are working up a DNA profile on her. Could be the same woman you saw him with. The desk clerk says he was alone when he checked in and paid with a federal credit card. Any idea what case he may have been working on?"

Mac shook his head. "I left the police department five months ago."

"What about cases that were still open when you left?" David suggested.

"They were all passed on to other investigators."

"How about cases that hadn't gone to trial yet?"

"There were a couple, but Maguire wasn't the prosecutor on record for those cases," Mac said. "I wasn't the only homicide detective in Georgetown. He could've been working on another detective's case."

"I don't think so," David said. "I think Maguire was on a business trip and I think it was one of your cases." He removed the yellow notepad from where it had been hiding under the accordion folder and slid it across the table to land in front of Mac. "This was found in Maguire's room next to this folder."

At the top of the notepad on the first line, in block capital letters, was the word *THEMIS.*

The lines below read:

VM. Emma Wilkes: RE: Dylan Booth
 # Cases. How far back?

Two lines below that note was the notation that Mac sensed had captured the police chief's interest: *Call M. Faraday?*

"What's Themis?" David asked.

"I have no idea," Mac told him. "Emma Wilkes might be the woman we saw Maguire with. She may also be the one who slipped between his sheets."

David said, "The same thought occurred to me. Jeff says there's no one registered at the Inn by that name. What about Dylan Booth?"

"Dylan Booth was one of my cases."

David sat back in his seat and pressed his palms and fingertips against each other. "Tell me about him."

"A law clerk I accused Maguire of killing," Mac said. "This was before he slept with my wife."

"What interest would Maguire have in a law clerk?"

Mac told him, "I had no doubt in my mind but that Maguire was capable of murder and the evidence made him a suspect."

"Do you mean like the other man being found dead in your private suite?" David asked.

"Touché," Mac replied. "I was certain Maguire was involved in something dirty having to do with this clerk, but I couldn't place him at the crime scene. Plus, I came up blank finding out what that dirty deal was. I came up with nothing."

While David sipped his cold coffee, Mac went on. "Dylan Booth worked for Judge Randolph Daniels, one of the most influential judges in D.C. He was in his last year of law school. One Saturday someone shot him in the parking lot when he was leaving his office. On the surface, it looked like a robbery. His watch and wallet were missing."

"Why do you think it wasn't?"

"The security guard at the building said that when Booth left he was carrying a folder box and that it was heavy. That was missing along with Booth's laptop."

"What was in the box? Case files?" David drew his attention to the note on Maguire's notepad about the number of cases.

"We assume so. Neither the laptop or box have ever been located."

"Why would someone steal case files unless there was something incriminating in them?" David wondered. "Did you ask the judge's staff if anything was missing from their records?"

"I'd been a detective for a very long time," Mac reminded him with a grin. "The staff said nothing was missing."

"Maybe the judge—"

"Would you believe the judge had committed suicide the night before?"

"Really?" The expression on David's face was one of instant suspicion.

Mac cleared that thought from his mind. "Judge Daniels was eighty-four years old. His doctor diagnosed him with brain cancer. He went home and said nothing. That night, after his wife went to bed, he went down to his study and blew his brains out with a Colt revolver."

"Any possibility of—"

"Nope," Mac interrupted. "He left a suicide note saying that he'd rather go out with a bang than chemo. Everyone who knew him said that was his style. There was absolutely no connection."

"If it weren't for this note, I'd think Booth went to the office to clean out his stuff because he knew that he was out of a job with no judge to clerk to. The box had his desk stuff in it."

"I don't think so," Mac argued. "Stephen Maguire was the last person Booth spoke to minutes before someone blew his brains out. He claimed Booth called him to ask for a recommendation for his application to the U.S. Attorney's Office."

"But you didn't believe that," David said.

"It was Saturday afternoon. People don't call lawyers' offices for job interviews on Saturdays. We never found any other suspects and the case went cold. It always bugged me. Maybe because I knew in my gut that Maguire was involved and got away with it." He looked down at the notepad resting between his hands. "This proves I was right."

"Or wrong," David said. "Maguire made that note to call you unless there's another M. Faraday you think he knows. At least he was thinking about calling you. Maybe he found evidence to prove that he wasn't involved and wanted to call you to tell you who was."

Mac concluded, "And that someone killed him and Christine."

CHAPTER SIX

"Are you going to show me what's in there?" Mac asked about the accordion folder that had been taunting him during the interview with the police chief.

"Since Maguire made a note to call you, maybe you can shed some light on it." David shoved the folder across the table in his direction.

Mac studied the front of the folder. One word was written in thick black marker with block lettering across the front: THEMIS.

"Could Themis be the name of a victim from one of your cases?" David asked him. "You said that you've investigated well over a hundred murders."

"I never forget the name of a victim," Mac said. "When you take on the responsibility of finding out who killed someone, you'll never forget their name or their face." He shook his head. "I've never run into the name Themis."

He opened the folder sealed shut with a rubber band. Inside, a single sheet of paper rested on top of four files.

"Where did you find this?" he asked David.

"On the table next to the window in his suite," he replied. "We found a mini-laptop, his cell phone, pen, and his car keys next to the notepad. It looked like he'd been working on something when he finally decided to answer Christine's calls and went up to the penthouse to get killed."

A list of names was written out in long hand. Freddie Gibbons. Sid Baxter. Jillian Keating. Leo Samuels. Gerald Hogan. Douglas Propst.

Mac turned the paper around so he could read it. "It's a list of killers. Most of these cases I've worked on."

He tapped the fourth name with his finger. "I arrested Leo Samuels. He was a pimp and drug dealer on his way up. Got some kid to kill a girl he'd snatched from Union Station who refused to go to work for him, even after he'd raped her and beat her to a pulp. The kid rolled on Samuels, then got knifed in jail before the trial. The guy was a monster. Not an ounce of remorse."

Seeing that the case still got under Mac's skin, David said, "I take it by the look on your face that he got off."

"His lawyer got everything suppressed since the kid wasn't alive to testify. According to everything that I got on Samuels, it wasn't the first time. He knew the way the system worked inside and out. The guy was smarter than some lawyers I know." He sighed. "But for all his smarts it didn't do him any good. Less than six months later he was dead and another gang member took his place in the hierarchy."

David said, "Sometimes I wonder why we bother wasting our time."

Studying the label on the top file, Mac opened the cover and read the first sheet of paper. It was a letter. "Look at this." He held it out to David.

"What is it?"

"It's a letter from the police in Paris." Mac explained the contents. "It says that according to the results of a DNA test made at Maguire's request, they have positively identified a John Doe found in a hostel in Paris as Frederick Gibbons Junior."

David spun the folder around to view the discovery. "Isn't that the rapist and killer that skipped the country less than an hour after the grand jury indicted him? The one that Maguire blamed on you for letting him escape? He's dead?"

Retrieving the report taken from him, Mac flipped the cover letter to study the sheet underneath. "This letter is from a private investigator hired by Gibbons's father to look for him."

"Didn't Gibbons fly out on his father's jet?"

Mac was still reading the private investigator's report. "A couple of months after they'd helped their son to escape, he disappeared. Their private investigator found an American John Doe matching Freddie's description murdered execution style around the time he stopped communicating with his parents."

"What would this have to do with Stephen Maguire's murder?"

"Gibbons was killed only a couple of months after he got away," Mac said slowly. "Maybe it was payback. Everyone on the inside knows Maguire was behind Gibbons's escape. It turns out Frederick Gibbons, Senior, and Maguire were friends. They used to be roommates in law school."

David almost spit out his coffee. "And Maguire didn't remove himself from the case?"

The police chief's shock amused Mac, who had seen more incidents of unfair politics played out in the justice system than he cared to remember. "If Maguire had done that, then he couldn't have stalled and blocked me as much as he did to keep Gibbons from getting arrested. It was only because I went over his head with the evidence I had against Freddie Gibbons Junior that Maguire finally took it to the grand jury. When they voted to indict, Maguire got word to Gibbons Senior to get his son out of the country. I missed him by less than an hour."

Mac shrugged his shoulders. "Of course, Maguire was so slick that it's yet another one of those things where everyone knows he did it, but no one could get enough proof to arrest or convict him of anything."

"But, if everyone knows he did it, why didn't his boss fire him?" David asked.

Chuckling, Mac said, "He was a Maguire. That's why. You really don't know anything about politics." He turned his attention back to Gibbons's fate. "Maybe the killer decided not to stop with Freddie, but the crooked prosecutor that let him escape."

"That's a lot of maybes," David said. "Gibbons ran off to Europe. If it was revenge, they would've had to find out what country he had run off to, fly overseas, and hunt him down in that country to kill him."

"Gibbons was murdered." Stunned, Mac repeated the word murdered over and over again while leafing through the reports in the file.

Peering at the bottom of his empty coffee mug, David said, "Granted, we don't have any of the evidence on hand for the Gibbons murder, but I can't help thinking it's farfetched to assume that it would be connected to our case."

Mac replied, "Most likely Gibbons's parents came to Maguire to find out who killed their son. I assume, since he was the one behind helping Freddie escape prosecution and getting out of the country, he's probably the only one who would have given enough of a damn to help them find out what happened to him."

"Did the P.I. find anything?"

"The clerk at the hostel said that Gibbons had a beautiful American woman with him when he checked in." Mac repeated, "She was American."

David argued, "There're a lot of American women in Europe. Gibbons was a sexual predator that'd killed one of his victims. This woman could have been getting even with him for a rape he'd committed over there after leaving here."

Mac shuffled the Gibbons folder to the bottom of the stack and read the label on the next one. "Jillian Keating. That's a name I haven't heard in a long time."

David's eyebrows met in the center of his forehead. "Another case in that folder rings a bell?"

"Eight years ago you couldn't turn on the news without seeing Jillian Keating." Mac thumbed through the pages in the file to refresh his memory. "Usual case. Andrew Keating was in his seventies. She was late twenties. Whirlwind romance. He married her in Vegas where she'd been a stripper. Days after the honeymoon ended, she poisoned him. I caught her. Defense got my evidence suppressed saying that the warrant wasn't valid." He laid his hand flat on top of the file. "Guess who her defense lawyer was."

"Who?"

"Natasha Holmstead," Mac told him. "Maguire's wife. The Keating case was the first time I got to see Holmstead up close and personal. She got Jillian Keating off."

He growled deep in his throat. "I can still see the smirk on Jillian Keating's face when she left the courthouse and climbed into the back of her limo after the case had been dismissed. I wanted to throttle her."

"The same way you wanted to do Gibbons?"

"It's cases like that, where you know who the killer is, and the killer knows you know, but you see them walk away..." Mac sighed. "When you actually see them walk away, and they look you right in the eye, and there's nothing you can do. There's no way you can make it right. Justice is completely out of your reach." He swallowed. "Cases like that haunt me."

"Who blew the prosecution? Maguire?"

Mac recalled, "George Vance was the prosecutor in the first chair on that case. This was a couple of years before he became Deputy U.S. Attorney. Vance is good, nothing like Maguire. He was as furious as I was when Keating got off. When Sutherland ruled to suppress my evidence, we ended up with nothing. Everyone knew she did it. But if the jury wasn't allowed to hear about the poison, then there was no way they'd convict. There'd be reasonable doubt. Makes me wonder."

David asked, "What makes you wonder?"

"Theoretically, Sutherland and Holmstead are on opposite sides," Mac said. "I remember back when Sutherland was a prosecutor. He was passionate about getting the bad guys off the street. Holmstead has gotten the slimiest of slime released. He tossed out my poison in the Keating case and now they're living together. I can't believe he's dirty though. Since they've gotten together, he removes himself from any cases that she's defense counsel on."

David stretched across the table to read the label for the next file, which was Leo Samuel. "You already told me about Samuels. What's in that last folder?" He slid the case file in Mac's direction.

"Hogan. First name Gerald." Mac turned the file around in order for him to read the label. "Gerry Hogan." He scanned the narrative until he recalled the case. "This wasn't my case, but I do remember it. Rape and murder following a college fraternity party. A freshman girl went to a frat party and had too much to drink. Gerry Hogan offered her a ride home. Only he slipped something into her last drink. He raped and strangled her. The case made it to trial. The prosecution had all the evidence they needed, but his lawyer put the victim on trial. They found where she'd uploaded some dirty videos of herself with S&M paraphernalia onto the Internet, and showed them to the jury. The defense claimed that she consented to the sex and the strangulation was an accident."

"Let me guess," David growled. "The jury refused to convict."

"It was hung. Prosecution saw no point in trying again since they knew the defense would trot out that video."

David spun the list of names around to read them over. "From what you're telling me, these are all cases of killers who got off."

Agreeing, Mac recounted Natasha's visit to Spencer Manor. "She told me that Maguire was investigating old cases in order to cause a scandal so that he could be appointed U.S. Attorney."

"Do you think something dirty was happening behind the scenes that got all these murderers off?"

Sitting back in his seat, Mac thought back over the events behind each of the cases.

While waiting for his answer, the police chief collected the files and replaced them in the accordion folder.

"Knowing the attorneys on each of these cases," Mac finally said, "the only one I would have suspected of taking a bribe to let a killer off would be Maguire. But he was the one digging this up and the one that got killed."

"He certainly wasn't any candidate for Good Guy of the Year," David said. "Even so, he had this list of cases for a reason. It looks like, if we want to find out who killed him and why, we're going to have to look back through them, too."

Keeping his hand on the list of names, Mac watched David seal the accordion folder. He wanted to smuggle the list home to ask Archie to research the cases in order to uncover the common thread between them. There had to be more of a connection than that they had all escaped justice.

"Give me the list, Mac." David held his hand out to him.

"What else have you got?"

"Hand me the list." David snapped his fingers.

"Before you let me see that folder you didn't know what this list of names meant. Now you know," Mac said. "I've cooperated with you. The least you can do is let me see the crime scene pictures and evidence box."

"I told you enough already." David snatched the paper from his hand. "As a matter of fact, I told you more than you have any need to know."

A tap at the door by one of his officers signaled the end of their interview. The police chief was needed outside. After unsealing the folder again to place the list inside and gathering everything he had brought into the room, they went out into the hall.

The commotion in the reception area could be heard throughout the station. Tonya stood back while Bogie, all six feet four inches of him, tried to contain Stephen Maguire's assistant.

"They belong to the office of the United States Attorney," Hamilton Sanders argued. His face was as red as his hair, which was so curly that it looked like he could bounce a ping pong ball on top of his head.

Based purely on a calculation of the number of years that he had been a lawyer with the U.S. Attorney's Office, Mac knew that Hamilton had to be in his mid-thirties. Between the freckles on his baby-face and his skinny frame clothed in an oversized suit, he looked like a teenager in his daddy's clothes.

Spying David with his gold chief's badge pinned on his chest, he rushed to plead his case while raising his voice in order to drown out any potential opposition from the deputy chief.

"Chief O'Callaghan, I am Hamilton Sanders. I have a letter here from United States Attorney Boris Hunter asking you to please turn over any case files you found in Stephen Maguire's room or otherwise in his possession." He waved his letter in front of David's face and chest in a non-verbal order for him to take and read it and do so now. "They're the property of the federal government and classified. We can't risk them falling into the wrong hands."

"Really?" David replied. "I was planning to make copies of them and post them onto the world wide web."

Not realizing the police chief was joking, the lawyer gasped. "You can't do that?"

"He's not serious, Ham." Mac shook his head at David to inform him that Hamilton Sanders didn't have a sense of humor.

Hamilton told him, "Lieutenant Faraday, you have no authority in this case. You aren't even a detective anymore."

"Stephen Maguire was murdered at my inn. That makes his murder my business."

"That plus him breaking up your marriage makes you a suspect," Hamilton countered. "Chief, I hate to be one telling you how to run your investigation, but it really isn't wise making suspects privy to the details of your case."

Hugging the accordion folder tight against his chest as if he feared the attorney would make a grab for it, David replied, "No less wise than handing over evidence to a suspect."

Hamilton gasped. "I resent that."

Instructing her to lock everything up, David handed the accordion folder and notepad to Tonya. The thick clumsy folder caused her to buckle under its heavy weight.

"About those files, Chief," the attorney said while watching them disappear up the stairs to David's secure file room.

"Tell your boss that he'll get them when I'm through with them," David said.

"I can't tell him that." Hamilton waved the unread letter in his face until David took it from him. "He sent me here with the express order to retrieve them ASAP."

Mac asked, "Why did Maguire take them and bring them to Spencer in the first place?"

Hamilton glared at Mac for his intrusion into their conversation, before turning back to David, who pointed out, "The man asked you a question."

Hamilton said, "I don't have to answer him."

David replied, "But you do have to answer me. If not, then I'll get the answer directly from your boss."

"Background work for an upcoming murder case, I suppose," Stephen Maguire's assistant said. "Mr. Hunter is asking you nicely for the return of those case files. He knows a lot of powerful people. One phone call and he can have me back here with a court order for you to turn them over."

"If he knows a Maryland judge who would put your runaway case files ahead of potential evidence in solving a murder, then tell him to go for it." David took a step toward Hamilton, who backed up at his advance. "In the meantime, they aren't going anywhere."

Wagging a finger in David's face, Hamilton's voice shook when he announced, "You haven't seen the last of me," before scurrying out the door.

CHAPTER SEVEN

Mac concluded there was something wrong with his psyche. When David finally agreed to permit him to see the crime scene photos and evidence collected for Christine's and Stephen Maguire's murders, his heart leapt, not unlike it used to when, as a child, he would wake up on Christmas morning in anticipation of unwrapping his presents under the tree.

Maybe it was genetic.

While reading his late mother's journal, Mac discovered that Robin Spencer expressed similar anticipation upon delving into a new murder investigation. Yes, she acknowledged the tragedy of someone's life being snatched away from them by another. But, she also marveled at the challenge of piecing together a puzzle which, in the end, could bring justice for the victim and closure for the family.

He wanted to have that closure for his children. He didn't want them to go through life not knowing what had happened to their mother.

"Did you know about someone trying to kill Stephen Maguire a couple of weeks ago?" Mac asked when he followed David into his corner office on the top floor of the police station. With a view of the boat dock and lake and a four-foot fish mounted over the stone fireplace, his office didn't resemble that of any police chief Mac had met in the past.

"I found that out the same day you found his body," David said. "I had a nice long talk with the investigating officer in Georgetown. He even sent me a copy of the file."

He set a black suitcase on the conference table. A slip of paper for the chain of evidence was connected to the strap. "This is the suitcase we found in Maguire's room." After checking the time on his watch, he signed the log slip.

"Why didn't you say anything to me about it?" Mac asked about the poisoning while opening the suitcase.

"I couldn't say anything until I officially cleared you as a suspect." David slipped the lid off the evidence box. "Here's what happened. A couple of weeks after he left Christine, Maguire went to a retirement party at some swanky club in Washington. Everyone who was anyone was there, including Christine. Around four in the morning, Maguire called 9-1-1. A couple of days later, the doctors figured out that he had been poisoned with arsenic. Luckily, it wasn't a fatal dose, but he was in the hospital for a week."

"Do the police in Washington suspect Christine of poisoning him?" Mac asked while examining Stephen Maguire's clothes. The suitcase contained a few changes of clothes. Nicely tailored ones. He didn't scrimp on his wardrobe.

"She was at the party and Maguire went to the trouble of getting a restraining order against her," David said. "Of course, she became a person of interest when the police heard about the scene she caused at the party when she saw him talking to another woman. It sounded very similar to the scene she caused in the Inn's lobby. Yet, they couldn't connect her to the arsenic."

Mac said, "His wife, Natasha Holmstead, who inherited all of his estate, was also at that party."

"Do you buy that bull she's selling about looking for an old watch?" David took a mini-laptop from the box and laid it on the table.

"Of course not," Mac replied.

"There's no gold pocket watch among Maguire's stuff. A gold watch, but not a pocket watch. He'd packed light."

"She's lying, like all lawyers—except Willingham and Fleming."

"No, they'd never lie," David said with a note of sarcasm.

"Holmstead is good at what she does," Mac admitted. "I know that there are innocent people who've been accused of murder. Our country's justice system is based on everyone getting a fair trial. Where would we be if the accused didn't have the right to the best lawyer that they can afford or get? But..." He gritted his teeth as faces of murder victims he had encountered during his career flashed through his mind. "Seeing and knowing what juries haven't been allowed to see and know because of the likes of Natasha Holmstead convincing some judges to suppress evidence, allowing killers to walk out—" He sighed while shaking his head. "But, she's just doing her job and making a hell of a lot of money doing it."

While gesturing at the other contents in the box, David held up a set of keys on a gold chain with a small pocket knife attached to it. "We found all this on the table in his suite. It looked like he was working on something when he left to go upstairs to the penthouse."

Mac took the keychain and studied it.

"The forensics lab searched all of his electronics inside and out." David showed him a picture of a cell phone. "They found something very interesting on Maguire's cell phone and laptop. His phone had a tracking program loaded on it. It was set up to send his text messages, call logs, emails sent and received, as well as its GPS location to a clone phone."

Setting another picture of a cell phone next to the first, David announced, "This cell phone, which we found in Christine's suitcase."

"Maybe it was planted," Mac said.

"It has her fingerprints on it," David replied. "If Christine had Maguire under surveillance, she had to know that he was staying at the Inn. Are you sure it was your idea that she stay there?"

"Positive."

David continued, "His laptop had a similar type of spyware that allowed someone with a laptop to monitor what he was doing, including check his email and examine what he had on his hard drive or flash."

"Did you find the laptop used to monitor him among her belongings?" Mac set the key chain in the box.

"No, we didn't."

Mac said, "Christine wasn't one bit technically inclined."

David hesitated before responding, "Two weeks ago, she purchased the clone phone and a new laptop, which we suspect was used to keep track of Maguire. I'm sorry, Mac, but between finding these surveillance programs, her arriving in town the same day he checked into the Inn, and finding the clone in her suitcase, it looks like Christine was stalking him."

"But someone else was in that room." Mac studied the pictures of the two phones. "Did you find any external hard drive or flash drives in the room?"

"Nope. Only the laptop."

Mac opened the laptop and hit the button to turn it on. "Both Archie and I have one of these. It's built for portability. You can't store a lot on the hard drive. You need a flash drive for file storage."

"Found none."

"Maybe the killer stole the flash drive containing information about what Maguire was doing here." He shut the laptop off and closed the lid.

"Maybe, but he didn't get this." David held up a business card for him to read the name.

While Mac didn't recognize the name, he did recognize the title. Private Investigator. The name was listed as Nancy Brenner. "Maguire had hired a private investigator."

"And I know her," David said. "I've got an appointment to see her later. Want to take a road trip?"

* * * *

After getting David's invitation to ride along for the interview with the private investigator, Mac swung past Spencer Manor to change out of the sports jacket and slacks he had worn for his breakfast meeting and into comfortable blue jeans and a sweater. After discovering that Gnarly had shredded one of the pillows on his bed, he realized that he hadn't taken the dog for a walk since the murders. Gnarly's trainer insisted that boredom was the root to his misbehavior. This being the case, the German shepherd was invited to go along for the ride.

"Have you met Sandy Bennett yet?" David asked Mac during their drive out to Nancy Brenner's home across the West Virginia state line in Morgantown.

As if he expected Gnarly to know the answer, Mac turned to look at the German shepherd filling the backseat. With the dark patches above his eyes knitted together into a questioning expression, he looked like he was replying that he didn't know either. The dog resumed peering out at the trees and cows in the hillside pastures along the mountain roads.

"The name sounds familiar," Mac replied.

"She's in a few of Robin's books," David said. "Robin based her on Nancy Brenner. She had the honor of being one of the first women sworn in as a West Virginia state trooper. Back around when I was born, Dad had met her when one of his cases spilled over the state line. He said she was the best and she was. He introduced her to your mother, who created the character of Sandy Bennett, based on Nancy."

The reference to Robin's books jogged Mac's memory. Sandy Bennett was a police officer that Mickey Forsythe would sometimes work with during his investigations. Her sexy beauty disguised a quick wit and deadly aim with her gun.

David recounted Nancy Brenner's story. "She retired around the same time Dad passed away. She's got five grandchildren. The same year Nancy retired, her husband got a doctor to sign off on some disease I've never heard of, and will never be able to pronounce, to be put on permanent disability. He sits in front of the television drinking beer all day long."

"What a life," Mac said with sarcasm.

"I think Nancy got her PI license and went back to work because she didn't want to join him."

Once he had crossed the state line, David took an exit onto a side road that wound through the countryside until he found Nancy Brenner's doublewide mobile home on a hilltop south of Morgantown.

"There she is." David climbed out of the cruiser and opened the back door.

Gnarly took off for the nearest tree to mark the property as his.

Nancy Brenner didn't look like any PI Mac had ever encountered before. Private eyes he had met during his career were hard-drinking men who wore a lifetime of battling the system on their faces. Others were opportunists who had retired and moved into the high-tech field of security work to sit behind desks and swap war stories with other mid-level management types.

Nancy Brenner didn't fit either of those profiles.

At first, Mac had expected Nancy Brenner to be inside the home. He thought the woman on her knees in an oversized men's work shirt digging in the dirt to plant mums was the retired cop's mother or aunt. She certainly wasn't the same woman which Robin Spencer had created into a female crime fighter.

With an order to Gnarly not to dig up the flowers as fast as she was planting them, David stepped across the lawn. "Hey, Aunt Nancy."

Nancy shaded her eyes with her hand and spade and squinted up at them. "My God!"

After hugging her, David introduced her to Mac. "He's Robin's son." While she shook his hand, she studied his face with an eye that he recognized as being that of a well-trained investigator.

Mac could see why Robin Spencer had been intrigued by the female police officer. Even on the wrong side of middle age, she was very attractive. The lines that had crept up onto her face only enhanced her cheekbones. The silver in her blond hair shone in the autumn sun.

"So you're Robin's son?"

Mac replied, "That's what the DNA tests say."

"What does your DNA say about your daddy?" She glanced from Mac to David and then back again. The corner of her lips curled into a knowing grin. "Don't need any DNA samples to know the answer to that. The eyes alone say it all."

When she finally released her grip on his hand, he turned to David. The eyebrow over David's left eye rose into an arch. If Nancy Brenner had been born a decade later, she probably could have worked her way up from patrol to investigations.

"Well, what do you two boys want to talk to me about?" She went over to the porch where she had a pitcher of lemonade and a plate of sugar cookies waiting. "I take it you're here about Stephen Maguire?" She took off her gloves and poured the lemonade into a glass.

Sticking his thumbs into his utility belt, David leaned against the porch rail. "How did you guess?"

"I'm retired, not brain dead." She looked him over. "I must say that gold badge looks as good on you as it did on your daddy." She reached out to brush her fingers across it. "You're every bit as handsome as he was."

"Thank you for the compliment."

"How are you adjusting to the rich life?" she asked Mac. "What's it like going from underpaid cop to big man on the Point?"

This wasn't the first time that anyone had asked Mac about adjusting from the middle class suburban lifestyle of pinching pennies to having more than he could ever need. Before, he would grin, chuckle, and say, "It's great."

That was before someone murdered Christine and Stephen Maguire. While David was in on every clue, Mac had been shut out. With all his financial worries gone and living in the stone manor on Spencer Point, he felt like the pampered pooch with the rhinestone collar cooped up inside the mansion watching the junk yard dogs chasing the cat down the street and so wanting to be one of them.

"Retirement takes some adjusting to," he said.

"Ever thought of getting a PI license?" Her tone was serious.

"I may do that," Mac replied.

"Mickey Forsythe, look out." She laughed before asking them, "What do you want to know about Stephen Maguire?"

"Did he hire you?" David asked.

She scoffed. "You know the drill, Dave. My files are confidential. If it gets out that I'm blabbing, especially to the cops, about one of my clients, then no one will trust me and I'll be out of business." She gazed at him with the prettiest expression she could muster while being on the wrong side of fifty. "A girl has to make a living."

"Maguire is dead," David reminded her.

"I know that all too well," she said. "Someone offed him before he paid his bill. Do you really think the Maguire family is going to care about the whining of an old lady?"

Mac grinned. "Suppose I paid his bill?"

That was enough to make Nancy take her eyes off David's handsome face. "Are you serious?"

"How much?" Mac took his billfold out of his back pocket. "If I pay his bill, that makes *me* your client. You give us the full report."

She craned her neck to count the bills he was taking from his wallet. After he extracted them from the billfold, she snatched them from his hand, folded them up, and stuffed them into her bra. "Deal." She tapped him on the chest while flashing him a smile. "I'll even give you a receipt."

"Maguire was seen with a young woman on the day he was killed," David said. "Do you know who she was?"

"You said young," Nancy noted. "Did she have copper-colored hair? Very skinny?"

David looked to Mac, who had seen her, to confirm the description, which he did with a single nod of his head.

"She says she's Maguire's long-lost daughter," Nancy answered. "Maguire hired me a couple weeks ago. About twenty years ago, he had a fling with a young woman named Connie Hughes while they were students at Ohio State University. They broke it off and she never told him that he was a daddy-to-be. She was a real independent sort and raised the girl on her own. Then, two weeks ago this girl calls up Maguire, calling him 'Daddy.' She says her mommy had passed away eight years ago and she had just found out about him. Real soon after that, she had her hand out asking for money. Since she was going to college here in Morgantown, he called me to check her out. I got the impression that he never parted with cash unless he had to."

David asked, "What did you find out?"

"The girl's story checked out up to a point. Yeah, the mom died eight years ago, at which point Connie Hughes's daughter, Rebecca, moved to Traverse City, Michigan, to live with her grandparents. She's currently a student at Michigan Tech."

Gnarly sat up. His nose pointed up the hill across from them. He growled deep in his throat.

"Easy, Gnarly." Mac observed, "That's a long way from Morgantown."

Nancy agreed. "According to the profile pictures on Rebecca Hughes's Facebook friend page, the girl that contacted Maguire is really Cameron Jones. They were friends in middle school. Cameron spent all of her time in college majoring in sex, drugs, and hip hop and flunked out real fast. Her parents still don't know. As soon as they do, they'll cut her off without a cent. I assume that's why she decided to look up Maguire and pretend to be his long-lost daughter."

David asked, "Did you tell Stephen Maguire all this?"

"The day he got killed," she said. "He told me that he was going to let Cameron Jones hang herself."

"Shortly after which he ended up dead," Mac said.

"She didn't do it," Nancy said.

David wanted to know, "How can you be so sure?"

"I'm not an amateur," she said. "No one goes killing my clients before I get paid. I checked into it myself. After the scene with Christine Faraday at the Spencer Inn, Maguire did confront Jones. He'd recorded the whole conversation on his phone. Got her trying to shake him down. Threatening to reveal his illegitimate daughter, which I'm sure wouldn't have gone down well with his high society family. The whole extortion. He produced the recording and told her that, on account of him being such a nice guy, he was going to let her off easy. If she turned around and walked away and never came back, then he wasn't going to have her arrested for fraud and attempted extortion. I guess Cameron Jones did have a brain in her head because that's what she did."

David said, "We found no recordings among Maguire's personal effects."

"He recorded it with his phone. She cried to my source about the whole thing."

Mac was impressed. "Who's your source?"

"The bartender at iPooli. It's a cyber café joint right off WVU campus. Students go in to drink themselves silly while being sucked into virtual worlds and games. Cameron practically lives there twittering on her laptop and snorting coke in the parking lot. That's where she was from shortly after seven until iPooli closed. She went home with her boyfriend who deals coke out in the club parking lot. If you don't believe that, check with the Morgantown police. Lover Boy has been a person of interest in the drug scene for quite some time. They've been watching him, which means they can alibi Cameron."

"Sounds to me like she might blame Maguire for ruining this dream she had of him bankrolling her way into the party life," David said.

Gnarly stood up and barked at the hill.

Petting the dog, Nancy peered up the hill. "What do you see, boy?"

Mac asked her, "Since this place is a hangout for such low-lifes, do you think Cameron may be twisted enough to hire one of her boyfriend's associates to wreak her revenge on Maguire by killing him?"

"Even if one of these geniuses had the smarts to figure out how to pull off a murder at the Spencer Inn, she had no money to pay for a hit." She reached around behind her back. "Excuse me. I think you boys had better duck."

"She was a college girl with a body. What more—" David was saying when Nancy drew a handgun from a holster she'd been wearing under her work shirt and plowed into him with her full body to knock him down to the ground into her freshly planted mums.

A potted mum waiting on the porch railing to be planted exploded.

Gnarly's bark sounded like a wild animal's roar in the jungle.

The next shot from the hillside shattered the lemonade pitcher.

Drawing his gun, Mac dove to take cover behind a tree.

"They're using an automatic rifle up there at the top of the hill," she called out to Mac. "I saw the sun reflect off the scope. That's what your dog was barking at."

While Mac covered them with a round of shots from his gun, David and Nancy rolled together through the flower bed until David was able to reach around her to get his gun out of its holster on his utility belt. They ended up behind the wheelbarrow, which David overturned for them to use for cover.

Gnarly charged down the sidewalk and out into the road.

Mac didn't need any more information. Gnarly led the way across the road in the direction of the hillside.

Sounding his alarm, Gnarly charged up the steep hill to a roadside park and playground. In the middle of a school day, it was vacant.

By the time Mac caught up to him, Gnarly was sniffing around a bench between two trees that looked out across the valley. The back of the bench provided a brace to rest the rifle in order to take two shots seventy-five yards down the hill to the house with the police cruiser in front of it.

Mac knelt down to examine the ground where Gnarly was sniffing. The two rifle casings in the grass were still hot to the touch.

"Good dog."

Gnarly didn't stick around for more praise. The scent was still hot. He took off again toward the parking lot on the other side of the playground.

The black Ford SUV barely missed the dog when it careened around the corner and hit the ditch before swinging out onto the road to make its getaway onto the interstate.

CHAPTER EIGHT

"Who does the caddy belong to?" David rolled the police cruiser between the stone pillars and up the circle driveway to Spencer Manor's front door.

A black Cadillac SUV blocked the entrance to the stone path from the driveway to the wrap-around porch.

There was only one person Mac knew that the Cadillac could belong to. She bought the latest model Cadillacs with the same frequency that Archie upgraded her technological gadgets.

"Christine's sister." Mac's tone alone conveyed everything the police chief needed to know about his ex-in-laws.

David couldn't hear the rest of his reply over Gnarly's barking, which erupted when the cruiser passed the oak tree at the corner of the manor's wrap-around porch. His snarling snout smeared dog drool on the back window in his fervor to get out. When Mac released him from the back of the cruiser, Gnarly charged as if he had forgotten that he couldn't climb trees.

"What's gotten into him?" David looked up into the branches to see the source of Gnarly's fury.

"Otis," Mac answered while bracing for the scene he suspected was awaiting him inside the manor. "Archie says there's some giant squirrel that's been tormenting him."

David pointed his finger up toward the top of the tree. "That's the fattest squirrel I've ever seen." When an acorn flew out of the tree to bounce off the top of the cruiser, he yelled, "Hey, did you see that? That piggy squirrel threw an acorn at my cruiser."

"Gnarly, I'm going to kill you." Between getting shot at, the shepherd's barking, and his ex-in-laws waiting inside, Mac was ready for an early cocktail.

"Well, it's about time," Sabrina immediately called out from the living room when Mac, David, and Gnarly stepped into the foyer.

He hadn't seen either of his ex-sisters-in-law since they had accompanied Christine to the courthouse in a show of support when their divorce became final.

After that hearing, Edward Willingham, senior partner of Willingham and Associates, had chased Mac three city blocks before convincing him that he had indeed inherited two hundred seventy million dollars from the birth mother he never knew.

In a black ensemble suitable for mourning, Sabrina Carrington filled the leather wing-backed chair in the corner of the living room. Dripping in ruby jewels, she resembled a queen on her throne holding court, with her surviving sister playing the role of princess in waiting on the sofa across the room.

In a black pantsuit void of any jewels to brighten it up, Roxanne Burton contrasted her sister. She wasn't only dressed the part, she was indeed in mourning. Her eyes were red and swollen. Her face was drawn and pale.

With only eleven months between them, Roxanne and Christine had been more than sisters. They were the best of friends. So close in age and similar in beauty and body type, they had served together as professional cheerleaders for Washington's football team. Signed by the same agency, they had worked together as models to pay for their college education.

Archie came in from the kitchen bearing a serving tray with tea for them after their long drive from Washington.

"I was beginning to think that you'd deserted your children in their time of need to go off on one of your crazy adventures with one of your friends." Sabrina directed Archie to leave her English tea on the end table. When unable to decide between the sugar cookie or the tea biscuit, she took both after Archie informed her that they had plenty.

After admiring the exquisite herringbone china cup, Sabrina took a sip of the tea, which prompted a sour expression and a squawk that resembled the honk of a goose. "This is nothing more than hot water. Don't you know to let tea steep?"

Archie turned around from where she was about to return to the kitchen. "We can let it steep a few more minutes."

"Do." Sabrina ordered the tea taken away with a wave of both her hands. "This is totally unacceptable."

The roll of Archie's eyes told the two men that the sisters were everything Mac had warned her about. She returned to the kitchen with the rejected tea pot. Having seen enough of the visitors, Gnarly, his tail between his legs, followed at her heels. When Mac heard a door slam in the kitchen, he guessed that she wouldn't be returning until after their visitors were gone.

The matter of the tea taken care of, Sabrina looked up to notice that both Mac and David were covered in soil after their run-in at Nancy Brenner's home. "What happened to you?"

"Someone took a couple of shots at us," Mac said.

"People are always shooting at you," Sabrina scoffed between bites of her cookie. "Your day isn't complete until you get shot at, at least twice."

"Oh, Mac!" Roxanne leaped off the sofa and threw her arms around his neck.

The embrace was so unexpected that a lock of her auburn hair went up his nose. Roxanne had never made it a secret that she believed he wasn't good enough for her little sister.

The last time Mac recalled them embracing was on his wedding day after Christine had ordered them to do so.

Roxanne continued to hold onto him while sobbing onto his sweater. "Chris didn't deserve to die like that. I was supposed to take care of her." She dissolved into incoherent blubbering.

Over the sobs, Mac introduced David to them as Spencer's police chief. When he added that David was investigating the murders, Roxanne erupted with a fresh round of sobs.

"I'm sorry you had to wait," Mac apologized. "I didn't know you were coming."

"That's okay. Your girl has been taking very good care of us. Though she's a little slow with that tea." When Sabrina waved her hand her jewels caught the rays of the sun streaming through the window. "I'm glad you're here, Chief. You were going to be my next stop. What progress have you made in finding the killer?"

Bracing to be interrogated, David stepped further into the room. With Sabrina refusing to budge out of the chair, Mac and he resembled army generals reporting on the war's progress to the queen. "We're making progress."

"Do you have any suspects yet?"

"A few," David answered.

"Who?"

"I can't say."

"Why not?" Sabrina demanded to know.

"Because I don't believe in showing my hand until it's time to show my cards," the police chief replied.

Sabrina's voice was low and threatening when she told him, "Christine was my sister. When you mess with one of us, you mess with all of us. I want to know what happened. Was it an accident or did someone kill her?"

"She was drunk," Roxanne said. "She had called me that night from the penthouse and she was out of her mind. I told her to get something to eat and to go to bed and sleep it off, but she was crazy out of her mind. She kept saying that she was going to kill Stephen." She sobbed. "I never thought she would've done it."

"Someone else was in that room," David told them.

"Who?" Sabrina asked.

"We don't know yet."

"Are you sure?" Roxanne's eyes filled with fresh tears.

David said, "We're finding evidence that others wanted Stephen Maguire dead. There's a possibility that Christine was in the wrong place at the wrong time."

"Someone did try to poison him a couple of weeks ago," Sabrina said.

David turned to Roxanne. "The Washington police told us that you were on the scene of that incident."

Mac hadn't thought it was possible for Roxanne's face to become paler, but it did.

"Only because I dragged Christine there," she answered the police chief. "I thought it would do her good to go out and meet other people."

Sabrina said, "They couldn't prove that Christine had any connection to whatever it was Stephen ate that was poisoned."

Roxanne explained, "I finally convinced the investigators that if they didn't have any proof she did it, then to leave her alone. They didn't, so they did."

"That was after I made a few phone calls." Sabrina caught David's eye. "It pays to have friends."

"Who else at that party could have slipped that arsenic to Maguire?" David asked Roxanne.

"Everyone was there," she said. "His wife Natasha was there. She hated the air he breathed."

"But Maguire didn't get a restraining order issued against Natasha Holmstead," the chief pointed out. "He got the order issued against Christine after he'd been poisoned."

Sabrina bristled. "That was a political move on his part. He did that to make Roxanne look bad so that he'd get appointed Deputy U.S. Attorney instead of her."

"Was there anyone on his enemy list named Nita?" Mac asked, thinking about the servant who had slipped into the Inn. "Mexican maybe. Didn't speak a word of English."

Sabrina let out a laugh. "Nita? That sounds like that girl I had working for us for a few years."

"Who?" David asked.

"A few years ago I had a cleaning woman working for me," Sabrina said with a wave of her hand. "It was purely charity on my part. She had family in South America that she was trying to bring to the United States." She pointed across the room at her sister. "She worked for you first. That's how she came to work for me."

Roxanne said, "Everyone felt sorry for her. She worked in housekeeping at the courthouse. She spoke very little English and was desperate for money to have her family brought here. So a bunch of us would have her clean our houses, and we'd pay her under the table."

"She worked for me for quite a few years," Sabrina said, "which she was totally inadequate at doing anyway. Then I had to drive her home and she would be talking at me and didn't speak any English. Thank God I remembered it from when we were kids. I tell you, her working for us brought it all back to me. We used to speak fluent Spanish when Big Daddy was the ambassador in Brazil. Then, after coming back to the United States and not using it—but when Nita worked for us, it all came back like riding a bike."

"But Portuguese is Brazil's native language," David said.

The glare Sabrina shot in the police chief's direction prompted a chuckle from Mac. The correction exposed the underlying message that Sabrina was truly relaying: She was a former ambassador's daughter and a woman of importance to be treated as such.

"Actually," Mac explained to him, "before they went to Brazil, Christine and her sisters learned Spanish from their nanny, who happened to be an illegal immigrant willing to work cheap."

"Big Daddy took very good care of Nonnie," Sabrina said. "She lived like a queen compared to the other illegals working for our friends' families. Money hasn't changed you one bit, Mac. You're still a bastard always trying to make us look bad."

He went on to explained, "When they were in South America, they never bothered learning Portuguese because so many people understood Spanish. Plus, their father sent them to an English-speaking private school."

"I did learn Portuguese. So did Roxanne." Sabrina pointed across the room to her sister. "She speaks both languages like a native."

"Nita spoke Spanish," Roxanne returned to the subject of the maid. "She was from tiny village—where in South America I don't remember. Extremely polite. I felt sorry for her until she went weird on us and you ended up firing her."

"She was weird." Gasping, she snapped her fingers at David. "This all happened after Stephen moved in with Christine. She accused him of raping her. He denied it. Of course, no one believed her. I fired her for making such an absurd accusation."

"Everyone fired her," Roxanne said. "She even lost her job at the courthouse."

"If he raped her, why didn't she report it?" David asked.

Mac knew the answer. "Because Stephen Maguire, with all of his powerful friends and connections, could have had her deported. I'm sure he made that very clear to her. Getting her fired was a warning of what he could do to her." He asked Sabrina, "If she was telling the truth and he raped her, and she lost everything, where did that leave her?"

Sabrina was indignant. "At that time, we thought Stephen was a good man. If we knew then what we know now about him..."

David turned to Mac. "It's very possible that if this Nita tracked Maguire down for ruining her life, and Christine, his mistress, happened to be on the scene..."

"What happened to Nita?" Mac wanted to know. "Do you know where she is now?"

Roxanne and Sabrina exchanged looks.

"I have no idea," Sabrina said. "The last I heard she got evicted from the apartment she was living in for nonpayment of rent."

"She could be anywhere," Roxanne said in a soft voice. "Even dead for all we know."

Clearing her throat, Sabrina continued on to the reason for her visit. "There are a few things that we need to discuss and I thought it would be best if we discussed them in person. Big Daddy used to say that it was very poor taste to bring up business at a funeral, and since we believe that this should be taken care of before Christine's service, I suggested to Roxanne that we come out to see you."

"About what?" Mac plopped down onto the sofa. "Christine and I were divorced. All of our business affairs were taken care of months ago."

"She never changed her will," Sabrina said. "You're still her executor and beneficiary."

Mac smiled broadly. "How about that?"

Roxanne said, "It's about the lake house. We agreed after Big Daddy died that I would buy Sabrina and Christine out of their shares."

Her sister interjected, "That share being the house and the grounds itself, not necessarily everything in it."

"Now is not the time to discuss this, Sabrina," Roxanne warned in a low voice.

"Discuss what?" she replied in a mockingly innocent tone.

Wordlessly, Roxanne glared at her sister across the room.

Curious, David asked, "What?"

"Big Daddy's Bug." Roxanne's annoyance was evident. "Our father had transferred the title to me when he was sick, before he passed away."

"Because he expected you would keep it in the family," Sabrina said. "He never would have given it to you if he knew you were going to sell it."

"It was a broken-down Volkswagen."

"It was a classic," Sabrina told David. "It was a 1978 VW Beetle convertible. We all learned how to drive in it. My children learned to drive in it. I loved that car. We kept it out here on the lake to use as an extra car to zip around in. We get out here today and I find that Roxanne has sold it without even offering it to any of us." She snapped her fingers in her sister's direction as if to make her point. "I would've bought it if you had had the common courtesy to ask."

"Will you just shut up about the Bug already?" Roxanne replied.

Mac jumped in to say, "My lawyer did tell me that Christine's name is still on the deed to the lake house."

"Because Stephen cheated me," Roxanne said. "I refinanced my house to pay both Sabrina and Christine for their shares of the lake house. Sabrina signed the deed transfer to me, but Christine never did it. She said she never got the money transfer. When I followed the money, I found when the bank transferred it. It went into her account. When I tried to show her where her account did get the money and suggested that maybe Stephen had transferred it out since she had put his name on all of her accounts, he convinced her that I was trying to manipulate her. She bought his lies and stopped speaking to me."

Sabrina said, "Christine was starting to believe us about what a monster Stephen really was when she got killed. Everyone he's touched has had their lives ruined."

"Where have I heard those words before?" Mac asked in a mocking tone. "Oh, I know. I said it to both of you when you let him slither into Christine's and my bed."

While Roxanne hung her head in shame, Sabrina refused to take any credit for her mistake in judgment. "You played a role in all this, too, Mac. So we got bought in by Stephen's good looks and charm. Most everyone in D.C. did. But Christine wouldn't have been so easily suckered if you had treated her right."

"I did treat her right," Mac claimed. "Okay, so I couldn't play 'keeping up with the sisters.' What underpaid homicide detective can? But I put a roof over her head and food on the table and the heat on in the winter. Our kids went to good schools and got everything they needed, including braces, and most of what they wanted. Not everything, but most. But, according to you, I never gave Christine enough, because I couldn't take her on cruises every season or buy her a lake house like Big Daddy's. You made damn sure that she knew that, every time you got a chance to flash your newest diamond in her face."

He pointed his finger at Sabrina. "You asked David here who killed your sister. Look in the mirror, Sabrina. You're the one who did it. You got her killed. You drove her out of a perfectly good marriage and into Stephen Maguire's arms."

Mac took pride in being fast and observant on his feet. Before he had retired, he was ready for anything. He didn't know if retirement had made him soft, or if he had let his guard down when it came to confronting a middle-aged suburban housewife dripping in rubies. Whatever the case, he wasn't expecting it when Sabrina shot out of her chair like a badger out of its den to deliver a handful of claws across his face.

Grabbing his bleeding cheek, Mac retreated backwards, while she advanced with her claws flying to strike any other part of him that she could rip apart.

"That's enough!" Suddenly David was between the two of them with his arms out like a traffic cop stopping traffic in every direction. "Step back!"

"What's going on in here?" Archie was at Mac's side, while Gnarly was barking as if to demand answers as well.

"How dare you talk like that to me? She was my sister! You have no right!" In spite of the uniform between her and the man who had dared to offend her, Sabrina continued to charge. With her arms flying in front of her in an effort to slap anyone who got in her way, she continued to advance.

Mac grabbed Archie in a bear hug and the two of them ducked.

"I said to stop it!" David charged toward her with his shoulders down like a football player taking out the quarter-back. His right shoulder catching her in the middle of her chest, he drove the heavy-set woman backwards and off her feet until she landed with a plop in the chair from which she had begun her assault.

Silence fell over the manor.

Her eyes wide, Sabrina's mouth hung open while she huffed and puffed.

Archie examined the scratches on Mac's face. "I've never seen a woman scratch someone so deep. And David said my scratches were impressive. I should put some antiseptic on those."

Roxanne's eyes were equally wide while she looked from her sister to David who straightened his clothes and smoothed his hair.

"Consider that a warning," the police chief told Sabrina. "Next time I won't be so nice."

CHAPTER NINE

It was officially off season on Deep Creek Lake.

In a matter of days, the autumn foliage had passed its brilliant height. In the setting sun, house lights that had been concealed by the green leaves in the summer now reflected on the lake. The effect was a colorful dimensional illusion visible all the way up at the top of the mountain.

Mac hoped he and Archie would have the restaurant to themselves with Deep Creek Lake's population in hibernation until ski season. For what they planned to be a night to remember, they both dressed for a dinner for two that Archie had called Antonio to prepare. Archie looked splendid in a sapphire colored cocktail dress with matching jewels. Mac wore a gray suit with a sapphire colored shirt to match her dress. Seeming to sense his desire to be alone with her, the servers disappeared after delivering the champagne and bread.

"I'm sorry for Sabrina and Roxanne," he apologized after sipping the champagne.

"None of it's your fault," she said. "You did warn me." She took another sip from her glass. "Who do you think did it?"

"Maguire had a lot of enemies," Mac said. "I think I was the least of his worries." He pulled the list of names that he had recreated from memory of the list that David had found. "Can you find out what this list means?"

She read the names before folding up the sheet of paper and slipping it into her handbag.

"Maguire had that list in a folder labeled Themis." Explaining about them being suspects and defendants in murder cases, he asked, "Can you find a common denominator besides that they were all murder suspects who got off?" He added, "I have no idea who Emma Wilkes is. David tried calling her number but her phone has been turned off."

Archie reminded him, "There were two murder victims in that room. How can you be so sure Stephen Maguire was the intended victim? What about Christine?"

"The only one who'd want her dead is you," Mac said. "Do you even want to go there?"

She cocked her head at him. "Why would I want to kill Christine?"

"So that you don't have to deal with an ex-wife on the scene," he replied. "You know how the security system works here at the Inn. You probably even had a hand in setting it up. Don't tell me that if you didn't set your mind to it, you couldn't plan and execute a murder. You've been trained by the best."

"You're the one who doesn't have an alibi," she reminded him.

"I have Gnarly," he said, "only he refuses to talk."

They looked at each other over the tops of their glasses while enjoying another sip.

"Do you really think I'm capable of killing someone?" A tremor slipped into her tone.

He took her hands into his. "Only if you had to." He kissed her fingertips.

"Can I speak to you?" Mac jumped when he heard Ed Willingham's voice in his ear. It was so abrupt and harsh that he could feel the lawyer's spittle in his ear canal. The lawyer's face was inches from his own. His expression was so stern that Mac felt like a schoolboy caught cheating by the principal.

In the far corner of the restaurant, he saw that Ed had been having a dinner meeting with Jeff Ingle. Mac had been so involved with Archie that he didn't notice them.

"I need to talk to you over here." With his eyes and a toss of his head, the lawyer gestured for Mac to follow him over to the other table. "Please, Mr. Faraday?"

"Now?"

"Now."

After Archie nodded her consent for him to leave her alone at the table, Mac, puzzled by the sudden intrusion on what clearly had all the earmarks of a private dinner, got up and followed the attorney across the restaurant to where he had been eating dinner with the Inn's manager.

Ed launched into the reason for the interruption as soon as Mac sat down. "What are you doing?"

"I'm having dinner with Archie. It's been a tough week."

"Dinner?" Ed's silver eyebrows seemed to reach half-way up to his receding hairline. "Hmm? She's dressed to die for. You're wearing a suit. You're drinking champagne. You've ordered a special dinner for just the two of you. You're kissing her fingers and look like you're about to start on her toes. Is this by any chance a date?"

The guilt Mac had felt evaporated. "Neither of us are married or otherwise engaged."

"I don't know if you're aware of this, Mac, but Robin Spencer was world famous for coming up with imaginative ways of killing people," Ed said. "By virtue of that, so are you. *Your* ex-wife and her lover were killed at *your* resort. The police chief is *your* half brother. Whether that's common knowledge or not, it's not hard to figure out. You don't know it yet, but you own Spencer, which was named after your ancestors who founded this town. Even though it's not true, it makes for a real sexy story that you had Christine and her lover killed, and your brother is covering it up to clear the way for you to begin a new relationship with a younger and notably much more beautiful woman."

"That isn't what happened," Mac objected.

"Doesn't matter," Jeff said. "It makes for a great story."

"You know that isn't what happened and I know that," Ed said. "Try explaining that to conspiracy theorists when they see you here at your five-star restaurant with your latest mistress."

"He's got a point, Mac," Jeff said. "It doesn't look good for you to be flashing Archie around in public so soon after these murders."

Mac glanced over at Archie, who was gazing back at him. She seemed to sense what they were talking about. "What would my mother have said to this?"

Ed looked over at Jeff. They both chuckled. "She'd tell me to go to hell," the lawyer finally replied. "But think about Archie, Mac. If the media saw you just now, how long do you think it would take for her to be tagged 'Mickey Forsythe's mistress'?"

"You make it sound like I was cheating on my wife," Mac said. "Archie and I have done nothing wrong. I didn't even meet her until after my divorce was final."

Ed said, "I believe you. I'm glad for the both of you. I like Archie. Robin loved her like a daughter. It's the timing. Take her home with you. Make love to her day and night. Just keep your relationship behind closed doors until after these murders are solved."

Jeff chimed in, "I've seen how the media and public react to these types of things. Do you really want to inflict that on Archie?"

"She's the last one I want to get hurt." Mac could see her looking at him with question in her eyes as he made it back to their table. In his mind, he rehearsed how he was going to tell her that the relationship they had been planning to take to the next level would now have to be taken there under wraps.

He made it only halfway across the dining room before he turned back to the table of his lawyer and hotel manager.

"Ed," Mac began, "you're without a doubt one of the best attorneys in the world and I pay you a very hefty retainer for your advice. It's because you know what you're doing. And Jeff, if it weren't for you, the Spencer Inn wouldn't have kept its five-star rating all these years. But, you two have to understand, I have a problem."

"Mac—" Ed tried to say.

Mac held up his hand. "Ever since I can remember, people have been telling me that I need to learn to do what I'm told. My adoptive parents, teachers, bosses—everyone. When I was a cop, officers I trained would get promoted over me even though my record was way better than theirs. My supervisors would tell me that I would go far if I'd just learn to do what I'm told to do."

Ed and Jeff exchanged glances.

"What I'm telling you, gentlemen, is that I respect your advice. You mean well and one of the things I pay you for is the benefit of your vast experience in these types of matters. But I wouldn't do what I was told before I was rich and famous; I'm certainly not going to start now."

As they watched Mac return to join Archie at his private table, Jeff sighed. "Well, we tried."

"I'm not surprised," Ed responded. "Between Robin Spencer and Patrick O'Callaghan, Mac Faraday's gene pool has been dealt a double whammy of bull-headedness."

"Problem?" Archie asked while he sat down next to her.

"None." Aware of the waiter serving their salads, Mac didn't want to go into the matter any further.

She brushed his cheek with her hand. "You're getting more like Mickey Forsythe every day. A man with a mind of his own."

Hector came rushing into the lounge with his mini-laptop under his arm. Seeing that the restaurant only had a few patrons, the security chief felt safe to raise his voice. "Mr. Faraday, I saw on the security monitor that you were here. We got something." Like a child bursting to tell about what he had found, he sat in the seat next to Mac and opened up his laptop.

Sensing a break in the case, Ed and Jeff rushed over to join them at the table. They all crowded around Hector in his chair to see the unveiling of the killer.

"This is one bright bitch," Hector said with a note of awe while opening up various screens on his small laptop. "I'm connecting us remotely to my computer in my office to show you what I've found."

Ed asked, "Why don't we all go over to your office?"

"This will only take a minute," Hector answered. "Plus, it will be easier with all of you. My office isn't that big."

Archie explained, "Remote connection is so much easier than it used to be, especially with mini-laptops and all the other gadgets that are available. Just one click and you're working on your computer which is someplace else. The speed and ease are virtually the same."

On the monitor was a paused grayscale image of the corridor, with a shot of the service elevator, the door to the stairwell, and down the hall at the end of the penthouse floor. The shot was too tight to capture the doors going into the suites. Since the cameras covered each end of the corridors and the only access onto and off the floor, none were necessary to cover the suites themselves. The key cards recorded the comings and goings of the suites.

Hector set up the sequence for his audience. "Our problem has been figuring out who our killer was."

"That's usually the problem in any murder mystery," Mac told him.

Archie brushed against him when she moved her seat in closer to see the monitor. With a rebellious glance at Ed and Jeff, Mac slipped his arm around her.

"You'd think it would be easy. Get her picture on the security video, blow it up. See if she has a record, get her name and address and pick her up. But this bitch knows about the cameras. She won't look up for us to get her." Hector hit the Play button. In less than a minute, the service elevator door opened. The server, a young man who Mac recognized as a service clerk who worked in the dining room, wheeled the cart off the elevator. A woman in a black house-cleaning smock held the elevator door open while he maneuvered the cart into the hall.

"That's Nita," Hector placed his fingertip on the monitor at the woman in the black smock. "At least, that was the name she'd given to the other employees."

Her bushy hair was tied back at her neck. Black plastic framed glasses covered her face. In her arms, she carried a pile of white towels and a black bag hung from her shoulder.

As Hector had pointed out, she never looked up or in a direction that the camera could capture a clear image of her face while she made her way down the corridor and out of the shot.

He tapped the monitor with his fingertip while telling them over his shoulder, "Now, it doesn't end there. You see, we have her getting onto the floor. Mike, the server, he said that she went to the suite across the hall from the murders. She was gone when he came out a few minutes later. The couple across the hall, the ambassador and his guest, said that she was delivering extra towels, which when the police and I talked to them, they realized they hadn't ordered. Each one thought the other had ordered them. She tried talking to them in Spanish, which neither of them knew. She left. They heard her knocking on the door across the hall after she'd left their suite."

Mac said, "She was stalling until Mike was gone."

Hector nodded his head. "Yeah, sure. And then she went into the suite across the hall. Christine had let her in. But, the question remains, how did she get off the floor with security cameras at both ends of the hall? We never see Nita leave."

Jeff answered, "And you finally figured it out."

"Yep," Hector said. "Do we have anyone leave that floor that we don't see come on?" He grinned wickedly. "And we sure do. It was around quarter 'til midnight."

He switched the image on the monitor to another screen and sat back in his seat with his thumbs tucked into his belt.

The image was that of the other end of the corridor at the guest elevator. A couple dressed for an evening out came into view. She had on a cocktail dress with high heels, while her companion wore a sports coat and slacks. The man pressed the call button for the elevator. When the door opened they stepped on, and the man pressed the button inside the elevator. As the door started to shut, he grabbed the doors to stop them. A woman with long black hair, dressed in slacks, tunic top, and stylish chain belt, ran onto the car and jumped to the back out of camera view. The doors shut.

Hector paused the video.

"That couple had spent the evening in the suite next door to the murders," the security chief said. "Three couples had booked the suite for the weekend. This couple had a cottage down on the lake. They came up for a party in the suite and had a temporary pass to get up to the penthouse floor. They said that when they left—well, you see it in the video. As soon as the doors opened, she flew faster than lightning out of your suite and onto the elevator out of shot. The man pressed the button for the lobby, just like he did the call button, so she left no fingerprints. When she got to the lobby she skipped out into oblivion."

Mac said, "But you did get a glimpse of her."

"Enough to know that nowhere in any of the videos do we have this woman arriving on that floor." Hector nodded his head quickly. "Just like we don't have Nita leaving. They have to be the same perp."

"That's more than an hour after the murders," Mac said. "That gives her plenty of time to clean up the murder scene and change from cleaning woman to hotel guest." He asked Hector, "Are you able to get a good picture of her leaving the Inn? Maybe in the lobby?"

Hector shook his head. "She knew about the cameras. Notice that her head is down and turned away. Not only that, but she ran too fast for us to get anything. All I can see is that she has long dark hair. I can make a guess about her height."

Archie said, "She's wearing a wig. I can tell."

"Of course it is," Mac said before ordering Hector, "Get these videos to Spencer police as soon as you can. You did good work."

* * * *

"Lieutenant Faraday, I didn't see you there. Good to see you again."

With a brandy in his hand, Judge Garrison Sutherland got up and trotted across the lobby from where he had been enjoying the fireplace with Natasha Holmstead to intercept Mac and Archie. The judge and lawyer were dressed casually in sweaters and slacks after having spent the evening out.

At his urging, Mac and Archie joined them. Since the judge and Natasha filled the chairs, they had to sit next to each other on the love seat in front of the fireplace. Mac was uncomfortably aware of his lawyer's glare at him when he came into the lounge to see that Mac had slipped his arm across her shoulders.

After ordering two glasses of wine, Mac asked the judge, "Have you and Natasha extended your vacation?"

Judge Sutherland replied, "We're still trying to find out what Maguire had with him here at the Inn when he was killed."

"From what the police chief said, he'd packed light."

Natasha asked, "Have you seen what he brought with him?"

"No," Mac lied, "but the police chief did tell me that they found no pocket watch. I also talked to Jessica, my daughter. She's staying at Christine's house in Georgetown. You're more than welcome to contact her to make arrangements to meet her at the house to look through whatever is left of Stephen's belongings for this watch you're looking for. I suggest you do it soon because as soon as I'm able to settle the estate, we're clearing everything out and I'm putting the house on the market."

Garrison and Natasha exchanged glances. He chose to respond, "We'll do that right away. Thank you."

"I would have thought the Maguire family would've swooped in to demand answers by now." Mac asked Natasha, "Are they usually this laid back about murder in the family?"

Her expression betrayed a great deal of puzzlement. "Granted, Stephen and I were married for a very short time, but they never chose to get involved in anything we did. No invitations to the Hamptons. Not even a Christmas card. Stephen said that everyone was very busy and that's why we never received any invitations to any of these family events you'd see on the social pages."

Archie said, "That's not the way the media pictures them. According to them, the Maguires are close. They always throw big family weddings—"

"We eloped, honey."

"Maguire funerals are massive."

Mac said, "David told me that no one has even claimed Maguire's body." He cocked his head at Natasha. "You're his next of kin."

"Let a Maguire take care of burning him up or dumping him in the ground," she replied cruelly, while glaring over at him. For the first time, Mac noticed how thick her eyebrows were. "All I want is what belongs to me."

"Nice young man. O'Callaghan. Spencer's police chief." The judge took a sip of his drink. "I was surprised to see he was so young. But then, I guess, considering the legend his father is around these parts, it would be expected that he'd step into his shoes."

"From what I've learned about Patrick O'Callaghan, they were big shoes to fill." Mac sipped his drink while Judge Sutherland watched him.

"And David fills them very nicely," Archie said.

"An interesting thing happened when Natasha and I met with him at the police station the other day," Garrison said to Mac. "Have you ever had one of those moments when you meet someone and they remind you of someone, but you can't put your finger on who it is they remind you of?"

"Yes, I guess that's happened to everyone," Mac replied.

"That happened when I met Chief David O'Callaghan." Judge Sutherland peered at Mac with his dark eyes. They were intense as he studied him. "The way he talked, his looks, especially around the eyes. I kept staring at him. It bothered me so much, trying to figure out who it was he reminded me of, that I couldn't even pay attention to most of our conversation."

Mac felt him studying him.

"It finally hit me when Natasha and I went to see you." After the server replaced his finished drink with a new one, the judge asked, "Have you ever found out the name of your birth father?"

Unsure whether to lie or not, Mac peered back at him. He felt Archie's grip on his thigh.

"There are websites all over the Internet with fans devoted to Robin Spencer and everything there is to know about her," the judge said. "Have you ever looked at them?"

Mac said, "Actually, I haven't."

The judge said, "Well, purely out of curiosity, I happened to google your mother's name and do you know how many websites came up?"

"How many?"

"Over three and a half million websites. That's a lot of information out there about her."

"Robin Spencer was a very popular author," Archie said. "Her books are in every language. She has fans all over the world."

"Everyone loves Robin Spencer." The judge went on, "Now, these websites aren't all completely devoted to Robin Spencer and her life, but some are. And a lot of them do go into her life back when she was young and do you know what they said?"

Knowing the judge's style, Mac sensed where he was leading and he didn't like it. Neither did Archie based on how tightly she had hold of his thigh.

"According to her biography, back when she was a senior in high school, her parents sent her to a girls' finishing school up in New England. Knowing now, since her death, about you, everyone knows that in reality they had sent her away to have you."

Chuckling, Mac replied, "That's not exactly a secret anymore."

The judge went on, "But then, on one of those sites, long before it came out about you, there was a woman who posted that she had gone to high school with Robin Spencer. It was one of those posts about how talented and fun and outgoing and curious she was. This woman also remembered that for over a year, Robin went steady with a certain boy who graduated the year ahead of them. This boy went on to the police academy. She even remembered the name of this boy. Do you know what it was?"

Mac and Archie glared at Judge Sutherland.

The judge grinned at Mac. "I think you do." He pointed at Archie. "And she does, too."

"What's your point, your honor?" Mac asked.

"I also think David O'Callaghan knows." He chuckled. "He's not stupid. All he had to do was look at you. The family resemblance about slaps you in the face."

"David has no problem with our relationship," Mac said. "We're friends."

The judge's laughter was sarcastic. "Oh, I believe that. You two must be more than friends. I mean, why else would he so quickly eliminate you as a suspect when your ex-wife and her lover got killed here in your private suite?"

"There's no physical evidence to indicate that I was at the crime scene during the murders."

Judge Sutherland said, "You know how the media works, Mac. The implication is so much more exciting than the truth."

"So I've been told." Mac sat forward. "Your honor, up until this moment, I had immense respect for you. I've considered you to be one of the few fair and honorable lawyers on the face of this earth. What's happened to you?"

"You can't possibly understand the importance of this whole issue," Natasha said.

"I was a homicide detective for over twenty years. I know precisely the importance of all this." Mac asked, "What do you want that's so important to you that you would stoop to extortion, which, I might add, I'm not giving into? David and I aren't broadcasting the identity of my father. True. But we aren't keeping it a state secret either. Like you just said. It isn't hard to figure out. Before I forget about you being a judge and beat you about the head and shoulders, I want the truth about what you two want so badly from Maguire."

Mac cocked an eyebrow at Natasha. "As a matter of fact, I just remembered that you know Spanish. I heard you use it when representing some Spanish clients. Our killer knew Spanish."

"Spanish?" Natasha repeated.

"She got onto the floor pretending to be a housekeeping woman by the name of Nita."

Natasha glanced at the judge and blurted out the name, "Nita."

Archie asked, "Did you know a Spanish speaking woman named Nita who wanted to kill Stephen Maguire?"

Natasha said, "I had a cleaning woman named Nita working for me a while back. She had some issues."

"With Stephen Maguire?" Archie asked.

Natasha replied, "Definitely with him, but then, everyone had issues with Stephen."

Mac told them, "There was a cleaning woman named Nita that worked for Christine's sisters who claimed Maguire raped her. Do you think that's possible?"

Immediately, Natasha nodded her head. "Certainly. He was a snake."

"When she told someone about it, she was fired."

Archie asked Natasha, "Does she still clean for you?"

"No," Natasha said. "She disappeared. She quit or maybe Stephen got her fired from her job. I lost contact with her. I mean I suddenly wasn't able to get in contact with her. She had no phone. She'd been kicked out of her apartment. One day she was there. The next day she was gone." She looked over at Mac. "Do you think she killed Stephen?"

"Or maybe you killed them and pretended to be Nita to throw us off your trail."

The judge raised his voice to pull Mac's attention from his companion. "Get any thought of Natasha killing Maguire out of your mind. She was with me at the Carmel Cove Inn during the murders." His affection for the defense attorney was obvious.

Seeing that he would have to tread gently in order to keep his cooperation, Mac softened his tone. "Like you pointed out, I'm not without influence with the police chief. If I knew what you wanted so badly, I could help."

The judge sucked in a deep breath that puffed out his barrel chest. He smoothed his hair and folded his hands in his lap. He looked hard at Mac for a long moment.

He had given Mac that same look before in the court-room when he was under cross examination by defense attorneys trying to twist the evidence in their clients' favor. Mac would hesitate too long and the judge would give that glare before ordering him to dignify the attorney's inane question with an answer.

"We told you what we want," the judge finally said. "I admit Natasha was foolish the way she went charging into the police station and demanding that O'Callaghan turn every-thing over to her. I told her that. Then we thought that if we talked to you about it that you could have some influence with him. Instead, we've only made you suspicious, especially since you know now that we were in the area while Maguire was getting killed."

Mac replied, "All I want is to clear my name and the Inn's reputation. In order to do that, I need to know what's really going on. First, Maguire is poisoned at a party with both you and Natasha in attendance."

"Half the lawyers in D.C. were there," the judge said, "most of whom would have loved to see Maguire dead."

"But none of them were in Spencer the night Maguire was killed," Mac countered.

The judge blinked. He shifted from one side of the chair to the other like a horse pawing the ground anxious to bolt.

Gesturing at the two of them, Mac asked, "Does this have anything to do with your relationship, your honor?"

The judge pointed out, "We've been together for a very long time."

"Did your relationship begin during or after your marriage to Maguire?" Archie asked Natasha.

"It began shortly after I married Maguire," the defense attorney confessed. "I knew almost immediately that I'd made a mistake marrying him."

With a smirk on his face, the judge peered into his drink. "Natasha and I became involved after I made bench during a case that she had before me. Vance was the prosecutor. We knew it was inappropriate and we kept it a secret because if it ever came out..." He sighed. "You can't tell anyone. And if you do, I'll deny it—unless you find the recording."

"Recording? What recording?" Mac asked.

"We became involved during the Sid Baxter case," said Natasha.

"It was my first major trial after being appointed judge. A child disappearance case." Judge Sutherland waited for Mac to recall.

"Andy Sweeney. Nine years old. Disappeared on the same street where he lived while bike riding," Mac said. "Sid Baxter confessed. You threw it out."

The lawyer's and judge's anger about the circumstances behind the suppressed confession was visible on their faces.

Immediately, Natasha raged, "Because Baxter asked repeatedly for his lawyer, and that idiot Lieutenant Fitzwater ignored it. I *had* to move to have his confession tossed. I had no choice."

"And neither did I," Judge Sutherland joined in. "It broke my heart to let Baxter go and it broke Natasha's to have any part in making it happen."

Mac could see that it was their common misery that had brought them together.

"Maguire began suspecting that we were involved during the Baxter case," the judge explained. "George Vance moved up to deputy not long after that, and Hunter started looking for his replacement. Maguire didn't have a lot of experience at that point and his record wasn't much to write home about, but his family connections were appealing to Hunter. Maguire started recording Natasha's conversations with me in order to get something to hold over my head so that I'd put in a good word for him."

"It certainly wasn't out of romantic jealousy," Natasha jumped in.

The judge confessed, "Maguire recorded us discussing Sid Baxter. Out of context, which is how he edited the recording, it sounds like I let Baxter off in exchange for sex, which isn't how it happened. We didn't become intimate until long after that case was over." Pleadingly, he reached over to grasp Mac's wrist. "Do you see what I mean?"

"Your honor, you do realize that Maguire holding something like that over you and Holmstead gives you motive for wanting him dead."

"Killing him wouldn't do us any good as long as we don't know where the recording is." Judge Sutherland waved his hand in dismissal. "Maguire has been holding that recording over our heads for years. Since Vance has been appointed judge, it's been between Maguire and Roxanne Burton to take the deputy slot."

Mac noted, "So you told me this morning."

Natasha said, "Roxanne has seniority and a much better conviction record. Rightfully, the slot should go to her."

Mac said, "But Maguire was a blue blood and his family connections could help Hunter get the attorney general appointment, something Roxanne's family connections can't."

"Exactly." The judge said, "Maguire wanted me to have a little talk with Hunter to help push him in the right direction. Hunter was torn, especially when Maguire blew the Garland case."

Mac said, "I heard he was in the dog house over that."

The judge said, "But then Burton got slapped with an ethics charge in the Parker case. Did you hear about that?"

Mac reminded the judge that he had been out of the loop for several months.

"A bunch of juveniles stole computer equipment from their school and sold it to a fence that the older brother of one of the juvies used for his own B&E business. Burton's key witness, the fence, accused her of paying him ten thousand dollars for his testimony against the juvies. Now, not only is she out of the running for the deputy slot—"

Natasha pointed out, "But now that Maguire's dead, I guess she's back in the running."

"Not if she's disbarred," the judge countered, "which could happen."

Mac said, "I guess that made the two of them even."

Garrison nodded his head. "I wouldn't be surprised if Maguire made it that way."

"He got the fence to lie," Mac said with certainty. It sounded so much like Stephen Maguire.

"I'd believe that before I believe that Burton paid him to testify," the judge said. "The fence came in with an envelope full of money. Someone paid him for something. I doubt that it's just a coincidence that this accusation came up right after the Garland incident," he scoffed. "Word around the courthouse was that Roxanne set Maguire up hoping that it would blow his chance for the promotion, and he made things even. The problem is that the ethics committee, which happens to be made up of a lot of Maguire's friends, isn't letting this accusation drop. They're doing a full investigation into the charge and Burton may end up being disbarred."

Mac wondered, "Do you think she set him up?"

"Garland's attorney belongs to some of the same committees as Sabrina, Roxanne's sister," the judge said.

Mac said, "Knowing that family, I wouldn't be surprised if it was Sabrina who set him up, and Roxanne knew nothing about it."

"Rightfully," Natasha said, "the deputy slot should have gone to Roxanne. If Hunter was torn, it wasn't very much.

The backing of Maguire's family for the attorney general slot was too tempting."

The judge groaned. "I hated myself for going to bat for Maguire."

"And him for making you do it," Mac pointed out.

Natasha said, "We never entertained the thought of killing him."

"Someone did poison him at that party," Mac said.

Natasha held up her hands with the fingers spread. "I can count on both hands other people at that party who wanted him dead—including Christine who was staying at your Inn when he was killed. Wasn't her death an accident? I heard she was drunk and fell and hit her head."

"Someone else was there," Mac said. "What kind of scandal was Maguire looking to uncover?"

"That I don't know," the judge said, "Of course if that tape was found and made public, both Natasha's and my careers would be over for letting a pedophile back out on the streets. So you see why it's so important that we get it."

Seeing the weight they were under, Mac sighed. "I see."

The judge asked, "Did O'Callaghan find it?"

Mac shook his head. "He did find a folder labeled Themis. Do you know what that is?"

While Judge Sutherland's face was blank, Mac did notice him sit up taller. Natasha gazed over at her companion. She put on her best poker face. He had seen that expression in court hundreds of times. It gave nothing away.

"I'm sorry," the judge replied after a moment. "What was that name again?"

"Themis. No first name or initial. It could have some connection with Dylan Booth."

"Who?"

"Dylan Booth. Homicide victim. I was the lead detective on the case. It went cold."

"What makes you think this particular victim is connected to this Themis?" Before Mac could answer, the judge glanced at his wrist watch. "I'm sorry, Mac, but we have to get going. We forgot that we have an appointment." After walking hand in hand casually out of the lounge, they both broke into a trot once they reached the lobby.

Watching them hurry away, Mac asked, "Do they look guilty to you?"

Archie replied, "They look guiltier than we do."

CHAPTER TEN

"Now you have me so excited that I'm speeding," Mac told Archie when he saw the Spencer police cruiser come up behind his sports car and turn on its lights. A glance at the speedometer showed that he had been going forty-two miles an hour on the twisting mountain road in a thirty-five-miles-per-hour zone in his hurry to take Archie back to Spencer Manor to enjoy their strawberries dipped in chocolate. He pulled over to the side of the road.

She laughed when she saw him reaching for his registration in the glove box. "That's David. He's not going to give you a ticket."

Before Mac could reply, the police chief knocked on his driver's side window. "Hey, don't you ever answer your cell?"

"Was I speeding?"

"A little," David replied. "You should watch that. I'd hate to give you a ticket. We got a call from the Morgantown police. They've picked up Cameron Jones for possession, and she's singing like a canary about Stephen Maguire's murder. Plus, one of my officers IDd the woman from the security video who Maguire was having dinner with on Saturday. Her name is Bonnie Propst. She's the president of Propst Security. The Inn has bought some security equipment from her company."

"Did the dinner Maguire was having with Propst look like a date?" Mac wondered if she was the one whose vaginal fluid had been found on Maguire's bed sheets.

"I don't think so. The tapes aren't the best, but I didn't see any lovey-dovey eyes." David added, "Not only that, but I noticed something else in the security video. Remember that couple I told you about that came into my office demanding Maguire's personal belongings? His wife and the judge?"

His last discussion with Judge Sutherland fresh on his mind, Mac replied, "I certainly remember them."

"Guess who was having dinner within camera range of Maguire," David said. "According to Ingle, they even had reservations for that evening. They were sitting three tables away from him while he was eating his last meal."

"They failed to mention that." Mac turned to Archie. "Do you recall them saying anything about that to you, dear?"

"Never said anything like that to me, darling."

David continued, "Anyway, I'm going out to Morgantown to question Cameron Jones and wanted to know if you wanted to tag along as my consultant. I've been calling you on your cell—" Noticing her dress and his suit, David stopped. "I'm sorry. Were you on your way to get your back scratched?"

Mac glanced over at Archie. He was torn. He so wanted to be with her, but he was also anxious to get answers about what Stephen Maguire was doing in Spencer. If he declined David's invitation, he'd have to wait until at least the next day to drag it out of him.

She grasped his wrist. "For that, you have to let me come along, too."

*   *   *   *

"I wasn't planning for this to turn into a field trip," David said while holding the back door to his cruiser open for Gnarly to jump up into what had become his seat directly behind the driver.

While Mac and Archie were changing into more comfortable jeans and sweaters, Gnarly had spied David's cruiser and saw that his family was going on an outing. According to Archie, he insisted on being included.

The next stop on the way to the Morgantown station was a diner across the state line in West Virginia, off Route 68, where David, who hadn't eaten dinner yet, knew the food was good and the service fast. Archie and Mac drank coffee while David ordered two cheeseburgers and fries. One of the burgers was plain and to go for the German shepherd cooling his jets in the cruiser in the parking lot.

It was a far cry from the elegant dinner Mac and Archie had at the Inn, but a good opportunity to go over what they had so far in their investigation and come up with a plan on which direction to go from there.

While waiting for David's dinner, Mac recalled, "Did you say that the woman that Maguire was having dinner with on Saturday was Bonnie Propst and she owned a security company in Morgantown?" After David confirmed that it was, he pointed out that there was a Douglas Propst on the list found in the Themis folder.

"Archie, can you look it up on your phone and find out if there's any connection between Bonnie and Douglas Propst?" Mac was glad to see that she had already pulled out her smart phone and was searching the Internet.

"There was no file labeled Propst in the Themis folder." David eyed a plate of delicious-smelling food passing their booth, but not coming his way. "What do you know about Douglas Propst?"

"I had been in homicide only a couple of years when it happened," Mac recalled. "Douglas Propst was a uniformed officer and a bully. He was the type of cop that gave us a bad name. Charged with brutality a couple of times. Really nasty bastard. One day, his wife disappeared. His story was that she'd left him a note saying she was going out for milk while he was out for a run. After her body turned up with a broken neck and his skin under her fingernails, family and friends started making statements about spousal abuse. His name was moved up to the top of the suspect list real fast."

When the server arrived with his tray of food, Mac could see that it took all of David's restraint to not grab the plate and devour his burger like a barbarian. It made him wonder if David had eaten since the donut he had earlier that day.

"I think I remember that case. I was like fifteen when that happened." David smiled his gratitude to the buxom server when she refilled his cup along with the others at the table.

Mac had noticed that David greeted her by her first name when they had come in. The grease on the burger and the soggy fries made him wonder if it was the service that David enjoyed as much as the food.

"If I recall correctly, Propst was arrested?" David asked after the server left.

Mac nodded his head somberly. "And tried twice. Both times it ended with a hung jury."

"Did he do it?"

"Everyone knew he did it." Mac shrugged. "It wasn't my case. I was in homicide at the time but not close to the investigation. I remember it was one of those cases where everyone knew he did it, but there was no real evidence."

"Except his skin under her fingernails," David said.

"Natasha Holmstead was his attorney. This case made her career. I didn't actually meet her until the Keating case," Mac said. "Holmstead argued that since they were married the skin had gotten under her fingernails during marital relations."

David shot Archie a naughty look. "I never actually had that happen."

"I saw that." Archie said with her eyes still on her smart phone. "I could say a few things about you, Dave."

Mac steered them back to the topic of Douglas Propst. "No other evidence could be found to use against him."

"What about the abuse?" David wanted to know.

Mac said, "Not once had the police been called to their home for domestic disturbance. Once she'd gone to the ER for a broken wrist. She said it was because she'd fallen off a step ladder. Some friends had seen her with a black eye. She said that it was an accident. The Propsts had argued in public, but he was never seen hitting her."

Mac grimaced. "Propst was a bully and abusive in the field. All that was kept from the jury. Holmstead pointed out how many couples have fights in public but the wife doesn't end up dead." He shrugged. "Both times, the jury got hung. The prosecutor finally said that until we got more evidence, they weren't wasting their time."

"Who was the prosecutor?" David popped a fry into his mouth. "Maguire?"

"That was before Maguire's time at the attorney's office," Mac said. "Garrison Sutherland was the prosecutor on the Propst case."

"The judge that Holmstead is sleeping with now?" David chewed a big bite of his burger and frowned at the same time.

"Douglas Propst is Bonnie Propst's late husband." Archie held up the phone for them to see the screen.

"Late as in dead?" Mac asked.

She went on to read the screen. "Douglas Propst was a retired cop. He opened Propst Security in Morgantown, WV, with the money from his late wife's life insurance. Two years later, he was killed when he walked in on a burglary in his office. Since then, his widow, Bonnie Propst, has made the company one of the most successful security firms in the tri-state area, according to the company bio."

Mac scratched his head. "Douglas Propst is dead."

"If the perp is dead, then it would make no sense for Maguire to re-open the case." David finished the last bite of his burger.

Archie slipped her phone into her purse. "Unless he had found new evidence while working on this Themis case that Propst didn't kill his wife."

Mac took out his wallet to pay for the bill. "I guess we'll find out when we talk to his widow."

* * * *

First, they had to go to the Morgantown police station where Cameron Jones, the college drop-out claiming to be Stephen Maguire's illegitimate daughter, was spending the night in a holding cell awaiting a bond hearing on possession of crack cocaine with intent to distribute.

In the station's reception area, David, Mac, and Archie met Master Sergeant Rick Bromberg, the trooper who had arrested Cameron. The tall, muscular, bald-headed officer shook David's hand so hard that he shook the police chief's whole arm. "David O'Callaghan, nice to see you. Congratulations on the appointment to chief. I always thought if anyone should take over your dad's slot, it should be you."

While shaking his hand, Sergeant Bromberg glanced down the corridor to the holding cells. "We're taking Jones into an interview room now. Like I told you on the phone, we busted her for possession with intent to distribute, and she immediately started talking about wanting to make a deal."

"We put out an APB on her as a suspect and witness in the Maguire murder this afternoon," David told him.

"It must have been about the same time that we busted her." The sergeant looked worried. "We're hoping she'll roll over on her boyfriend, who is a person of interest in the drug community here in Morgantown. Instead, she wants to roll on the murder in your neck of the woods." He confessed, "I really don't want to give her up with what we have against her. This is the best break we've had in nailing the boyfriend."

David cocked his head at Mac and Archie. "Why don't you let me hear what she has to say first?"

Mac and Archie watched from the observation room while David went into the interrogation room where Cameron Jones sat at the table.

Mac's memory of their brief meeting days before was unclear. At the time, he had been focused on calming Christine down. After learning that she was trying to con Stephen Maguire out of money, Mac's perception of her

140

created the image of a hard young woman willing to say and do whatever it took to keep up her party lifestyle.

That image was a far cry from the little girl shivering in her thin sleeveless top over a short skirt with only sandals to cover her bare feet in the cold interrogation room this late in the night.

She looked like a frightened animal.

"What do you think?" Mac asked Archie while comparing Cameron to the woman running onto the guest elevator in the security video.

"She could be the right height and build," Archie answered. "But would she know enough about how security works at the Inn?"

"If she's involved with drug dealers, she knows enough about security, period."

"Cameron, I'm David O'Callaghan, the police chief in Spencer, Maryland. Tell me what you know about Stephen Maguire." Taking on a casual attitude to put her at ease, David straddled the back of the chair across from her. He had laid his pen on top of the notepad in the middle of the table.

"I want a deal," she said forcibly.

After all of his years of experience dealing with suspects from all walks of life and criminal experience, Mac saw that her harsh demand for a deal was a cover for her fear.

David said, "You don't seem very broken up about his murder. That's surprising since you claimed Stephen Maguire was your father."

"That was all a misunderstanding," she said. "I didn't kill him, but I can tell you who did. All I want is a deal."

"I already know you weren't on the scene," David said. "My sources tell me that you have an airtight alibi. That makes me wonder how you would know who did it."

"Because I saw her try to kill him before."

"Are you talking about the woman who attacked you in the lobby?"

She sat back in her seat. "I'm not telling you anything else until I have a deal."

David started to rise out of the chair. "I can see I'm wasting both our time. I'm sorry, I must have misunderstood. I thought you had some useful information on this case."

"Wait!" She jumped out of her seat and grabbed his arm. "I saw her try to kill him the day before. I can identify her. All I need is for you to give me a deal."

"I don't help drug dealers."

"I'm not a dealer. My boyfriend's the dealer. I don't even use drugs. When I don't help him, he beats me up. I had no choice. I had told him about my friend Rebecca from school and her daddy, and it was all his idea that I contact this Maguire guy and get him to pay me off to go away." Clinging to David's arm, she pleaded, "Please. You have to help me. Please don't let them send me to jail."

"He's going to sit back down," Archie whispered.

David lowered himself back down into the chair.

"Told you." She grinned. "David's always had a soft spot for the ladies, especially if she's a lady in distress."

David told her, "First off, Morgantown is out of my jurisdiction. The only thing I can do is put in a good word with the prosecutor here. If you cooperate with me and the police here about your boyfriend's drug activities, then they'll be more inclined to help you than not."

Without a reply, she stared at the two-way mirror while seeming to consider his advice. After they sat a long time in silence, David told her, "What do you know about what Stephen Maguire was doing in Spencer?"

"Nothing," she answered. "He said he had some business in the area. On Friday, we met at some restaurant on the lake. It was closed for renovations. There was a big pool table on the lower level. It was really cool. He was really cool. He had gotten some burgers from the take-out place on the corner. We played pool. We even had some beer. Then, I made my move. I told him about flunking out of school, but now I was getting my act together and wanted to make a new start, but since things are so tough, that I needed some money; or I could follow him back to D.C. and meet all his friends." She stopped.

David urged her to continue, "To which Maguire replied..."

"He said he'd have to think about it and wanted to get together for drinks at the Spencer Inn the next day to discuss it."

"Then what?" David urged her to continue.

She asked, "Are you talking about at the place with the pool table on the lake or the Spencer Inn?"

"The place where you saw some woman try to kill him the day before he ended up dead."

"Yeah, right," she said. "At the lake. After he put me off about giving me any money, I had to go take a leak. I was in the bathroom and I heard this big fight. It was, like, wild. I went back downstairs and there was this crazy woman there and she was screaming like a witch at Maguire. I couldn't believe he was laughing at her."

"What was she screaming about?"

"She called him a liar and he laughed even more. That pushed her off the deep end and this bitch grabbed a screwdriver and went at him with it."

David sat up straight. "A screwdriver?"

"I don't think she's talking about the drink," Archie said.

Cameron continued, "Maguire took it off her and slapped her down. She took off running out of there."

David frowned. "Did Maguire tell you who she was?"

She shook her head. "He didn't give me a name. He just said that she was some crazy bitch who couldn't take a joke. But I saw her. I could identify her if I saw her in a line up."

"What did she look like?" David leaned toward her.

In the observation room, Mac and Archie pressed up against the glass.

"She had long black hair..."

* * * *

"Mac, I hate to tell you this, but Christine had been in Spencer at least two days before Stephen Maguire got killed." David glanced over his shoulder to the back of the cruiser where Mac was sitting in the back seat behind Archie.

Except for the occasional squawks over the radio, the inside of the cruiser had been so quiet since they'd left the police station to find their way to Bonnie Propst's condo complex that all they could hear was Gnarly breathing in the seat next to Mac. Little had he envisioned his romantic evening with Archie would end with him in the back seat with a hundred-pound German shepherd with bad breath.

"I checked with the security cams at the main intersections in McHenry, coming in and out of Spencer," David said. "We have her car on Route 219 Thursday, Friday, and Saturday. Roxanne Burton stated that Christine had told her that she was coming out to the lake house to clear her head."

David continued gently, "I'm beginning to think that maybe she did kill Maguire. We don't have any actual evidence to prove she didn't do it. The clone phone with her fingerprints on it was in her suitcase. This other person that was on the scene could be a witness to the murder. Afterwards, they got into a fight. Christine fell, hit her head, and died. The witness panicked, cleaned up the scene, and ran."

"Even before her illness, Christine wasn't clever enough to have thought up anything like Maguire's murder," Mac said. "It was planned. The wig and smock and getting up to the suite by way of the service elevator. Christine has been out of her mind ever since she took up with Maguire. That's what made her such a good target for a snake like him. No way could she have planned it well enough to have pulled any part of it off."

Their silence made him turn to the only one he could turn to. "What do you think, Gnarly?" He stroked the dog's back. Gnarly answered with a tongue that went into Mac's ear.

Bonnie Propst lived in a high-rise condominium on a hill overlooking West Virginia University's campus. Her condo was on the eighth floor of a twelve-story building. Late in the evening, they were lucky that many of the residents were coming and going. Most of them looked like academic types from the university. With the coming and going, it was easy for David in his police chief uniform to get a resident on the way out to hold the door of the main entrance open to allow them, with Archie leading Gnarly on his leash, into the lobby of the secure building.

"The same way Nita got up to the penthouse floor," Mac noted.

David checked his notes. "Bonnie Propst lives in unit 812."

On their way up to the eighth floor, Archie petted Gnarly, who sat obediently for her in the back of the elevator. His ears were up at attention. "I think Gnarly likes police work."

"He's not on the payroll," David cracked.

"He was trained by the United States Army," Archie reminded them.

"He also got a dishonorable discharge for what, we don't know," Mac said.

They found Apartment 812 to be a corner unit. After answering the door on the first knock, Bonnie Propst looked displeased when she saw David flash his badge and identify himself as the police chief investigating the murder of Stephen Maguire in Spencer, Maryland.

Blocking their entrance into her condo with her door, she stated, "If you have any questions about Stephen Maguire's murder, you'll need to talk to my lawyer." She reached behind her to snatch a business card from a table and thrust it into David's hand.

While David tried to negotiate for some information, Gnarly looked up and down the hallway like a censor on duty.

Having met Douglas Propst, Mac remembered him as a vain, antagonistic man who hated not having control, especially over his women.

Bonnie Propst was overweight, something her late husband would have abhorred. In spite of her weight, she had a pretty face. Her clothes and make-up were tastefully applied and she was stylishly dressed in a business suit.

"Stephen Maguire is dead," David said. "He was killed after having dinner with you. If there's anything that you can think of—"

"It wasn't a date," she said. "That was the first time I had even met him."

Mac interjected, "If it wasn't a date, what was it?"

"Business," she said quickly. "I own a security company. He was opening a business in Spencer and wanted to know about our services. It's important to have a good security service, especially for a restaurant on the lake."

"Do you always meet potential clients at five-star restaurants on Saturday night?" Mac asked.

"He set it up," she answered. "I don't get invited to the Spencer Inn very often. Who was I to argue?"

Mac and David exchanged glances. Mac chose to toss out the next question. "Did Stephen Maguire mention your late husband during the interview?"

"No," she answered too quickly.

"Stephen Maguire was the prosecutor in D.C. where your late husband was tried twice for killing his first wife." Mac said. "Maybe he had some questions about what your husband may have told you about his wife's murder or the trials."

"He's dead. Long gone," she responded in a firm tone. "Look, I'm sorry Mr. Maguire is dead, but my dead and forgotten husband doesn't have anything to do with it." She tried to slam the door shut but found the police chief's foot in the way.

David explained, "Since you work in security and with the police, you have to understand that since you were the last person to see Stephen Maguire alive, we need to know what took place when you met him. What did you talk about? Did anything happen? Did anyone come to the table to talk to him?"

She hissed at him. "Surveillance cameras. Motion detectors. Police and fire alarms. That's all we talked about. As for what we did, we met at the Spencer Inn for dinner at seven o'clock. I ate shrimp scampi over linguini. He ate the filet mignon. He paid for dinner. I came home. That's all that happened." After kicking David in the shin to get him to remove his foot, she slammed the door shut.

David turned to Mac who was petting Gnarly. "What do you think?"

"I think the woman doth protest too much."

Gnarly exploded into a round of snarling barks. Archie held onto his collar while he lunged at the elevators.

The woman in the car jumped back from the hundred pounds of fur and teeth straining against the collar holding him back from getting at her. Keeping her eye on the dog, she moved slowly to get off the elevator.

Mac noticed that, at first glance, she appeared much younger than her true age. The red curly hair that fell to her shoulders and her athletic figure made him think she was more youthful than the hardness in her face revealed.

This woman has had a hard life.

"Sorry," Archie gasped at her. "I guess he doesn't like your perfume."

"What's gotten into him?" Mac joined her in grasping his collar.

David muttered, "I knew we should have left him in the car."

The red-haired woman backed up against the wall to get as far away as she could from Gnarly, who continued to strain to get at least one tooth into her while Mac and Archie dragged him onto the elevator. Her glare said that she was unforgiving of the dog's anger.

"What's up with him?" David whirled around to glare at the dog once the doors were shut.

Archie suggested, "Maybe she had a particularly nice dog biscuit in her pocket that he wanted to steal."

"I thought he was a B&E type of dog," Mac said, "not an armed robbery sort."

Whining, Gnarly pawed at her.

"He didn't like her," she explained. "Not everyone likes everyone."

"Just because he doesn't like someone, he doesn't have to rip her throat out," David said.

Once they stepped outside into the parking lot, Gnarly exploded again into a fit of snarling barks. He lunged on his leash with such force, trying to charge across the parking lot, that Mac had to grab the end of the leash from Archie in order to drag the dog in the other direction to the cruiser.

"Gnarly has lost his mind," David told Archie as she climbed into the front seat while Mac played tug of war with the dog to get him into the back. "I can't take him with me anymore. He's too unpredictable."

"He was fine until he ran into that woman that came out of the elevator," Archie said. "Gnarly has a good sense of people. Maybe she's a bad person."

"And maybe he's nuts." David fastened his seat belt and turned on the engine. "He's stolen from all of your neighbors and has started shoplifting from the stores on the other side of the lake, damn it."

They waited for Mac, who had to lift Gnarly up to set him in the back seat. "I don't know what's gotten into him." He climbed in next to the dog and closed the door. "Something's gotten under his skin."

David put the cruiser into reverse.

Suddenly, Gnarly was in Mac's lap. Barking and snarling, Gnarly pressed his nose against the window.

With the dog blocking David's view in the mirror, he pressed his foot on the brake. "Mac, do something about him. I can't see."

"What are you so upset about?" Mac looked through the window to determine what Gnarly wanted so badly.

They were looking at a parking lot. It was only half filled with a variety of vehicles. Recalling that Gnarly was trying to get to the other side, Mac peered in the direction that the dog had tried to drag him. On the other side of the parking lot, far away from the main entrance, where the lighting wasn't as bright, there was only one vehicle parked in the last space next to the rear exit, which provided easy access to the side roads out of town.

It was a black Ford SUV.

Where did I see a black Ford SUV?

"Mac, do something about Gnarly," David was saying. "I can't see to pull out."

"Wait!" Mac pressed his index finger against the glass. "I think Gnarly is trying—"

The police cruiser jarred with the impact of a blow from overhead.

Archie screamed.

Mac would later recall thinking that he had never realized she was capable of reaching such high notes.

David whirled around to see what had shattered the windshield. He only caught a split-second glimpse of it before the front airbags exploded. The shock caused him to hit the gas pedal, which shot the cruiser backwards straight into the path of a van carrying a group of senior citizens. With no time to stop, the van plowed into the cruiser's driver's side, which set off the side airbags.

Gnarly, who seemed to be as stunned as everyone else, held Mac pinned against his seat while he cried into his ear. "Gnarly," Mac moaned while patting the top of his head, "you're a good dog, but I'm going to kill you."

The inside of the cruiser seemed to take on the atmosphere of an electrified nightclub with the lights flashing and the sirens going off. The police operator's voice called out from the radio to confirm notice that the cruiser had been in a collision and needed emergency response. In Mac's aching head, she sounded like she was calling from another planet.

After David confirmed that they had indeed been in an accident, she asked, "What did you collide with?"

"A dead body."

CHAPTER ELEVEN

Smirking faces flashed before Mac in his dreams.

Freddie Gibbons Junior sneering during Mac's interrogation about the seven innocent women he had raped in Rock Creek Park. Each attack escalated in violence. He won the status of killer after strangling his last victim.

He taunted the detective. "Yeah, I did it. What are you going to do about it?"

Then, there was Leo Samuels. The gold and diamonds he wore on every part of his body cost more than the house Mac would later lose to his wife. All had been paid for with blood money collected from his business of drugs and prostitution.

The day Samuels strutted out of the courthouse after Mac's evidence against him had been tossed out, the gang leader made a point of plowing into the detective. "Later, sucker." His breath felt hot against Mac's face.

For an instant, Mac wanted to press his gun against Samuels's stomach and pull the trigger. He wanted to give his victims the justice denied to them by the system. The same type of justice that someone had given Sid Baxter.

"There's the bastard," Mac's partner cursed.

He started out of a sleepy trance he had fallen into while staring at a spot on the lid of his coffee cup to gaze across the street to where the creature posing as a human being going by the name of Sid Baxter had climbed out of his car. He was clutching an armload of what appeared to be mail to his chest. A plain brown envelope was tucked under his arm.

At the back door of his house in the lower-middle-class neighborhood, Sid Baxter looked around while digging in his pockets for his keys.

Mac put the binoculars to his eyes to close on Baxter's face. "He looks worried."

"He should be."

Detective Paul Grove was Mac's senior partner. During his long police career, Detective Grove had seen it all. Some detectives grow from what they see; others become bitter, like Grove.

"I still can't believe they let that bastard back out on the streets," he muttered.

"He won't be for long," Mac said. "We'll get him."

Sid's dark little eyes darted around until he saw Mac watching from the sedan across the street. Spotting him, Sid clutched the package tighter to his body and hurried inside.

"He spotted us," Mac told his partner.

"So what?"

They made no move to conceal themselves. They didn't have to. Since Sid Baxter had been released after confessing to killing eight-year-old Andy Sweeney, the prosecutor and police chief had ordered two units to keep the pedophile and child killer under constant surveillance until they could find some way to get him behind bars.

"He actually confessed, damn it." Detective Grove wasn't alone in his anger.

The detectives in homicide were outraged that Judge Garrison Sutherland had tossed out Sid Baxter's confession and released him. It wasn't expected of a judge who had been so passionate about justice when he was a prosecutor.

After four nights of listening to Detective Grove's complaining about the justice system and tailing a man who did nothing at night except watch television, Mac snapped, "If you want to blame anyone for releasing the likes of Sid Baxter back out on the streets, blame Fitzwater. He's the one who blew it. Not Sutherland. Fitzwater."

Grove argued, "Listen, I know you and Fitzwater don't get along, but he did his job. He found out who snatched the kid. He got a confession, damn it. And the court let him go. Fitzwater did what he needed to do."

Mac resumed staring at the small house tucked toward the back of the bare lot to leave only a small backyard. While the other homeowners did what they could to make their cozy spaces as inviting as possible, Baxter did nothing. There were no shrubs or trees. The backyard was confined behind a chain-link fence.

"You're aware that Andy Sweeney was about the same age as Tristan." Grove aimed for Mac's vulnerable spot. "If it was your son, you wouldn't be sitting here making excuses for Sutherland letting Baxter go. Baxter'd be dead already."

"No, it would be Fitzwater that'd be dead for screwing up the whole investigation and sending us all back to square one."

Detective Grove was right. Detective Fitzwater and Mac had mixed like oil and vinegar ever since Mac got promoted to the homicide division right out of uniform, an unusual appointment for a detective so young. Fitzwater didn't like the young officer. He was openly insulting and more than once hurried to their lieutenant to take credit for Mac's theories on cases.

Mac could see Sid Baxter going through the mail at his kitchen counter.

"Have you ever watched National Geographic?" Mac asked his partner.

"What?" Detective Grove's doughy face screwed up at the notion of wasting his time watching anything so educational. "Nature shows?"

"Tristan's into science." Mac didn't want to confess that the shows captured his interest as well. "Anyway, on these shows, when a pack of wolves go chasing after a jack-rabbit, if the rabbit's lucky, he can jump into a hole where the wolves can't reach him. When that happens, the wolves have a couple of options. Some wolves waste their time banging their heads trying to get the rabbit by following the path it took to hide. The smart ones will look around and find another way to get to it. Some will even double back around and come up behind the rabbit to snag it from behind."

Mac took his eyes off Sid Baxter to glance back at Grove. "I don't like to waste my time banging my head against a rock trying to get into a hole that I can't fit into, or coercing confessions that aren't going to be worth the paper they're written on. I'd rather spend my time doing something worthwhile, like doubling back and finding another way in to nail my suspects—ways that are going to stick."

Mac turned back to watch Sid Baxter at his kitchen window. With excitement that resembled a child on Christmas morning, he unwrapped the package sealed in plain brown paper.

"And what about when those legal weenies at the courthouse decide to block that way in because it's infringing on some poor pervert's rights?" Grove asked in a mocking tone. "Frankly, to tell you the truth, if that Sweeney boy's dad came over here right now with a shotgun to blow Baxter away, I wouldn't be inclined to stop him."

Mac brought the binoculars to his face to watch their suspect more closely. "Baxter got something in the mail."

"What?"

With his eyes glued to the glasses, Mac caught sight of the object clasped in Sid Baxter's hand when he stuck a cigarette between his lips. "It looks like a tape." He felt his blood rise. "It must be a sex tape. Child pornography."

Mac adjusted the focus on the binoculars to get a closer image of the tape before Sid Baxter left the room to go view it in the living room. He didn't want to leave the warmth of the car to crawl into the bushes on the other side of the house to look in the window.

His grin broadening in what had to be anticipation, Sid Baxter brought the lighter up to the end of his cigarette and flicked the end—

Still hearing the roar of the bomb that blew Sid Baxter to pieces, Mac sprang up on the gurney.

David was on the next gurney flirting with the nurse bandaging his shoulder.

Hearing Mac's cry, she whirled around to ease him into lying back down onto the gurney. "It's okay, Mr. Faraday, you're all right. You're in the hospital. You suffered a blow to the head. You need to rest."

Mac laid his head back down on the pillow and floated back to the boat dock off Spencer Manor.

Spencer, Maryland, had been founded by Mac's ancestors and was populated with residents who made up the listing of Who's Who. Mac's neighbors were rich and famous, like Andrew Keating had been. His life had been one of fame, luxury, and achievement, until Jillian Keating ended it.

Once again, Mac found himself outside the courthouse while Jillian Keating swam through the sea of journalists with Natasha Holmstead at her side. Wrapped in her fur coat, she had flipped her blond hair over her shoulder and smiled for the cameras in all her glory after getting off for killing her husband.

She slowed her pace when she saw Mac, the cop who had captured her. A brilliant smile crossed her face. Her driver opened the back door of her limousine. Before getting in, she paused to look Mac in the face. With a wink, she puckered her red lips and blew him a kiss. Without a word, she climbed into the back of the limousine and sailed away.

As the car faded from sight, Mac turned away to see the killer's defense attorney, Natasha Holmstead. Her smile of triumph matched that of her client.

"How can you even look at yourself in the mirror?"

Mac's grip cutting into the flesh on her arm turned her triumph into fear.

Judge Garrison Sutherland appeared at his side. "Let her go, Mac."

"He was a lonely old man and she used him," Mac hissed at her. "Jillian made him fall in love with her, and then she killed him. For what? His money? He thought she loved him and she killed him."

"Let her go," Garrison ordered the detective.

"Parasites and monsters," Mac fumed. "That's who you work for. Parasites and monsters. How can you look at yourself in the mirror, twisting the system around the way you do to let them back out on the street?"

"Detective!" Garrison snapped out the title like a whip.

It was the only time Mac saw fear in Natasha Holmstead's face. His grip on her arm seemed to shut off the usual strong-willed demeanor that had become her trademark.

"We're the ones who have to clean up the messes your clients make after you open the door to let them back out on the streets."

"Mac!"

He felt a firm grip on his shoulder.

"Mac, wake up." David's voice broke through his dreams.

Mac opened his eyes. The white ceiling above him, and the call for a doctor in the corridor outside his room, reminded him of where he was. He sprung up in his bed.

He remembered Archie's screams. "Archie!"

"It's okay, Mac. Everything is okay." David pressed him back down by his shoulder. "We're at WVU hospital. You hit your head, but you're going to be okay."

Feeling his forehead, Mac could feel the puffy bruise over his right eye. As his vision cleared, he saw that David's left arm was in a sling. "You?"

"It's only a dislocated shoulder. Hurts like hell, but I walked away. Not bad for getting hit in the driver's side door by a van. Airbags did their jobs. Archie walked away without a scratch. She'll be having nightmares about a woman landing on her face right in front of her, but other than that..."

The more Mac woke up, the more his head hurt. "What happened to me?"

He was surprised by David's laughter. "Your airbag went off like it was supposed to. Luckily, the impact was perfectly cushioned by Gnarly's head. You got head butted by a dog."

"Gnarly, I'm going to kill you." The pounding lessened when he laid back down to rest his head on the pillow.

"It didn't feel much better for him. He was staggering around after the emergency crew got him out of the cruiser."

"Where is he now?" Mac wanted to know.

"Bogie's driving them home. Archie and I have given our statements to the police about last night. They'll be wanting to talk to you."

Now it was coming back to him. Gnarly's barking. His attempt at attacking the red-head in the elevator. Her deadly eyes. The black Ford SUV.

Mac grabbed David's wrist. "I remember now what got under Gnarly's fur. It was the black Ford."

"What black Ford?"

"SUV parked on the other side of the parking lot." Mac was clinging to David's good arm and shirt. "It was the same black Ford SUV that the shooter escaped in after shooting at us at Nancy Brenner's house. I recognized it. Gnarly must have recognized the scent. And that woman who got off of the elevator. It had to have been her."

"Someone threw Bonnie Propst off her balcony." David pried Mac's fingers off from where they were digging into his arm. "The police told me that her place was wrecked. She put up quite a fight before going over the balcony railing."

"It was the same person who was shooting at us. She didn't want Bonnie Propst talking to us."

David said, "She has to be Nita."

Mac agreed. "If she went after Bonnie Propst because her late husband's name was on that list, then his murder has to be connected to Themis, whatever that is."

* * * *

They were on their way back to Spencer in the back of a state police cruiser when the state forensics lab emailed to David's phone their report on fingerprints found in Stephen Maguire's suite.

"Her name is Justine Kable," David said while reading the report. "We found her fingerprints all over Stephen Maguire's room, including the headboard. I think it might be a good bet that DNA tests will show that the vaginal fluid we found on the sheets was hers, too. Her prints were in the database from when she used to be a schoolteacher. Now she's a bartender at your inn."

Clutching the bruise over his right eye, Mac moaned, "I'm beginning to hate the sound of that."

"Sound of what?"

"Your inn."

David chuckled. "We'll drop you off at the manor and—"

"No," Mac said. "I want to know why my bartender is slipping between the sheets with my guests. I'm not running one of *those* types of establishments. Take me to the Inn. While I'm there, I want a drink." After calling Jeff Ingle to ask when Justine would be working next, he told David, "She's on duty now."

During the mid-afternoon lull before the early dinner hour, the lounge was empty except for a couple nuzzling in the corner booth by the fireplace. A curvaceous woman wearing thick make-up, Justine Kable was cleaning the last of the glasses to get the bar ready for the happy hour crowd.

When David stepped up to the bar in the civilian clothes he had changed into at the hospital after their accident, she snapped, "Lunch time is over. We won't start serving the dinner menu until four o'clock." When she saw Mac turn from where he was admiring the view of the mountaintops on the horizon, her attitude softened. "Unless you want us to open earlier, Mr. Faraday."

"I'm not interested in lunch. I need a drink."

Noticing the bruise on his forehead, hospital ID bracelet, and his disheveled appearance, she agreed. "What happened to you, sir?"

"I was in a head-on collision with a German shepherd." Mac climbed up onto a stool and slapped David on the back, hitting his dislocated shoulder. "What do you want? It's on the house."

"Anything?" David hesitated.

"You do like cognac, don't you?"

"Yeah, but—"

Mac turned to Justine. "Two snifters of cognac from my special reserve. Make it Camus Jubilee."

David grinned. "Jubilee. Dad's favorite. I was only allowed to have it a couple of times."

"Then this should be a treat."

Camus Jubilee was a special blend of the oldest cognac. Robin Spencer had a special collection of the most expensive and decadent wines, champagnes, and spirits reserved for herself and her special guests. Now they belonged to Mac. He still didn't know the complete inventory. Archie had been gradually introducing it to him and his taste buds.

Mac feared that he was becoming horribly spoiled.

After Justine delivered the drinks, Mac held up his snifter to David's in a toast. "To murder. The ultimate puzzle."

"Some people do crossword puzzles. Mac Faraday solves murders." David swirled the liquor in the snifter before savoring a sip of it.

Both men groaned with pleasure while the smooth spirit slid down their throats.

"Better than sex," Mac declared.

"Equal to, but not better," David countered.

Mac chuckled when he thought about how long it had been since he had been with a woman. "When I was your age, I thought the same thing. Funny how age has a way of shifting your priorities."

"Now you prefer cognac to a fine woman?" David asked. "Tell me the truth. If you had to choose between a snifter of

Jubilee and an evening alone with Archie, which would you choose?"

Mac grinned. "You've forgotten that I spend most evenings alone with Archie."

"Have you forgotten about Gnarly?"

"Gnarly doesn't count."

"Do you want me to tell him you said that?" David laughed.

Out of the corner of his eye, Mac saw Justine listening to their conversation while trying to appear busy completing her inventory check list. She was good at appearing nonchalant. The tilt of her head in their direction gave her away.

"How long have you been working here, Justine?" he asked so abruptly that she dropped her pen to the floor.

After retrieving the pen, she smiled broadly at him. "Four years."

"Are you married?"

"Divorced."

"Did you know Stephen Maguire?" David held up his badge for her to see. "The man killed here at the Inn."

"No," she said quickly. "I served him a couple of drinks, but that was it. I didn't know him."

In silence, they sipped their drinks. Mac set his drink down on the bar and peered up at her. "You are aware that we have security cameras all over the place, Justine."

Her cheeks turned a bright shade of pink. "All we did was have sex. That was it. Nothing else. I didn't know him—except in the biblical sense. I didn't really know him. I mean, I knew nothing about him, except that he was a big lawyer and knew lots of important people and was great in bed. That's all." She waved her hands and the bar's dishrag like it was a flag, while repeating, "It was sex. Nothing else."

Mac nodded his head. "Okay, I get it. You had sex with Stephen Maguire and nothing else."

"He was in here for drinks Friday night and we hit it off," she rambled on. "He invited me up to his room and we were attracted to each other." In a choked voice, she asked, "Am I going to get fired for this?"

"Were you on the clock when you had sex with him?"

"No."

"Good," Mac answered, "because I don't want a reputation for running that type of hotel. We can have murder, but no sex on the clock."

David asked, "Where and when did you have sex with Stephen Maguire?"

"His room. Saturday afternoon," she said. "I went up to his room around one o'clock. I went on duty at four. I was there a few hours. We made the date for lunch. He'd sent for room service. Fruit and cheese and strawberries dipped in chocolate." Giggling, she twisted the dishrag in her hands. "But we didn't eat that much. He was really great."

Uncomfortable with her discussing the sexual prowess of the man with whom his wife had cheated on him, Mac shifted in his seat, took a large sip of his drink, and rubbed his aching head.

David resumed the interview. "Did he talk to anyone while you were there? Get or make any phone calls or texts?"

She shook her head before changing her mind. "I take that back. He did get a phone call. They got into an argument. I remember thinking he sounded like those hardball lawyers you see on television."

Mac asked, "Do you remember the conversation?"

She proceeded to wipe down the bar with the dishrag. "It had to be a woman, because they were talking about her husband."

Mac and David exchanged glances.

"He was telling her that he wanted to talk to her about her husband's case," she said slowly while recalling. "I guess she wanted to know why, and he said because the case had come to his attention, and he thought there had maybe been some irregularities about it. That was the word he used. Irregularities. I guess she didn't want to talk to him because then he said—and this was when he started talking hard ball, it was a real turn on, too—"

"Focus on what was said," Mac directed her.

"He asked her if she knew Randolph Maguire. I don't know who that is," Justine said.

"He's a high-ranking official with the IRS," Mac told her.

"Oh," she said. "Well, he told her that this Maguire dude was his uncle, and one phone call from him and he could have her company come to a grinding halt with audits, and she'd be up to her eyeballs in IRS agents. Then they made an appointment to meet later on for dinner."

"Dinner?" Mac repeated. "And this was Saturday?"

She nodded her head quickly.

David clarified. "They met for dinner on Saturday night?"

"I guess," Justine said. "I saw him having dinner with some woman. She didn't look like she was having a good time either. Is that any help?"

Mac jumped when he felt a strong hand clasp his shoulder. "You look like you've been hit by a truck."

Garrett County prosecutor Ben Fleming had decided to make his presence known. With his blond good looks and upscale style, he resembled a golf pro more than he did a lawyer. Judging by his athletic togs, he'd been visiting the club on the ground floor. He looked the Inn's owner up and down. Even with a layer of sweat, Ben Fleming's breeding was several degrees more evident than Mac's.

"As you can see, Mac went several rounds with Gnarly and lost," David explained.

"And you?" Ben touched the sling on David's arm. The curl in his lip told them that he had already heard via the Spencer grapevine.

"T-boned by a van filled with geezers," David said. "You should see the van."

Ben gestured for Justine to serve him a snifter of the same cognac they were having. After getting his, he invited them to join him in the sitting area around the fireplace.

"By the way, Chief, I got a call about you this morning," Ben said before slipping into a pub chair.

They could only imagine which suspect had called the county prosecutor to complain about David. It could've been anyone from Judge Sutherland to Natasha Holmstead to Hamilton Sanders.

"Sabrina Carrington," Ben announced.

"My sister-in-law?" Mac corrected himself, "Ex-sister-in-law."

Ben smiled into his snifter. "She claims she was assaulted by our chief of police."

Before David could reply to the accusation, Mac argued, "In defense of me." He showed Ben the scratches on his cheek, which the bruise on his forehead had made him forget. "David told her to stand down and she refused. He had no choice but to shove her back and that's all it was."

The prosecutor said, "She claims he tackled her and manhandled her breasts in the process."

"It's like Mac said," David replied. "She was out of control. I warned her to back off and she continued the assault on Mac. I ended it."

"How big was this woman?"

David hesitated, then revealed that while Sabrina wasn't very tall, she was a hefty weight, which caused the prosecutor to chuckle at the image of the athletic young police chief taking down a heavyset middle-aged woman in defense of Mac.

"You haven't met this woman," Mac told him. "Sabrina Carrington can be as mean as a snake when she's riled, which happens frequently."

"In that case, don't worry about it." Ben dismissed the matter with a smirk. "I'll handle it. Other than Mac's out of control relatives—"

"Ex-relatives," Mac corrected him. "Ex-in-laws."

"Ex-relatives," Ben repeated. "How's it going otherwise? Any headway we can speak of?"

"We're making some headway." Relieved that the prosecutor wasn't taking Sabrina's complaint seriously, Mac sat back into the chair. "We have an APB out on Hamilton Sanders. He was Stephen Maguire's assistant."

David explained, "He has to know what this Themis is. Archie is searching the Internet to find a common denominator about all the names on the list we found in Maguire's folder. We believe it has to be more than that they all got off for murder, especially since someone took a shot at us and killed Bonnie Propst, the widow of one of the defendants on his list."

"Do keep me informed about any developments." In a casual tone, Ben announced, "I got an interesting phone call from a friend of mine. Broderick Maguire."

"Broderick Maguire is a friend of yours?" Mac sensed, rather than knew, that Ben, who came from old money, was well connected. He appreciated that the prosecutor didn't indulge in name-dropping. Even so, he would've thought that if his friend was connected to billionaire Broderick Maguire, he would have mentioned it at some point.

"So you're the one he called," David said. "We've been wondering why we haven't heard anything from the Maguires wanting to know the status of our investigation."

"I went to college with Broderick's youngest son," Ben explained. "Straight up guy. You never would have known that he came from so much money and political power."

"What did you tell Broderick?" Mac asked.

Ben scratched the side of his head. "Don't you want to know what he was asking me about first?"

"Okay. I'll bite," Mac said. "What did he want to know?"

"He wanted to know why he and his family have been getting all these calls from the media asking how they felt about some dude they'd never heard of getting killed at the Spencer Inn."

Forgetting about his aching head, Mac jerked upright in his seat. "What? Some dude they'd never heard of?"

Ben chuckled. "I don't know where you got the idea that Stephen Maguire was any relation—Broderick said he has no grandson named Stephen. He's got twenty-three grandchildren, but none of them are named Stephen. He's got a nephew named Stephen, but he's a retired dentist in Florida. To Broderick Maguire's knowledge, he's never even been to the Spencer Inn."

Mac spat out, "He lied. Maguire lied about belonging to the Maguire family."

"Is his name even Maguire?" Ben asked.

"David ran a background check on him." Mac pointed in David's direction in an accusing manner. "It said that he'd gone to Ohio State University. I thought that was odd, because I was told that he went to Oxford."

Ben said, "Then his name may be Maguire, but he's not related to *the* Maguires."

"That's why he never introduced Christine to his family, because they weren't his family." Mac felt as if the wind had been knocked out of him. All the years that he had known Stephen Maguire, he'd bought the lie as well. He put up with Maguire's arrogance because of the family connections he believed he had. "Who lies about things like that?"

"Con men," Ben answered.

"And the con worked," Mac said. "Hunter put Stephen Maguire on the fast track, specifically because he wanted his family's endorsement for attorney general. Wealthy women supported him in the life style of the rich and famous, with the promise of being part of high society as soon as Grandpa Maguire kicked the bucket and he came into his share of the family dynasty."

"It happens all the time," Ben said with a shrug of his shoulders. "Con men say they're from money, but it's tied up in a trust or an overseas bank. They flash enough cash around to convince you that it's true—"

Mac said, "The U.S. Attorney bought it. Washington bought it. Maguire had a lot of influence. I was ordered by my supervisors to walk on eggshells around him for fear of his wrath against them."

Mac's fury rose. "Maguire has probably been playing this con ever since hitting Washington. It probably started when someone asked if he was any relation to those Maguires and he said yes. When he saw people bowing down to kiss his feet without actually checking to see if he was telling the truth, he took a liking to it and decided to start living it. Then he conned women like Christine into supporting him in that lifestyle with the promise of being introduced into high society."

Ben held up a hand to study his manicured fingertips. "Living the debutante life has a high overhead." He gestured at Mac's worn and discolored jacket. "If you got more into it, you'd see that for yourself."

"I prefer my jackets broken in, thank you." Mac brushed his fingers over the worn leather of his three-year-old jacket. "If Maguire wasn't already dead, I'd fill him full of bullets and dump his body in the lake."

"What did I just hear?" David asked.

"Hey, I'm only now finding out about this," Mac said when he recalled that he didn't have an alibi for the murders.

"Think about it," the police chief suggested. "Look at how mad you are about this fantasy pedigree that Maguire pulled over everyone's eyes. Imagine if you were one of his mistresses who got taken for a ride, or a colleague who had spent years kowtowing to him only to discover that he was a fraud."

"Like when Maguire's so-called illegitimate daughter calls his office saying that her mother and he were friends at Ohio State instead of Oxford," Mac said.

"Maguire was stabbed twenty-seven times," David said, "which points to his murder being a crime of passion."

Mac nodded his head with a grin. "If Cameron told any of Maguire's enemies about his pedigree being a fake, then I can imagine the blow-up it would have caused in the U.S. Attorney's Office." He added, "There's one thing that I can't figure out. The federal government runs background checks on all of their employees."

Ben agreed. "In order for Maguire to have pulled this off, he had to have someone working in the Office of Personnel Management to go along with it. He would have had to have falsified transcripts and they run checks on all of that. He had to have an accomplice."

David asked, "Who?"

Mac shrugged his shoulders. "In all the years that I was a homicide detective, I thought I'd seen it all. But this, conning the United States Attorney's Office into believing that you were local nobility..." He shook his head. "I can't believe he pulled it off."

Taking his cell phone from his pocket, David rose up out of his seat. "I think I'm going to have another conversation with Cameron Jones to find out who she contacted in Stephen Maguire's world and what she told them."

CHAPTER TWELVE

Archie met Mac at the door with a hug and a kiss after David dropped him off at the manor. For a moment, Mac imagined that he was coming home to a lovely wife who smelled of roses...and their dog, who was hiding under the coffee table.

"Don't tell me." Mac sniffed.

A familiar odor met his nostrils. Instantly, he knew what it was. It went with the Cadillac parked in front of the manor. It was the sisters, who were making something overcooked and bland in his kitchen.

"Sabrina said that it was your favorite," Archie told him.

"English pot roast," Mac said. "Why are they cooking it here?"

"Mac Faraday, whose wife and her lover had been found dead last week in his penthouse, was in a car accident. It made the news," Archie explained. "They wanted to do what they could since we've been dodging dead bodies while sorting out their sister's murder. I have to admit, I was surprised when Sabrina told me that pot roast was your favorite. I've never seen you eat pot roast."

Aware of them nearby in the kitchen, Mac whispered, "I didn't hate pot roast until I ate Sabrina's. Christine told her about how it was my favorite as part of a cruel joke."

He pointed at Gnarly who was still hiding under the coffee table. "What did he do?"

"He came running out here with his tail between his legs when Sabrina tried to feed him a bite."

They could hear Sabrina and Roxanne quarreling in the kitchen. Mac assumed the argument was about cooking techniques and other culinary tidbits. Suspicious about why the sisters-in-law who had always hated him would be cooking dinner for him, he wondered if the pot roast was a bribe to get him to sign over Christine's share of the lake house. Ed Willingham was adamant about Mac not promising anything to Roxanne until he had time to ensure she had paid Christine.

Taking his hand, Archie led him into the living room, where her mini-laptop was set up on the coffee table. "I've made some progress. I'm still working on the other names on your list, but I found out about Emma Wilkes, whose name was listed next to Dylan Booth's."

Before he could ask for more details, Sabrina screeched from the kitchen. "If Big Daddy could see you right now, he'd slap you across the head, bitch!" Her curse was followed by a crash of what sounded like a pan against the wall.

Archie jumped up off the sofa. "I hope she's not throwing our good pans."

"Sounds like she is." Bracing for a fight, he hurried into the kitchen.

"I'll wait here for backup." Archie's quip wasn't a joke.

Sabrina was shaking a paring knife in her sister's face when Mac barged into the kitchen. Tears were streaming down Roxanne's face.

"Drop that knife, Sabrina!" he ordered.

Sabrina scoffed. "I was only making a point."

"Make it without the knife," he said. "I mean it. Put the knife down."

In a huff, she laid the knife on the counter and returned to the sauce she had on the stove.

"Is everything all right?" he asked Roxanne.

"Other than the fact that her sister was murdered and you haven't caught her killer yet, fine," Sabrina answered. "But we Burton girls are tough. We'll muddle through somehow. We always do."

"Is that what Big Daddy used to say?" he asked. "To muddle through somehow or he'd slap you across the head?"

"Something like that," Sabrina replied.

Sympathy for Roxanne was a new thing for him. When he asked her a second time if she was okay, the words didn't sound natural coming from his mouth.

"She's fine," Sabrina answered for her. It sounded more like an order than an answer. "We've been taking care of Christine for so long, that Roxanne is feeling lost right now. I felt the same way when Big Daddy passed."

She reminded him, as she had often to whoever would listen, that when their father's health began to decline, he had come to live with her. She would never mention in those reminders that she had also hired two private nurses, who cared for him and drove him to his doctor's appointments.

"You don't realize it when you're caring for someone, even when they become a burden, the guilt that you feel when they pass. You end up feeling like they died because you didn't do enough for them." Sabrina glared at her sister. "That's what Roxanne is feeling like right now. Guilt over Christine's death when it wasn't her fault."

"Is that all it is?" Mac asked Roxanne.

Roxanne had a pleading look in her eyes.

"Did Archie show you Robin Spencer's study?" He gestured to the door on the other side of the kitchen. It led to the hallway and steps, at the bottom of which was the room where the author had penned eighty-seven books and five plays, one of which was in its twelfth year on Broadway.

Sabrina was casting them the evil eye from the end of the hall when Mac shut the study door behind them.

Robin Spencer's famous mysteries had been written in the most cluttered room in the manor. Built-in bookshelves, containing thousands of books collected over many generations, took up space on every wall. Robin had left her son first editions of all her books. First editions of famous authors personally inscribed to her, and books for research in forensics, poisons, criminology, and the law also lined the shelves. With every inch of shelf space already in use, the author had taken to stacking books on her heavy oak desk, tables, and the floor.

Portraits of Spencer ancestors filled wall space not taken up with books. Mac was still learning their names and places in not only the Spencer family history, but the histories of the state of Maryland, Garrett County, and the town of Spencer. Some paintings appeared to be from the eighteenth century. Others were dressed in fashions from the turn of the twentieth century. The most recent portrait was a life-sized painting of Robin Spencer, dressed in a white strapless gown.

"Jessica," Roxanne gasped when she saw the portrait.

"That was my reaction, too," Mac said.

The portrait of the demure-looking author filled the wall between two gun cases behind the desk. One case contained rifles and shotguns, while the other had handguns. Some of the guns had been handed down through the Spencer family. Others Robin had purchased for research.

Robin had acquired many weapons during her murder mystery writing career. The coat rack sported a hangman's noose, and a Samurai sword hung on the wall.

In a chair in the far corner of the room, Uncle Eugene watched all the comings and goings. A first aid training dummy, Uncle Eugene had been stabbed in the back, tossed off rooftops, and strangled on numerous occasions, all in the name of research. When he wasn't being victimized, he sat in an overstuffed chair in the corner, dressed in a tuxedo with a top hat perched on his head. With one leg crossed over the other, Uncle Eugene, an empty sherry glass next to his elbow, looked like he was taking a break while waiting for the next attempt on his life.

After they had finished the tour with Mac pointing out facts that he had uncovered since taking ownership about the room and its most famous occupant, Roxanne surprised him with a question he had never expected, "Do you ever think that Robin Spencer left you all of this out of guilt? To make up for what you missed out on being raised here?" She gestured at the view through the study window of Deep Creek Lake. "Robin Spencer's son. Think about what she deprived you of, by putting you up for adoption. Private schools, traveling all over the world. You could have—"

"I had a good childhood," Mac said. "I had the best adoptive parents any kid could want. I wouldn't change a thing."

"But how can you be so certain that she left you all of this because she did love you as the son that she gave up, and not as some sort of a payoff for in case you decided to come looking for her."

"Maybe if I hadn't met her, my cop side would have thought that, but Robin Spencer came looking for me. I met her, even though it was only for one day. She also left me her journal. I got to know her." He said firmly, "Robin didn't pay people off. She wasn't perfect. She admitted that in her journal. She had made some mistakes, but she was never wrong."

"You forgave her."

"Maybe if I hadn't met her, and seen for myself what a warm loving woman—" He gestured to the living room out front. "Ask Archie. Ask David O'Callaghan. Ask anyone in this town. It was impossible for anyone to not love her. For me to hold any bad feelings for her." He smiled broadly. "Especially when I saw this house, the Inn, and all the money she left me."

"Nobody will ever feel like that about me when I'm gone." She was rubbing the binding of a hundred-year-old book on autopsy techniques.

"What's going on, Roxanne?"

"It's my fault," she sobbed softly.

"What is?"

She raised her eyes to his. "I was the one that suggested to Christine that maybe there was some remote possibility that

171

the two of you could get back together. It never occurred to me that you would check her into the Spencer Inn the same weekend that Stephen Maguire was staying there."

"Why did you plant that idea in her head?"

Roxanne opened her mouth, but then, seeming to think better of what she was about to say, shut it again. There was fear in her eyes, something he had never seen there before.

"I was trying to get her to go into rehab," Roxanne blubbered. "I'd told her that if she went into rehab, dried out, and made a real effort to get herself together, that maybe, ideally, that you might forgive her and maybe get back together again."

Mac swallowed the anger he felt rising. "Did it ever occur to you that there's no way in hell that reconciliation between us was ever going to happen? Why did you plant that thought in her head?"

Wiping her nose on her sleeve, Roxanne stood up tall in her defense. "As an incentive for her to go into rehab. Did you know that I had to file a petition to have Christine declared incompetent? That's how bad it'd gotten. After Stephen left, she was too lost to even handle her own checkbook. I had to go through her books and pay her bills. That's when I found out how he'd been ripping her off all along. Meanwhile, she was drinking away, running up bills with money she didn't have, and wallowing in misery and anger and resentment. I thought that if I got her into rehab she could be saved."

She admitted, "Yes, Mac, I used you as bait. It never occurred to me that she'd come over here and throw herself at you and that you'd take her to the Inn where she'd end up on a direct path with Stephen Maguire."

He asked, "How did she get here to the lake house?"

Roxanne shrugged. "She drove her car."

"The kids told me that she'd stopped driving months ago. She was afraid of getting a DUI."

"I guess miracles do happen," she said. "Now you see why I feel so horrible. I planted that seed in her mind two days before she suddenly took off here to the lake house and came after you. If I'd never done that, then she'd have stayed home drinking away, while I'd continue cleaning up her messes, but at least she'd still be alive."

"And Stephen Maguire?" he asked.

She said, "I don't give a damn about Stephen Maguire."

"From what I hear, you certainly don't."

Her tears now dry, she asked, "What do you hear?"

"Your name's right up there on the list of those Stephen Maguire screwed over."

The purse of her lips brought on by the clench of her jaw signaled the return of her usual resentment of him.

"It's a very long list," she replied. "I already told you about how he ripped off the money the mortgage company had sent Christine to buy her out of the lake house. When I tried to tell her, she called me jealous and stopped speaking to me for months. It wasn't until after he was gone and she had no one to turn to that finally..."

Mac countered, "But you didn't tell me about how in addition to that, during those months that your little sister wasn't speaking to you because of what Stephen Maguire did, he had the nerve to frame you for bribing a witness, which now has you on the path to disbarment, as well as taking you out of the running for Hunter's deputy."

He didn't expect her to be surprised by his discovery. Roxanne had been around the courthouse and criminal cases for too long. She had to know it was coming. It was only a matter of when.

"Did your sources also tell you that I am no longer out of the running?"

He wondered, "Did Maguire's murder open that door again?"

"As more and more of Maguire's dirty dealings are coming to light, Hunter is looking to select someone as unlike him as possible."

"Which means you benefitted from his murder," he pointed out. "You know the term for that. Motive. You had motive for killing him."

"But not my own sister."

Mac ticked off on his fingers. "Motive. Means. Your family has been coming out here since you were a little girl. You've been regular visitors to the Spencer Inn. You knew how security there works."

"Opportunity," Roxanne said. "I wasn't here. I was in Washington until yesterday morning."

"Can you prove it?" Mac shot back.

She uttered a squawking sound from deep in her throat. "Do I have to?"

"Yes."

"You're not the police anymore, Mac."

"Then you can answer that question for David. He knows everything that we're talking about and he'll be asking you himself. So you might as well tell me."

She answered, "I was home, alone, in Washington. I was working on my computer throughout the day, sending out emails and working on case files until six-thirty, at which time Sabrina brought me her homemade chicken soup for dinner. If you don't believe Sabrina when you ask her about my whereabouts, I'm sure your forensics investigators can check my laptop and the emails that I had sent and received to confirm that I'd been working from home the same day my little sister was killed." She dared him. "Any other questions you want to ask me?"

"What other dirty dealings do you know Maguire was into?"

For the first time since Christine's death, a smile crossed Roxanne's face. "Rumor around city hall is that the high society Maguires are shaking their heads and saying, 'What? What one of our relatives got killed at the Spencer Inn? We never heard of any Stephen who worked for the United States Attorney's Office. He's no relative of ours.' A lot of brown-noses who kept him on the fast track because of his last name are now very embarrassed. Serves them right."

Mac wanted to know, "If that's true, how do you think he managed to get into the U.S. Attorney's Office without his lies being discovered in the background check?"

"How do you think?" She held up her hand and rubbed her fingertips together.

"Someone in the Office of Personnel Management," he said. "Which means that someone would have known all along that he wasn't who he said he was. Can you imagine the frustration of seeing someone that you know is a fraud moving up the chain of command, bypassing you when you work hard, because of something that you know for a fact is a lie? Are the feds going to investigate to find out who was responsible for letting Maguire get away with all this?"

"I'm sure some heads are going to roll," she said. "I have no doubt that it was Hamilton Sanders. He worked for OPM. Maguire brought him over to the U.S. Attorney's Office to be his assistant. Sanders wasn't qualified. Took him three tries to pass the bar. But Maguire got what he wanted, per usual. He seemed to owe Sanders for something."

"And now Sanders is in town lying, cheating, and stealing trying to retrieve what Stephen Maguire had brought up here." Now that he had her alone, out of Sabrina's presence, he asked her, "Do you have any idea what Stephen Maguire was doing in Spencer?"

"I assumed he was seducing his latest young woman," she said.

"He had some case files with him and was interviewing witnesses."

Her expression shifted from cocky to worried. "What kind of witnesses? What kind of case files? Were any of them from family court cases?"

"No," he answered. "What can you tell me about Themis?"

"What?"

"Themis," Mac repeated.

"What's that?" Her confusion appeared genuine.

"I was hoping you'd tell me."

"Could it be a name of a defendant or victim, or maybe an organization? It almost sounds like an acronym."

Sabrina called to them. Her voice holding a note of annoyance, Roxanne called back that she was coming. Before going out the door, she turned to him. "I hope you understand why I feel guilty about Christine. I loved her. Do you think she knew that?"

"Of course," he said, "She had no doubt."

With a weak smile, she left. At the end of the hallway, she turned left to go into the kitchen, while Mac continued to the living room where Archie was tapping away on her mini-laptop.

"How are you doing?" he plopped down next to her and dropped his head onto her shoulder.

Archie hit a button to bring up a news item on the screen. "I'd put Emma Wilkes's name in a search engine and found a news item dated this morning. Her body was found in the trunk of her car parked at the airport. The last time she was seen alive was Saturday night."

"Emma Wilkes is dead?" Mac asked.

"That's right," she replied. "The police report I hacked into said that time of death was Saturday night. COD is a shot to the head."

"Then they couldn't have been killed by the same perp," Mac said.

"Unless Themis is a big conspiracy and there's more than one assassin."

"I don't know about you, but I still don't know what Themis is. Did you do a search of it on the Internet?"

"Themis was the Titan goddess of law and order."

Mac waited for her to continue. When she didn't, he asked, "Anything else?"

"Do you know who the blindfolded lady holding the scales of justice is?"

"Themis?"

"The blindfold symbolizes that justice is blind." She wondered, "What would a Titan goddess have to do with this?"

"In each one of those cases that Maguire was going over," Mac said, "the defendants got off even though we had conclusive evidence that they'd done it. Maguire wanted to make a bid for U.S. Attorney. Most likely he was gathering information on these cases so that he could claim Hunter and the attorneys working under him have been incompetent because of all these known killers getting off."

"Makes one wonder if his boss is behind his murder."

"He was at the party where Maguire was poisoned," he said.

She said, "Well, I also found out why Bonnie Propst was so reluctant to talk to Maguire and us."

"Besides that someone wanted to kill her and succeeded, by the way?"

She pointed at the computer monitor. "I've discovered an interesting timeline. Douglas and Bonnie Propst got married and moved to Morgantown around a year after his last trial, which ended in a hung jury. Less than a year after that, Bonnie was admitted to the WVU hospital emergency room with a broken arm and black eye. She said that she fell."

Mac was already nodding his head. "But you don't think so."

"I believe in giving people the benefit of the doubt, except that in this case, less than two weeks after she got her arm broken, Douglas Propst was shot dead, execution style. The police report says that, according to Bonnie, her husband had come home that night and got a call from the police saying that they caught someone breaking into his office and asked him to go down to make a statement. The police found his body a few hours later. They said that call never came from them."

"It was a lure." Mac looked at her.

Her eyebrow was arched in a seductive way.

He asked, "Do you think she realized she had married a monster and arranged to have him killed?"

"Think about it," she said. "He got away with murder before."

"Why did she marry him then?"

"Easy," she explained. "These lonely pathetic women believe these poor misunderstood brutes claiming to be victimized by the system and the media—It's you and me against the world, babe! Then when they get behind closed doors, they discover that they've climbed into bed with Jack the Ripper. But, it's too late. Now, they're trapped. She probably thought having him killed was the only way out."

Mac agreed. "And then when Maguire calls her out of the blue asking questions about Propst's case, she panics."

Archie said, "And owning a security company, she would know how to get up to the penthouse suite."

"But Bonnie Propst had no way of knowing he was going to be in the penthouse," he reminded her. "He wasn't registered in the suite. Not only that, but, according to the security tapes, the killer was in the penthouse while Bonnie was having dinner with Maguire in the restaurant."

"You're right," she said. "But who killed Bonnie and why? Maybe it has nothing to do with Maguire. What do you think?"

"I'm more interested in who killed Dylan Booth. His murder was my case and Maguire had written a note to call me. I assume about Booth." Patting her knee, he leaned over to kiss her on the cheek. Saying that he was going to take a nap in hopes of getting rid of his headache left over from Gnarly's head butt, he stood up, but she cut him off.

"Don't forget garbage day is tomorrow."

Banging his head on the underside, Gnarly scampered out from under the table. He loved escorting Mac in taking the garbage bin from the garage out to the curb. It gave him a chance to check the perimeters and remind Otis who was boss.

Gnarly started barking as soon as he hit the sidewalk. He was barking so hard that he bounced all the way to the stone pillars marking either side of the driveway.

"What's wrong with you? Otis isn't out there." Being the only one who hadn't seen the fat squirrel, Mac was beginning to think he was the butt of a joke.

After twirling around in search of his master, Gnarly spied him in the garage getting the trash bin. His bark took on an urgent tone when he ran over and jumped up as if to "tag" Mac on the back with his paws, before turning back to lead him to the end of the driveway.

"Okay, I'm coming." Mac followed him to the end of the driveway to see if he could catch sight of the infamous Otis, who had turned Gnarly's outings into such crazed adventures.

He wished his sense of smell was as acute as the dog's. If it had been, he would have had some sense of the danger Gnarly was trying to warn him about.

As soon as Mac saw the back of the black Ford SUV, his hand flew for the gun he kept in the holster under his shirt. At the same time, he felt the barrel of the red-head's gun press into his side when she stepped out from where she had hidden behind the stone pillar when she heard Gnarly coming.

"Don't do it! Don't even think of doing it." Pushing him back up the driveway, out of sight of his neighbors with both her gun and body pressed against his back, she reached around from behind him and held out her hand. "Now, using only two fingers, hand it to me slowly."

Meanwhile, Gnarly was standing beside them sounding the alarm for all to hear. It was like the boy who cried wolf when it came to Gnarly's barking. Archie and the neighbors were all used to his barking at Otis and every other animal on the Point.

Mac slowly drew his gun out of his belt.

She grabbed it and aimed it at Gnarly, who responded by raising the pitch of his bark a notch. "Tell that damn dog to shut up or I'm going to shoot him."

"Don't!" Mac yelped, not pleased with the panic that had crept into his tone at the thought of her shooting his dog. "Gnarly!" he snapped. "Quiet! Listen to me."

To his surprise, Gnarly stopped barking and sat. Concentrating on the months of sessions they had had with the dog trainer, Mac recalled what she had been drumming into his mind with every session. Gnarly wanted his master to be in control. If they were to get out of this alive, Mac would have to convince the dog that he was in control of the situation.

His tall ears poised for his master's next command, Gnarly gazed up at him.

"Good," she hissed into Mac's ear.

"Gnarly isn't going to give you any trouble," he told her while keeping Gnarly's eyes on him. "Okay, boy, do as I say." Mac made two hand gestures at the dog.

Gnarly cocked his head at him. He seemed to ponder the wisdom of Mac's order.

Hoping he was giving him the right command, Mac said, "Go," before repeating the hand gestures that the dog trainer had taught him.

Without a look back, Gnarly raced up the driveway and around to the back of the house.

"Where's he going?" she asked when the dog that had previously threatened to tear her apart disappeared out of sight.

"I gave him hand signals to go lie down."

"You better be telling me the truth and that bitch had better be listening because if he so much as sniffs me, I'll blow him away."

Shoving him face first into the side of the garage, she patted him down after holstering her gun into the waistband of her pants. While pressing his gun into his ribs, she ran her hand over his body in search of other weapons that he could use against her. Her moves were thorough and efficient. She didn't miss a spot. Mac sensed that she wasn't your average, run-of-the-mill perp.

Finding him clean, she spun him around by his shoulder. "I guess I got you pinned down, Faraday."

With her face close to his, he could see that it was not so much the years that had aged her, but the mileage. Her eyes were yellowed, grayed out, and glazed—and crazed—from years of chemical abuse. When he had first seen her the night before, he'd thought she was slender and youthful. Up close, he saw that she wasn't slender, but skinny, with her flesh hanging off her bones.

"Now here is what we're going to do—"

"Are you going to kill me?" Mac surprised her by interrupting to ask about his fate. "Considering that you've already killed Bonnie Propst and shot at Nancy Brenner, I believe it's most likely that you intend to kill me, whether I cooperate or not. That being the case, I won't waste either of our time. If you're going to kill me, kill me now because you'll be wasting your breath lying to me about how I need to do what you say or you'll kill me, or do what I say and I won't kill you. I believe you do intend to kill me no matter what I do." Patting his chest, he stepped back. "So you might as well shoot me now and go on about your business."

Her darting eyes and working mouth indicated that his unexpected challenge knocked her off guard. She hadn't expected such a bold move on his part. It took a full moment for her to regroup. She charged forward with his gun and jabbed him directly below his ribs with it.

"If you don't do exactly what I want, I'm going to kill everyone in that house, including that crazy dog of yours, in front of you, one by one, before I kill you. If you get me what I want, then I might just let them live."

Mac wanted to tell her that he doubted it. Instead, he asked, "What do you want from me?"

"We're going to go into the house. You're going to introduce me to everyone as Emma Wilkes, a journalist that you're giving an interview to about your dead wife and her lover. Then, we're going to go into your study and you'll close the door. There, you'll call that stubborn police chief and convince him, I don't care how, bribe, whatever, to bring you the evidence box with everything he's got on the Maguire murder."

Mac scoffed, "He won't do that."

She held the gun up to his face and pressed the muzzle up against the bridge of his nose between his eyes. "Convince him. You have a lot of power in this town. Use it. If you don't, a lot of people you care about are going to die right before your eyes."

"Okay, you're the boss."

He turned around to start up the driveway to the house. The muzzle of his gun pressed against the small of his back, her breath hot on his neck, she warned him, "Remember, your gun will be aimed at your spine the whole time."

Taking the steps up to the wraparound porch one at a time, Mac prayed that for once, Gnarly would do as he had ordered him. Ever since he had inherited the German shepherd, the dog was intent on doing everything his way. The trainer claimed it was due to his high intelligence. Gnarly was smart and he knew it. He preferred to come up with his own plans.

If Gnarly had decided to disregard Mac's order and come up with his own plan, Mac prayed it would work.

When they stepped through the foyer, Archie called to him from the living room. "Hey, Mac, what's wrong with Gnarly? He went tearing through here like a bat out of hell."

With her gun in his back, the red-head steered him toward the living room.

Seeing the unexpected guest, Archie looked up from her mini. "Excuse me, I didn't know we had company."

The armed visitor called out, "I'm Emma Wilkes, an investigative journalist. Mac was kind—"

"But Emma Wilkes is dead," Archie blurted out before she had time to rethink her response.

Mac's scream was drowned out by the wave of emotions and actions that flooded the room like a tidal wave.

Instantly, the intruder drew the gun she'd been holding against the small of Mac's back and aimed it at Archie, who, realizing the stupidity of what she'd said as soon as the words had come out of her mouth, dove for the floor.

The second before the gun shot went off, the red-head's arm was taken into a toothy vice that sprang from the closet behind her. Catching her forearm directly below the elbow, like a whale nabbing a seal at the surface of the ocean from down below, Gnarly dragged her down to the floor.

A single bullet killed Archie's mini-laptop.

Mac joined the German shepherd in the wrestling match when he saw the red-head reach for the gun in her holster under her shirt. The man and woman struggled to get a hold of the weapon while Gnarly shook her arm as if to rip it from her body.

The red-head howled like the wounded animal she was.

Grabbing her free arm, Mac attempted to force her to release her grip on her weapon by pressing her forearm against the upper arm with all his weight while trying to keep her finger off the trigger.

"What was that?" Sabrina ran in from the kitchen. "Roxanne said it was a shot." She stopped when she saw Gnarly and Mac wrestling on the floor with a woman. They were all covered in blood.

Archie plucked Mac's gun from the floor where it had been dropped in Gnarly's attack, while jumping to her feet. "It was a shot."

Roxanne told her sister. "See, I know a gunshot when I hear it."

"You're dead!" the red-head howled. "I'm going to kill all of you and hack you all into little pieces."

"What!" Sabrina clutched her breast.

"Call the police, please?" Mac gasped out.

Archie tried to take aim at the intruder while keeping Gnarly and Mac out of the shot.

Sabrina pointed at the woman writhing on the floor. "Don't you see? She stabbed Stephen with a steak knife and then killed Chris." She ordered Archie, "Shoot her. Now. She's a killer."

"I'm trying to, but I don't want to hit Gnarly!" Archie called out.

The intruder let out a high-pitched screech when Gnarly's fangs found and punctured an artery that sprayed blood into Mac's eyes.

Blinded, Mac clutched at his face, which allowed her to regain her grip on the gun and its trigger.

"Bastard!" Before she could pull the trigger, he grabbed the gun with both hands and plunged it down into her gut with the weight of his full body on top of her.

The gun went off.

Archie screamed.

His tail between his legs, Gnarly jumped back and ran to hide behind Archie.

Sabrina and Roxanne resembled twins with both covering their mouths with their hands.

The room was silent while they waited for someone to say something or move, or to simply do something.

Archie ran over to the two people lying motionless in a pool of blood in the middle of the floor. "Mac!"

Gnarly dug his muzzle into his master's ear.

Taking a deep breath, Mac rose up to reveal his stomach and chest covered in blood. He clutched the gun in his hand.

The intruder's stomach and chest were covered in blood around the hole where the gun went off while plunged up and under her ribs.

Both horrified at the sight and relieved that Mac was the survivor, Archie threw her arms around him. Seeming to sense a family hug, Gnarly jumped up onto them, smearing them in the intruder's blood while licking Mac's face.

"You didn't want to shoot Gnarly?" he whispered into her ear. "What about me?"

Suddenly aware of what she had said, she smiled. "I knew you could take care of yourself. I never doubted it for a second."

CHAPTER THIRTEEN

"I can't believe Gnarly ambushed her," David marveled at the shepherd, who sat obediently while the crime scene officer took mouth impressions for their investigation. "I've never heard of a dog actually ambushing an intruder."

Mac was meeting with David outside while the officers investigated the scene inside the manor. Meanwhile, two officers were searching the Ford parked on the opposite side of the stone wall. Bogie was gathering information from the police database about Emma Wilkes on his laptop in his cruiser. Archie had already discovered much of the information he was uncovering.

For the second time in a week, Mac's clothes were confiscated by the forensics team for evidence to confirm his account of how he had come to kill a woman who had taken him hostage outside his home. After changing his clothes, he had met with David outside, where they supervised Gnarly, who was threatening to lose his patience with the forensics officer and bite off his fingers.

Admitting that he was equally impressed, Mac said, "He wanted to take her down when she first got the drop on me, but I knew he'd be dead before getting one bite in if I let him. Luckily, he listened to me when I told him to hunt and then kill."

"You told him?" David was doubtful.

"Did I tell you that the dog trainer discovered that Gnarly knows sign language?"

David corrected him. "You mean hand commands."

"I mean sign language," Mac said. "I didn't believe it myself until she showed me. She'll tell him in sign language to get the banana off a table that has about ten objects on it, and not bring it to her, but to take it into another room and put it on a desk, and he'll do it." He muttered, "But let me tell him verbally to do it and he'll pee on my leg."

"But when the chips were down and you needed him, he listened," David said.

"Gnarly is a rebel," Mac agreed. "He had to get her from the rear or she'd have shot him. I gave him two signs. Hunt and kill. He understood and did what I told him for once. When he took off around the house, I was afraid that he may have misunderstood and thought I was giving him permission to hunt and kill Otis. Archie said he came tearing into the house through the back door and hid in the foyer closet, where he waited for us to come in so he could ambush her."

"You never can tell what he's going to do," David said. "Last week, he was the neighborhood shoplifter. Today, he's a hero." Seeing Bogie climb out of his cruiser, he called to him. "Did you get anything that might tell us what this woman wanted from me?"

Bogie shook his head. "The SUV is a rental, rented in the name of Emma Wilkes, whose body was found this morning in the trunk of her car. The Washington police told me that the last time she was seen was Saturday night, which the ME puts as the time she'd been killed. She was last seen in a restaurant in Washington with a woman with curly red hair." He gestured toward the inside of the house where the intruder with red hair was lying in a pool of blood on Mac's living room floor. "There's no ID or anything on her. Maybe we'll get something from her fingerprints."

"She's a cop," Mac stated without doubt. "Or at least she used to be. She was probably suspended for drug use."

"How can you be so certain?" David wanted to know.

"She patted me down," Mac said. "She knew what she was doing to be able to overcome and pat down a man who was bigger than her. You don't just learn that on the streets. She'd had training and experience. At some point, she'd been a cop, which means her fingerprints are in the system."

Rubbing his forehead as if to physically force everything to make sense, David paced the walkway in front of the house. When he reached the corner, he turned around to see that Mac was still sitting on the porch steps. "You're sure she said she wanted everything we got on Stephen Maguire?"

"Everything."

"If she had said the case files, I would think Hamilton Sanders was behind this. No one has seen Hamilton since yesterday, by the way. He's staying at a motel in McHenry and their housekeeping said that his room wasn't slept in last night. I think he skipped, which would make sense if he's behind all this."

"Great," Mac muttered with sarcasm. "Most likely, this woman wanted you to bring everything in order to conceal what it was she really wanted. If she wanted a watch, and she said she wanted you to bring a watch, then we would know that the watch was what was significant and could trace it to who was behind it. By saying everything, it leaves us guessing like we're doing now."

"Hamilton is after the case files," David said. "Natasha and the judge want some tape. I say we bring them all in for questioning."

*   *   *   *

Natasha's back was to Mac when he stepped up to the back of the love seat in the Inn's lounge where she and Garrison were having their afternoon cocktails. As he came closer, he saw that she was checking for messages on her cell phone. "Dead people don't leave messages, Natasha."

Garrison splashed his drink on the front of his sweater.

Natasha whirled around.

Seeing Mac and David behind them, they gasped.

"Faraday, you look horrible," the judge said upon seeing Mac's unkempt appearance. "What happened to you?"

"I had a head-on collision with an assassin," Mac said.

Natasha regained her composure. "I don't know what you're talking about."

"I'm talking about the one someone sent to my home to retrieve Stephen Maguire's belongings. She killed a potential witness in Morgantown last night. Today, she tried to take me and guests in my home hostage in exchange for all the evidence collected in the Maguire case. I killed her." He leaned over the seat toward them. "Now you two have been very anxious to get your hands on his stuff."

"Not anxious enough to break the law," the judge said.

"All we want is a recording," Natasha said. "Garrison told you about it. We came clean. Why would we send someone to go after you after admitting what it was we wanted?"

"I don't know," Mac replied. "You tell me."

Natasha waved both hands in a gesture of innocence. "Whatever Stephen got into and got killed over, has nothing to do with me. This assassin you're talking about is something completely different."

"Mac," Garrison said, "you have to believe us. That recording might be embarrassing, but it certainly isn't anything worth sending a renegade cop to kill for it."

Chuckling, Mac shook his head as he whispered to them, "I said nothing about her being a renegade cop."

The judge's face turned red.

Mac turned to the defense attorney. "You're losing your touch, Natasha. You used to be the best liar in Washington. You slipped up when you said anyone could have slipped that arsenic into Maguire's champagne. The police never determined what the arsenic had been in. He drank more than champagne that night. He also drank martinis and ate a lot of different foods. But you, for some reason, knew that the arsenic was in his champagne. How is that?"

For the first time in all the years Mac had known Natasha Holmstead, she was speechless.

They locked eyes in a stare down, each one daring the other to blink.

Behind him, Mac heard David speaking in a low tone into his radio.

The stare down ended with David's hand on Mac's arm. "Mac, we've got to go."

Mac leaned in close to her as if to kiss her on the cheek. Instead, he whispered into her ear. "We'll talk more about this later."

David waited until they were across the lobby and out of earshot of the judge and Natasha before he announced to Mac, "A fisherman found Sanders's body in the lake."

* * * *

"He's been in the water for about twenty-four hours," the medical examiner announced from where he was still examining Hamilton Sanders's body on the dock behind the lakeside restaurant and lounge formerly known as Sully's.

Since the business had been shut down, with no one to care for the establishment, fallen leaves had blown across the dock to fill up crevices and corners and behind the steps that led down from the parking lot along the side of the building.

Between the sun setting behind the mountains, the long shadows of the trees along the shore, the chill in the air, and the rustic décor of the abandoned outdoor café on the dock, the crime scene took on an eerie atmosphere.

"That's why he didn't go back to his hotel." David asked the medical examiner, "Have you come up with a COD?"

She showed them Sanders's bare stomach where she had opened his button-down shirt. Three stab wounds were visible above his navel and below his ribs. "He was stabbed before he went into the water."

Mac searched around on the dock until he found a brown stain, which he pointed out to David. "Could be blood."

David stepped closer to the back door of the restaurant. "Here's another one."

Like following bread crumbs in the woods, they followed drop after drop until they arrived at the back door.

"Do you think?" David laid his hand, encased in an evidence glove, on the door lever. When he pressed down, the door opened. It had been unlocked.

They stepped inside the darkened room that had only months before been a lakeside bar and game room. Two pool tables rested in the middle of the floor. Tables with chairs, some on top of the tables, others stacked, still others in their places next to the tables, lined the room along the wall.

"I used to come here to drink beer and play pool with my buddies." There was a wistful note in David's voice. "I think I even met a few of my old flames in this room."

"Everyone has a Sully's in their past." Mac stepped up to one of the pool tables. "Didn't Cameron say that she and Stephen Maguire played pool?"

"She said that she met him at a lakeside restaurant," David said. "This was where they met."

"It was also where some crazy woman went after Maguire with a screwdriver."

One of David's officers came in carrying a clear evidence bag. "They found this in the water, Chief." He handed it to David.

David held up the bag for Mac to see the contents.

The bag held a screwdriver.

*   *   *   *

The Spencer police station was busier than Mac had ever seen it. With two murders at the Spencer Inn, an attack and shooting at Mac Faraday's home, and a body found in the lake, the media was swarming for information to explain how everything was connected.

"Has Spencer, Maryland, gone to hell in a handcart since the death of its undeclared queen, Robin Spencer?" some concerned journalists were inquiring of their experts in the studio.

In either case, all twelve officers on the Spencer police force had been called in to do whatever they could to restore order to the resort town.

Bogie seemed to be waiting at the door with his notepad and a case file for David and Mac when they arrived from Sully's. "They got an ID from the fingerprints on that whack job that tried to kill you, Mac. Her name is Celia Tennyson and you were right. She used to be an undercover cop."

"Celia Tennyson?" Mac repeated the name.

"Did you know her?" Mac didn't like the hint of accusation in David's tone.

"Not personally," he answered. "I knew of her. When an undercover cop's cover gets blown and people get killed, it gets talked about on the force."

"What's her story?" David asked Bogie to fill them in on the way up the stairs to his office. He had been keeping the evidence from the murders locked in his personal safe.

"Like Mac said, she'd worked deep undercover." Bogie raced up the stairs while referring to his notes. "Her and her partner's covers got blown. A gang working for an organized crime syndicate tortured and killed her partner and gang raped her. After the police caught the gang leader, he turned around and swung a deal with the feds in exchange for information on his bosses. The dirt bag got full immunity and went into the witness protection program."

"This much I knew," Mac told them.

They were waiting for David to unlock his office door. Usually, when the police station was open for office hours, he kept it unlocked; but since so many people had shown so much interest in getting their hands on Stephen Maguire's belongings, David was keeping everything under lock and key.

"This is what you don't know," Bogie went on. "Less than a year after this bastard struck his deal with the feds, he was killed along with the two U.S. marshals protecting him. His privates had been amputated pre-mortem. The feds were, and are, furious because without the dirt bag they lost their case against the crime bosses. There's been a federal warrant out for Tennyson for the last couple of years." He tapped Mac on the shoulder. "They love you and Gnarly right now."

Inside his office, David knelt next to the box safe he kept hidden behind his desk and pressed his thumb against the reader before keying in the combination. "A psycho cop. She was a psycho killer."

Bogie continued, "Not only that, but forensics matched the bullets from her gun to the slugs they found in Emma Wilkes's head. Since Wilkes was killed Saturday night, that eliminates Tennyson for the Maguire and Faraday hit."

Mac stepped back to allow David to set the evidence box on his conference table and remove the lid. "Someone sent her to eliminate everything connected to what Maguire was investigating here, including Bonnie Propst. This has to be connected to Themis, whatever that is."

Bogie said, "Wasn't Themis a Greek goddess?"

"Titan goddess," Mac corrected him.

"Whatever," was Bogie's reply.

David unpacked the evidence from the box. The largest items were the accordion folder and the yellow notepad. He slapped down the folder and proceeded to open it to review its contents. "What connection can a Greek goddess have with these cases that Stephen Maguire had listed on that sheet of paper? And why did he only have these case files and not all of them?"

Mac was busy re-reading the list of names Stephen Maguire had written in long hand: Freddie Gibbons, Sid Baxter, Jillian Keating, Leo Samuels, Gerald Hogan, Douglas Propst.

"A list of killers." Sitting down at the table, he stared at the names.

David repeated his question about why Maguire didn't have all of the files.

"Could the ones he didn't have have been archived?" Bogie tore his eyes from the list he was reading over Mac's shoulder to look up at David. "If big old Washington is anything like little ole Spencer, after so long, closed case files are scanned into a database and the hardcopy folders get shipped off to the county seat warehouse, where they're archived." He glanced down at Mac. "We're talking about physical space. What are the oldest cases that you know of on that list?"

"Sid Baxter and Douglas Propst are both over a decade old," Mac said while glancing into the accordion folder. "And those are the two case files that Maguire didn't have." He turned to David. "I think Bogie has a point. Now we need to figure out what connection these cases have with Dylan Booth."

With one of her laptops tucked under her arm, Archie burst through the door. "I found the connection between Emma Wilkes and Dylan Booth." She added in a breathless tone, "I'm going to bust this case wide open."

Waiting for her answer, they fell silent.

A smile filled her face. "I've always wanted to say that."

David asked, "Are you just saying that, or do you really have information?"

"Oh, do I." She plopped down in the first empty chair at the table and opened her miniature laptop. "First off, about Emma Wilkes." She pointed at the screen on her laptop. "Five years ago, Emma Wilkes was a journalist at a network news show, and she did a story about Gerald Hogan."

Mac said, "He was one of the names on the list. Accused of raping and murdering a woman after a frat party. The defense tried the victim and insinuated, without any real evidence, that she got herself killed after she and Hogan had consensual sex and her death was an accident. Judge Daniels was the judge on the case. While he didn't allow her dating history admitted, the defense managed to get S&M sex videos and pictures that she'd uploaded onto the Internet admitted by claiming that they were already public. The trial ended in a hung jury. The prosecution chose not to retry."

Archie read the story she had found in her research. "A year after the jury was hung, Hogan was found hung to death in a motel room up in Philadelphia."

Mac said, "I didn't know that."

"The medical examiner ruled it a suicide," Archie said. "Emma Wilkes did a story suggesting that Hogan had been murdered and the police were covering it up because he was a rapist and murderer that got away with it."

"Emma was investigating Hogan's death," Mac pieced together the connection. "Judge Daniels presided over Hogan's trial. Dylan Booth worked for Daniels. Then they would have met—"

"Better than that," Archie said. "According to my background checks on both of them, they lived at the same address in the same apartment when they were both undergrads at Georgetown University. They were either roommates or lovers. I prefer to think they were lovers."

Mac wanted to know, "Why didn't she come forward when he was killed?"

"They had stopped living together years before Hogan's death. Wilkes didn't get anywhere with the Hogan story and it went cold. I called her news station and they told me that she'd first started investigating the Hogan case after getting an anonymous tip that he'd been murdered. Then, less than a month ago, she picked it up again after getting another anonymous tip from a different source in the U.S. Attorney's Office."

David grinned. "I wonder if Stephen Maguire was that second informant."

"Booth was the first," Mac said. "He knew Emma from before and when he happened onto his story, he called her. But he kept what he knew close to the vest until he got a job guarantee from Maguire for blowing the whistle."

"How do you know that?" David asked.

"I investigated his murder," Mac replied. "Booth was a Stephen Maguire wannabe."

Archie picked up the scenario. "After the Hogan story went cold, Wilkes got assigned to an affiliate in the Midwest and had pretty much dropped the story because it was going nowhere. Booth was killed while Wilkes was in Chicago." She wondered, "Maybe they had a lover's quarrel because Booth knew the truth but was afraid to tell it."

Mac said, "Or chose to hold out for the highest bidder: a choice slot in the U.S. Attorney's Office or a bribe to keep his mouth shut."

Bogie said, "Too bad none of these people are around to tell us which it is."

Mac sat up straight in his seat. "That's it."

"What's it?" David asked.

"The common denominator." Mac picked up the list of names and studied it.

After a long moment of waiting for Mac to fill them in, David urged him to tell them what he had discovered.

"Freddie Gibbons Junior." He tapped the name scrawled on the sheet of paper. "Found shot to death in a hotel in Paris. The American Embassy believes he was killed and robbed by a prostitute. Killer unknown."

"Maybe it was Tennyson," Bogie said.

Mac tapped the next name on the list with his fingertip. "Leo Samuels arranged the murder of a girl he had abducted and raped. He walks free and his lackey is killed in prison. Less than six months later, he's killed in a drive-by shooting."

David said, "You told me he led a street gang. It's not uncommon—"

"But wait. There's more." Mac jumped out of his seat and began pacing. "Gerald Hogan is arrested for rape and murder. Defense tries the victim. Trial ends in a hung jury. One year later, he's found hung to death in Philadelphia. Dead."

David and Bogie exchanged looks of concern.

"Douglas Propst." Mac grabbed the sheet of paper from the center of the table and held it up to show them the name on the list. "Wife is found dead in the river near where he'd been jogging. She'd been beaten to death. Tried twice. Jury hung both times. Shot to death. Murder unsolved. Dead. Just like the others on this list. D-E-A-D, dead."

"It gets scarier." Archie went to the next name on the list. "Jillian Keating."

Mac reminded them, "She killed her husband for his money. I found the poison she used to do it. Maguire's wife was her lawyer. She got the poison suppressed and Keating walked away with all of her husband's money."

Archie tapped the laptop to display Jillian Keating's beautiful face along with the news items from the Internet. "Found dead in her Las Vegas penthouse of a drug overdose less than a year after she walked out of that courtroom. Las Vegas police have classified it as suspicious."

"Sid Baxter gets blown up while under surveillance months after getting off for murder." Mac's head was spinning. "It's too much to be a coincidence. All of these people, they all committed crimes and the evidence was strong that they did it and—"

"Themis is the goddess of law and order," David said. "Justice. That's what Themis is. It's a vigilante group."

Mac asked Archie, "Can you find any common denominators in who handled these cases?"

Archie shook her head. "I'll keep looking."

"Judge Daniels?" Mac said, "Booth must have found out about this secret group of theirs while working for him."

Archie said, "Here's another piece of information. I found an obscure item on the Internet, an interview dating around the time of Vivian Propst's death, with her godfather, who was none other than Judge Randolph Daniels. He had no children of his own. According to the interview, she was everything to him."

"That's the judge's connection to Douglas Propst," David said.

Mac said, "Judge Daniels had been a judge for forty years. Maybe he snapped after his goddaughter was murdered and her killer managed to escape justice. Dylan Booth found out about what he'd done, or was doing, and tried to sell Maguire evidence about them in return for a prime slot in the U.S. Attorney's Office. I bet that folder box that disappeared when Dylan Booth was murdered contained evidence about Themis."

"But who's involved in this vigilante group?" Bogie asked. "They sent out a whacko ex-cop to cover up their tracks. Sounds to me like they're organized."

Mac continued pacing. "Daniels killed himself the night before Booth was murdered. The last thing Booth did before he left that office was call Stephen Maguire, which was why I insisted that Maguire was the killer. Maguire stated that he never spoke to Booth, and that his call went to voice mail."

David asked, "Could Dylan Booth have called someone else when he wasn't able to get through to Maguire?"

"There weren't any other recent calls listed in his log."

"How about his email or IM?" Archie suggested while peering into the evidence box.

"Or maybe this Booth kid didn't call anyone," Bogie said. "Think about it. This judge was involved with this secret vigilante group. You're suggesting this box had evidence in it, that the kid was stealing it for whatever reason. Wouldn't you think that if there was incriminating stuff in the judge's office, as soon as word got out that he was dead whoever else was involved in this group would hightail it to his office to get it out of there?"

Mac said, "Crime of opportunity. Booth got there first and whoever else was involved ran into him in the parking lot and killed him to get it back."

"Good thinking, Bogie," David said. "All we have to do is figure out who that someone is." Noticing Archie going through the evidence box, he slid it away from her. "You don't belong in there. You're as bad as Gnarly."

When he slid the box away from her, her hand came out with Stephen Maguire's keychain dangling from her fingers. "Hey, I've been wanting one of these." She pressed the side of the pen knife and a flash drive sprang out, not unlike a switchblade knife springing out of its shield.

"What's that?" David grabbed the flash drive from her hand.

"It's a flash drive disguised as a pen knife," Archie took it back. "Isn't it cool? You hook it to your keys. That way you're less likely to lose it."

"Never mind that," Mac said. "Show us what's on it."

She slipped the flash drive into her laptop. "There's an audio file and a folder on here. It's named Themis."

"We got it," Mac said. "Let's see what this evidence is. It must be good to kill for it."

"I'll start with the audio file." Archie turned up the volume on her speaker.

"Hello, Natasha?" a male voice came out of the speaker.

"That's Judge Sutherland," Mac told them over the feminine reply.

The judge went on, "I was calling to find out how you were doing after last night."

There was a titter of laughter before she replied, "I've never felt so good. It's like a big weight has been lifted off my shoulders. This morning, when I went out to get my coffee and the newspaper, I noticed the color of the flowers and the sound of the children laughing. They sounded happy and I felt like I'd played a part in that goodness." She laughed again.

"Ah," Archie cooed, "they're in love."

Mac said, "This must be the recording that Sutherland said Maguire had of their affair during the Baxter trial."

Judge Sutherland jumped in. "I know exactly what you're talking about. After last night, I feel like I've given something back to society. I haven't felt like that in a long, long time. I feel like I've personally fed ten thousand men, women, and children, all by myself."

"That's not sex they're talking about," David said.

Natasha asked, "Did you see the paper?"

"It's on the news, too," he replied. "George Vance called me at one o'clock this morning."

She sounded worried. "You're certain they can't trace the bomb back to you?"

198

He replied, "Don't worry, Natasha. You know how it is. Sid Baxter was a plague that threatened the lives of every innocent boy in the city. We've tried everything we could, within the stifling constraints that the justice system has set on us, to get rid of him and protect the rest of society, but because of all the laws they created to protect *him*, there wasn't any other way to protect the rest of us."

"I know, Garrison."

"I hope you're not having second thoughts about what we did."

"No," she said forcefully. "I'm just worried about you. What if—"

"They aren't going to spend enough time and energy on his case to trace it back to us. Sid Baxter was a pedophile. Homicide is already suspecting the Sweeney boy's father. As soon as he lawyers up, the case will find its way to the back burner."

"Maybe we should have thought about this a little bit more before doing this," she said. "Suppose Mr. Sweeney gets arrested for killing him?"

Judge Sutherland laughed. "I did think about that. I have enough pull, that if that happens, I'll make a couple of calls to some old friends and suggest how poor it would look publicly to go after the victim's family when the system had let them down. I assure you. They'll *find* a reason to drop the case."

"Oh, Garrison," she swooned, "you thought of everything. To think that only two weeks ago I felt like I'd climbed into bed with the devil. Now, after personally swinging the sword of justice and making one less demon out on the streets, I feel like—Ah, I can't describe it!"

"You don't have to," he said. "I know precisely how you feel. Listen, I need to go. Can we meet later for drinks? I think this occasion calls for champagne."

Natasha ended the call saying that she agreed and would meet him later at the club.

Mac told Archie to stop the recording. "They were having more than an affair."

"No wonder they've been so anxious to get Maguire's personal effects," David said. "If this recording got out—"

"We have more," Archie said from where she stood over her mini. "There's a file inside the Themis folder called Emails." She clicked on the first email listed. "This first one is from Natasha to Sutherland. Based on the name on their accounts, I assume they're their private email accounts. Natasha tells Sutherland that she's sick and tired of this. She heard about how Maguire had made him call Hunter to give his recommendation for making him his deputy and that they needed to do something to put an end to it."

"What's the date on that?" Mac wanted to know.

"Five weeks ago."

"That's before Maguire was poisoned," he noted.

"And then, in the next email, Natasha says," Archie turned the mini around for them to read, "I think it's time that Themis meets to discuss the matter of Stephen Maguire. He may be a prosecutor, but he plays a bigger role within the system to let the real criminals back out onto the streets to hurt the innocent citizens than defense attorneys. Let us not forget Freddie Gibbons. He's more of a threat to society than the criminals."

Archie read out loud, "Then the reply from Sutherland, 'That's your frustration talking. Stephen is a bottom eater, but he's no criminal.' She replied, 'He's a direct threat to Themis. When I think of all the good that we've done society by getting rid of the likes of Freddie Gibbons, Lee Samuels, Jillian Keating, Gerald Hogan, Douglas Propst, and last but not least, Sid Baxter. If I didn't have Themis, I would've killed myself a long time ago. Themis is the only thing that keeps me going and we can't let Stephen threaten us anymore.'"

"That list of names." Mac grabbed the sheet of paper that had the list of names. "This email is where Maguire got this list of names from."

Archie continued, "Then Judge Sutherland replied to that email with, 'Stephen hasn't a clue about Themis. As long as he thinks it stopped with Sid Baxter, then we're okay. The less we say and do, the better.' To which she replies," she paused for dramatic effect, "'If the court won't do anything about him, then I will. I'll be careful and promise that I won't do anything if I'm caught to let it be connected to Themis. For the sake of justice for the people, I believe that it is best if Stephen Maguire is executed.'"

She pointed at the screen on the mini. "Now the next email is a couple of weeks later. Judge Sutherland is writing to Natasha Holmstead, 'What did you do? I heard in court today that Stephen is in the hospital. Someone poisoned him. I saw you talking to him the other night. Did you slip something into his drink? He could have died.' She replied, 'I only did what I had to do for the good of the people.'"

She paused to scroll down. "Sutherland then asks what would she have done if the poison had been traced back to her, to which she says that she is one of the top defense attorneys in the business and she could defend herself. Don't worry. She says that the mission of Themis is more important than any one person."

They all sat back to digest the information in the emails.

Archie said, "Maguire must have suspected her when he was poisoned. So he hacked into her email, and when he found this thread, he copied it to the flash drive to use for additional leverage against them."

David asked, "What else is in that Themis folder?"

"Two PDF files," she replied. "One is called Propst. The other is Baxter."

Bogie said, "Maguire must have downloaded those from the archives."

Mac said, "The emails don't really come right out and say what Themis is or does. They also don't say who is directly involved in the group. So Maguire took the names they listed and started investigating the cases to gather evidence against them. Can you imagine the publicity he would have gotten if he busted a vigilante group that involved a judge and one of the top defense attorneys in the country? He would've been assured of getting appointed U.S. Attorney then."

David said, "That's why he and any witnesses he talked to had to be killed."

Mac said, "That's why Themis has to be stopped."

CHAPTER FOURTEEN

It was between the lunchtime rush and the evening crowd that Mac waited at his private table in the lounge at the Spencer Inn, which provided a magnificent view of ski slopes and the lake down below.

He had asked Judge Sutherland and Natasha Holmstead to meet him alone to discuss the return of something that belonged to them.

The view of the mountain was changing almost daily. The dead leaves hanging by threads on the trees across the mountain would get snipped lose by the wind to dance to the ground and lake below. Now that "leaf-peeper" season was over, the staff at the Spencer Inn kicked into high gear.

There was a lot to do and a short time to do it.

The off season between height of autumn and winter was no time for rest. The staff was rushing around like Santa's elves changing the Inn from summer resort status to that of a winter sports resort. Ski equipment had to be taken out of storage, inspected, and set up. Cross country ski trails had to be cleared.

Since Mac was no longer on duty, he was able to enjoy a drink while waiting for his guests. It was one of the perks of being retired. For this meeting, he had chosen a snifter of Camus Jubilee from his private stock.

Believing enough people had died in Spencer in the last week, Mac ordered Justine the bartender took a break while one of David's officers filled her post behind the bar. Two more officers were cleaning and setting the tables on the other side of the lounge.

David, Archie, Bogie, and Prosecutor Ben Fleming were up in the security office watching on the monitor.

How will this go down? Mac wondered. *Considering that they've already sent a renegade cop after me... Will they come with guns blazing?*

With all the tension, Mac was surprised when Sutherland and Natasha came in and almost scurried across the lounge to his table.

"Lieutenant Faraday," Garrison greeted him in his usual friendly manner. "I was so glad when you called. Can't believe it was still in Maguire's room after all this time."

Mac felt his back tense up when he saw Natasha slip her hand into her purse. "How much do you want for it?" she asked.

"Not cash." Mac slapped the flash drive he held in his lap onto the table. "I want the truth."

Garrison rubbed his chin while looking over at Natasha. "I guess this means you listened to the recording."

"With all the bodies dropping here in Spencer, did you really think I wouldn't?"

The defense attorney and the judge exchanged looks of disappointment.

Natasha Holmstead whirled around to the officer behind the bar. "Did they teach you how to make a pitcher of martinis at the police academy?"

Garrison asked, "What are you drinking, Mac?" After learning that he was drinking Camus Jubilee, the judge also turned to the bar. "I'll have what he's having."

Uncertain of where anything was behind the bar, the officer began rummaging to fill their orders.

"Drinks are on me!" The judge craned his neck and looked around in search of the security camera. "Come on in and join the party." He turned back to Mac. "He went down not with a bang, but with a whimper."

Who would have thought?

No guns. No accusations.

Judge Garrison Sutherland plopped down in the seat across from Mac with the pleasantness of someone drinking with an old friend, not an ex-cop about to have him arrested for murder. "Your friends are free to join us. Don't worry. We're not armed." He sat up when he saw David and the rest of the officers come into the lounge. "Ah, Chief, sit down. Take a load off. Looks like a good night for a binge."

"Ah, nice that you could join us." Natasha took the first martini from the pitcher that the officer had delivered to the table. "Have a drink." She raised her glass in a toast.

Mac was in awe of how the showdown appeared to turn into a party. Archie slid into the booth next to him. David preferred to stand with his hand near the gun on his hip.

After introducing himself to the judge as Garrett County's prosecutor, Ben Fleming slipped into a chair he pulled over from another table and accepted the martini Natasha offered to him.

The judge accepted the snifter from the officer posing as the bartender. "When you told me about the cleaning crew finding that flash drive with the recording somewhere in Maguire's room, I knew it had to be a lie." He raised the snifter in a toast. "The jig is up. It was great while it lasted."

Martini in hand, Natasha had the same smug expression that most of her clients in the past wore before, during, and after their arrest. Mac wondered if she had taught them that expression.

He guessed that this wasn't her first drink. She'd probably been seeking courage ever since he told her about Celia Tennyson's death. She sensed they were closing in.

"I guess you know why we're here." David glanced over at Ben. "We're arresting you and Ms. Holmstead on several counts of murder. I must inform you of your rights. You—"

The judge waved his hand at him. "I know my rights already and waive them. Don't you, Natasha?"

Caught in the middle of sipping her martini, she waited until swallowing and letting out a breath of satisfaction. "Sure. I've done nothing wrong."

Garrison sighed with resignation. "I knew this day would come. Hell, I even half expected it to be Mac to put it all together three years ago when Dylan got himself killed."

Their lack of remorse amazed Mac. "You do realize that you killed people."

"No, we didn't." Natasha shook her head. " *We* killed no one." She gestured at the judge and herself. "We're no more guilty of murder than the juries who find defendants guilty of murder and sentence them to death."

"We found the recording that Stephen Maguire had been holding over your heads for years," Mac said. "You and Judge Sutherland blew up Sid Baxter. I was there. I saw him blown into pieces."

Judge Sutherland said, "That was in defense of another."

Natasha explained, "I was his lawyer. He had told me in no uncertain terms that he had no intention to stop preying on other little boys. He killed the Sweeney kid. That idiot so-called detective Fitzwater blew it. We couldn't let Baxter go out there and kill again."

"So you blew him up?" Mac asked.

Natasha said, "Only because Garrison pulled rank on me. I wanted to poison him with strychnine."

"We had Baxter under surveillance," Mac argued. "We would've caught him. Then he would have been tried and convicted."

"He was tried and convicted in our court," the judge said.

Not understanding, David repeated, "Your court?"

"Our court," the judge said. "We have our own system. It is a court very much like yours, except that it's completely free of political agendas. All of the evidence is seen in our court."

"Themis," Mac said.

"Our court is completely fair and just. We look at the facts as they are," Garrison said. "The good, the bad, and the truth with no political agendas."

"Yes," Natasha said. "The court of law and order. No evidence gets suppressed because it was unfairly acquired. We don't try the victim and we don't make deals. We try the defendants—purely and simply."

"I suppose it's purely coincidence that after you sentence someone to death in your little court, they suddenly die," Mac said.

"The cases that we would go over during our trials were very public cases. These defendants led high-risk lives. They were bound to meet violent ends, which is *coincidentally* what happened." Natasha Holmstead was in defense attorney mode.

Ben said, "Tell us exactly what goes on during your trials."

She replied, "We're not going to answer that without our lawyers."

"Put a cork in it, Natasha," Judge Sutherland said before answering the prosecutor. "Therapy." He gestured at all of them. "You all know how frustrating our business can be, especially when you know precisely who did it, when you have all the evidence, you have everything but the jury isn't allowed to see it. Or maybe you can't get *any* of it before a jury because of a roadblock in this system that seems to protect the killer more than it does the people."

The judge's anger rose as he spoke. "Like Leo Samuels." He waved a hand in Mac's direction as he reminded him, "We knew damn well that he intimidated that kid into doing the shooting, but the system let *him* right back out onto the streets and the kid went to jail where he got knifed by one of Samuels's men. The system should have been protecting that kid."

"Themis tried Samuels in their court. He was found guilty and got gunned down in a drive-by shooting," Mac surmised.

"He was a gangbanger," Natasha reminded him. "It was bound to happen."

"You killed your husband," Mac said.

Natasha sat up in her seat. "I didn't kill him."

"He was on to you," Mac said. "He'd stolen copies of your emails and had names of those Themis had convicted and executed. He was on to Themis."

Garrison and Natasha gasped in unison. "What do you mean he stole copies of our emails? What emails?" she asked.

"That's where he got the list of our cases," Garrison told her before turning back to them. "Maguire had given the list of cases to Hamilton to get him copies of all the case files. That journalist had started nosing around again. We thought Maguire got the list of names from her."

"Emma Wilkes," Mac said.

"Yes," Garrison said. "We thought she'd gotten the list from Dylan Booth before he was killed. Couldn't figure out why she waited so long before she started investigating the case again."

Mac said, "We think it was Maguire who called her when he got the list of names from your email. Hogan's name was on the list. Since his death was what had first prompted her investigation, he may have contacted her to compare notes with what Dylan Booth may have told her, or to see if she had uncovered anything new that might be connected to Themis."

"Not so much to give information," Archie said, "but to get it."

"Sounds like Stephen," Natasha said. "I can't believe he broke into our emails."

"They were the ones where you told Judge Sutherland that you were going to kill Maguire and not to worry because you'd rather go to jail than testify against Themis," Mac argued. "Then later he emailed you to ask if you'd poisoned Maguire and you said not to worry."

She told Mac and the others, "I knew nothing about that. Stephen said nothing to us about knowing about Themis."

Judge Sutherland said, "He must have wanted to figure out exactly what he had before blackmailing us."

"Your alibi for the night of Maguire's murder didn't check out," David told them. "According to the Inn's security video, you were sitting three tables away while he was interviewing Bonnie Propst."

"We had nothing to do with his murder," the judge said. "We went back to Carmel Cove Inn as soon as we'd finished dinner."

Natasha added, "And we certainly didn't want to hurt Christine Faraday. She was no threat to us. What do you think we are? A bunch of heathens?"

"Sort of. You sent that crazy cop to kill Emma Wilkes and Bonnie Propst for talking to Stephen Maguire," Archie said. "Then you sent her after us. All we wanted was to figure out the truth about who killed Maguire and Mac's ex-wife."

"That was Hamilton," Natasha said. "He had a tendency to get nervous."

"You're telling us that Hamilton was part of this?" Mac scoffed. "How convenient for you to pin the blame on someone who's dead and unable to defend himself."

Natasha said, "I guess next you're going to blame us for Ham's murder, too."

"We didn't kill Maguire. We didn't know what information he had," the judge said. "All we knew for certain that he had on us was an audio recording of a phone conversation between Natasha and me about killing Sid Baxter." He added, "A recording that he never, in all these years, used against us."

Natasha told them, "It was worth more to Maguire to use for extortion purposes than turning into the police."

"But you did know that Maguire knew something about Themis," David said. "If, after all this time, he hadn't turned in that recording then you had to have felt fairly safe. So, the next question has to be, what motivated you to follow him out here to Deep Creek Lake?"

Natasha explained, "When Maguire gave Hamilton that list of case files he wanted, Ham stalled in getting them. Not long after that, he saw that Maguire had gotten the files himself and put them in a folder with the name Themis on it. That was the first time any of us suspected that he actually knew about Themis."

"Until Hamilton saw that folder," the judge said, "for all we knew, Maguire could have been looking into another common element between those particular cases."

"Maguire never said anything to any of us about Themis," Natasha stated again with a firm tone. "But when Hamilton saw that Maguire was collecting information on our cases and putting them into a folder labeled Themis, then we started getting nervous. Hamilton was trying to find out exactly what he knew when Maguire was killed."

"Hamilton's name isn't mentioned in any of those emails that we found on Maguire's flash drive," Archie pointed out to everyone. "Since Maguire probably had no idea that he was involved with Themis, Hamilton must have been able to nose around to see what he had without him being any the wiser."

"You'd think," Natasha said. "But Maguire wasn't very forthcoming with Hamilton. We never fully knew what he had put together."

"We knew that if anyone was able to figure it out, it had to be you, Mac," the judge said. "Since you'd worked on most of those cases and were familiar with the outcomes, we were afraid that you'd be able to put it together. When you started asking about Themis, then we knew that it was only a matter of time before the jig would be up. But Maguire said nothing to us. We certainly didn't intend to kill him until we knew that he was a threat. We're not a bunch of animals."

"How long has all this been going on?" Ben asked.

Judge Sutherland sighed deeply before answering. "About a dozen years. It started with the Doug Propst case. The victim was Judge Daniels's goddaughter. It was a nightmare that we couldn't put that bastard away."

Natasha nodded her head quickly while refilling her glass. "He killed her and there was nothing anyone could do about it."

Mac reminded her, "You were his defense attorney."

"How do you think I know he killed her?" She gazed up at him. "Do you remember during the Keating trial when you asked me how I could look at myself in the mirror in the morning doing what I do to let monsters that I know are monsters back out on the street?"

"Yes, I do." The less-than-proud moment flashed through Mac's mind.

She went on to answer his question almost a decade later. "It became easier when we started the Themis Society. Do you think I liked taking money covered in blood? Granted, it was a lot of money, but all the same—Do you know how I live?"

Mac didn't answer.

"I drink a pitcher of martinis every day. I live on sleeping pills, valium, and anti-depressants." She chuckled. "Believe it or not, it was worse before the Themis Society."

David asked, "If defending animals was making you miserable, why didn't you quit?"

The question from someone she regarded as a lowly police officer caused her to look David up and down with disdain before answering, "Because I liked the money. I'm sorry, but I'm not a woman of principle. I wish I was."

"If you didn't have any principles you wouldn't be so bothered by what you do," Mac told her.

She went back to her drink.

Garrison resumed answering the question about how the Themis Society came together. "It was on the second anniversary after the end of Propst's second trial that ended in a hung jury when we all ended up together at the club. Hamilton and I had gone out for drinks after losing an appeal hearing. The idiot judge overturned our conviction of a rapist and let him go. Natasha was at the bar. Judge Daniels came in. One thing led to another and we all ended up together rehashing the Douglas Propst case. By the time the club closed, we had held an impromptu trial. We had everyone we needed." He gestured at Natasha who raised her glass to those in the room. "The defense attorney. The prosecutor." The judge patted his chest. "And Judge Daniels."

Natasha said, "We went over all of the evidence that the jury never saw."

Garrison said, "And we found him guilty."

Mac said, "And shortly after that someone shot him to death."

"Yes," Garrison sighed, "we did sentence him to death. But we had no intention of carrying out the sentence. It was only by coincidence that a couple days later Propst's second wife called Judge Daniels. Not only did Propst beat her to a pulp, but he threatened if she ever tried to leave him, that he'd do the same to her that he had done to his first wife, only better. He said no one would ever be able to find her body in the mountains."

"That's a confession," Mac said. "Why didn't you take that to a grand jury?"

"For a third trial?" The judge shook his head. "She was scared to death that she wouldn't live long enough to testify."

Natasha agreed. "Douglas Propst was an animal."

"We discussed our options and decided that for the betterment of society, and to save the life of this poor woman, we'd have our sentence carried out."

"But *we* didn't shoot him," Natasha said.

Mac said, "You got a renegade cop to do it for you."

Garrison told them, "With his connections, Hamilton was able to find cops on the brink who were more than happy to carry out our sentences."

Shushing him, Natasha said, "Hamilton did all that on his own. We didn't have any idea about what he was going to do until later, after Propst was dead."

Garrison added, "But we couldn't deny it. After we found out that Propst had been killed less than a week after we found him guilty, we all felt..." He sighed. "Even after I found out that it happened because of our verdict."

Natasha insisted, "It was purely coincidence. Everything Hamilton did was on his own without any direction from us."

"But this Themis Society," Ben pointed out.

"Judge Daniels came up with the name of Themis," Judge Sutherland said. "He came up with our code of conduct and bylaws. He was our founder."

Mac asked Sutherland, "After Judge Daniels died, did you take over as the Themis Society's leader?"

Garrison nodded his head. "Hamilton took over as the prosecutor."

"Who killed Dylan Booth?" Mac asked. "Hamilton?"

Natasha and Garrison exchanged glances before the judge answered, "Hamilton. Maguire told him that Booth had been trying to sell him what he'd uncovered about Themis's hearings. Booth kept dangling that he had something big, but wouldn't give Maguire enough details for him to figure it out on his own. According to Ham, Booth never even told Maguire the name of Themis. He refused to turn over anything that he had until he got a plum position at the U.S. Attorney's Office and a guarantee that he'd be on the fast track. Maguire wasn't about to do that until he knew what he would be getting. Unfortunately for Booth, Maguire told Ham, who quickly figured out that he was on to us. Booth was smuggling our case files out of Daniels's office when Ham intercepted him in the parking lot."

Ben had to ask, "Why did you even keep records? You must have known that they risked ending up being evidence against you."

Garrison said, "We aren't a bunch of wild uncivilized vigilantes. We had a process. We used common sense, something our current justice system has lost."

CHAPTER FIFTEEN

"They had to be stopped." Archie slipped onto the sofa next to him. Brushing her fingers across his cheek, she forced Mac out of his stare into the flames in the fireplace to look at her.

They were having a quiet moment in front of the fire in the living room at the Spencer Manor. The clean-up crew had finished their job of removing all signs of the violent death that had happened eight feet away in the same room. Gnarly was lying in wait at the deck doors for Otis or any other squirrel or critter that dared to enter his territory.

With Christine's funeral days away, Mac didn't feel like going out. The weather seemed to sense his dark mood. It had been storming since sunrise. Between the torrential rain and high winds, any leaves not strong enough to hold on were ripped from their branches.

He'd settled for a quiet dinner at home with her. She'd prepared veal marsala and linguini served with a rich bottle of pinot noir. Mac had learned not to ask how expensive the wine she served with her gourmet dinners was. The answer was guaranteed to ruin his appetite, even though he was able to afford it.

The day after the arrest of the surviving members of the Themis Society, the news was buzzing about the vigilante court, even though details were minimal.

In her defense, Natasha Holmstead was claiming to have believed the Themis Society was a social club that held mock trials. She claimed she had no idea about Hamilton Sanders hiring psycho ex-cops to execute their convicted defendants.

Meanwhile, Judge Garrison Sutherland intended to put the justice system on trial. The Themis Society came about as a result of the deficiencies in the justice system.

"It sounds like their rationale for starting their vigilante court was noble, but they had no right to take it upon themselves to decide who's guilty and innocent." Archie continued her assessment while spooning away in delicate bites at a bowl of chocolate mousse. "Look at where it led. Their psycho ex-cop killed both Emma Wilkes and Bonnie Propst. Neither of them had done anything wrong. Then, their vigilante cop tried to kill us, and all we were trying to do was find out who killed Christine and Maguire and clear the Inn's reputation. It got completely out of control, which is where vigilante justice goes."

Disgusted with the rain that had driven away the enemy, Gnarly came up from the dining room to join them. He jumped up onto his love seat and lay down with a groan of disgust.

"You're right." Mac accepted her offer of a spoonful of the mousse. "They talked a good talk, but when you take all that away and look at the facts, it came about out of vengeance. Judge Daniels wanted revenge on the man who got away with killing his goddaughter. Plain and simple."

"He didn't seek that revenge until he got a call from Propst's second wife after he threatened to kill her," she said. "And their motive for killing Stephen Maguire wasn't noble. I don't think so. They wanted to get rid of a blackmailing lawyer."

"I don't think Maguire's murder had anything to do with that."

"Because?"

"Did you see Natasha Holmstead's face when I mentioned Maguire breaking into her emails?" he recalled. "I caught her completely off guard. They said all that they thought Maguire had was a list of names and the name Themis. They were still trying to find out what else he had when he was killed."

Waving her spoon in the air, she laughed. "Natasha Holmstead got paid a lot of money for being a good liar."

Mac took the bowl of mousse from her. "I've seen her lie and, yes, Natasha is a very good liar. I've also seen her blindsided. When I mentioned those emails, she was blindsided, and so was Judge Sutherland. They didn't have a clue about Maguire breaking into her emails." He took the spoon from her hand. "That got me to thinking. Knowing his wife, wouldn't Maguire want to have everything all together before confronting her and Judge Sutherland? If he let them know about what he had in those emails before investigating Themis, he'd be showing his hand." He finished the chocolate mousse in three spoonfuls.

"Whether Maguire had shown them his hand or not," Archie argued, "Natasha confessed her intention to kill him to get him off their backs and confirmed in her email to Sutherland that she'd tried to poison him."

"Sutherland's claiming that if Maguire had stolen the emails that came after those we'd found, he would have read where Sutherland had talked Natasha out of finishing the job." Mac shrugged. "Frankly, I believe him. They put up with Maguire without killing him for years. I believe that Sutherland and Holmstead had enough morals about them so that they wouldn't cross the line to commit murder for selfish reasons, which includes the murder of Hamilton Sanders."

"They're using him as their fall guy." Taking the empty bowl, she went down into the dining room to return it to the kitchen.

"Because his murder has provided a good opportunity," Mac called out to her as she left the room. "I don't think they created it. I think it's second nature for Natasha to use Hamilton's murder to pin her guilt on. I don't think she killed him."

When she returned to the room, he lowered his voice. "I completely understand the emotions behind it. They weren't right in what they did, but I can understand completely."

She slipped onto the sofa and curled up against him. "If Judge Sutherland and Natasha Holmstead didn't kill Christine and Stephen Maguire, then who did?"

"I'm afraid of that answer," Mac muttered.

The doorbell chimed throughout the house.

Delighted at the prospect of some action, Gnarly jumped over the back of the love seat to race Mac to the door. With his valise tucked under his arm, David greeted him with a serious expression on his face.

Mac asked, "What's wrong?"

"Remember that crazy woman that took a screwdriver after Maguire?" David wiped his soaked shoes on the doormat before stepping in to get warm by the fire.

Archie answered, "Wasn't that Natasha?"

David said, "She says it wasn't her."

"Of course," she replied with a raised eyebrow. "And since she says it wasn't her, then we know she didn't do it."

"There's a security camera at the service station across the street from Sully's." David dug into the valise tucked under his arm to pull out two case files. "I checked their cameras for about the time of Hamilton Sanders's murder, and we got a vehicle leaving Sully's parking lot." He pulled out his cell phone to show Mac a picture of a black Cadillac SUV. "Recognize this car?"

Mac recognized the parking lot as well as the black SUV. It was Sabrina's Cadillac leaving the parking lot outside Stephen Maguire's lakeside business.

"I also checked the station's tapes for the night of Stephen Maguire's murder. It's the first service station you hit on the way out of Spencer to the city." David worked the cell phone to bring up another picture. "The other day when I was here, Christine's sisters were squabbling about a VW Bug that their father used to have."

Mac recalled, "Sabrina was upset because Roxanne had sold it."

David held up the cell phone for him to see a picture of an old white VW Beetle at the gas pump in the service station. The date stamp on the picture was close to one o'clock the night of Stephen Maguire's and Christine's murders.

"Turns out Christine wasn't alone in Spencer," David said.

Mac took the cell phone from him and studied the picture. "I knew Christine was incapable of planning to kill Stephen Maguire on her own." He sat down on the sofa next to Archie, who looked over his shoulder at the image. "I also couldn't believe that she was able to drive all the way here from Georgetown on her own. The kids told me that she'd stopped driving months ago because she was afraid of getting pulled over drunk."

"The problem is a picture of a Bug at a service station doesn't prove murder." After taking the case files from the valise, David urged Gnarly over to allow him room to sit next to him on the love seat. "We're clearly missing something. Show me what it is."

"Let's start back at the beginning." Mac opened the case files and thumbed through the reports and pages. "Using what we know, let's recreate the murders."

David took a yellow notepad out of his valise along with a pen. "Where do you want to start?" Before Mac could respond, he answered his own question. "On Thursday, we have Christine's car coming into Spencer. According to Roxanne, she was staying alone at the lake house. We know that wasn't the case."

"But we don't know for certain which sister it was," Mac said.

Archie asked, "How did whoever it was that filled up the Bug pay for their gas?"

"I have the service station manager checking on that," David said.

"Filling up a gas tank on Route 219 in McHenry doesn't prove murder at the Spencer Inn," Mac said. "Roxanne and Sabrina alibi each other. Roxanne says she was sick with the flu and Sabrina brought her dinner. We have to put whoever it was that killed Maguire and Christine in that penthouse at the time of the murders. Now, the security camera at the traffic light in McHenry first records Christine's car coming into town on Thursday, the same day that Stephen Maguire checked into the Spencer Inn. Late that afternoon, employees at the Inn noticed Nita lurking around."

"Nita, who knew hardly any English, told no one anything about herself," David said. "Most people's natural reaction is to avoid someone who doesn't know their language because talking to them is so difficult. No one asked and she didn't tell."

Mac recounted, "Then Friday noon, Cameron Jones sees a crazy woman who has the same long black hair as Nita attacking Stephen Maguire with a screwdriver."

David recalled, "This crazy woman was telling Maguire that she wanted him to tell the truth."

"Which truth?" Archie asked. "The truth about his real family? Truth about everyone he's screwed over throughout the years? There're so many truths to choose from."

"About four-thirty on Saturday afternoon, Christine shows up here," Mac said. "I take her to check into the Spencer Inn shortly before five-thirty."

David said, "That's where Christine and Maguire collide. He's with Cameron Jones."

"I did just remember something," Mac chuckled. "Even if this crazy woman was wearing a wig, Jones most likely saw her face. She showed no recognition when she saw Christine. She even asked who she was." He shook a finger at David. "That proves she hadn't seen Christine before."

"Not conclusive since the crazy woman was wearing a disguise." David checked Christine's cell phone report. "At five-forty, Christine used her cell phone to call Roxanne. They spoke for seventeen minutes. According to Roxanne,

Christine told her about you shooting her down and booking her in your private suite."

David referred to his notes. "At six-thirty-seven, Christine ordered two filet mignon dinners and a bottle of red wine from room service. We assume the second dinner was intended for Stephen Maguire. But he met Bonnie Propst for dinner in the restaurant at seven o'clock, about the same time room service delivered the two filet mignons."

"Give me Christine's autopsy report." After checking Christine's stomach contents, Mac asked, "Who ate the second filet mignon? Christine only had what amounted to one in her stomach. It certainly wasn't Stephen Maguire. He was eating down in the restaurant."

David said, "And Christine didn't start calling him until after eight o'clock. If dinner arrived at seven, why did she wait so long to call him?"

"She wasn't calling him for dinner," Archie said. "Maybe it was Nita, since she came up in the service elevator with the food."

"That's possible," David said. "Which proves again that Christine wasn't Nita because, according to the hotel security, the penthouse phone and Christine's key card never got used. That tells us that she never left the suite. However, Nita is seen arriving with the server when room service brings up her dinner at seven o'clock."

"Wait a minute!" Mac called out. "What did you just say?"

Confused by his reaction, David paused before replying, "I said that the penthouse phone and Christine's key card were never used from the time she checked in until you found the bodies."

"I thought that was what you said." Mac dug out his ex-wife's cell phone log. "From the time Christine checked in, she used her cell phone right away to call Roxanne. And then the next time Christine's cell phone is used is after eight o'clock to call Stephen Maguire. Yet, at six-thirty-seven, she ordered two dinners and a bottle of wine from room service."

He cocked his head from David to Archie. "How did Christine order room service if she didn't use the phone in the suite or her cell phone?"

When they had no response, Mac answered, "Christine didn't order room service. It was whoever ate that second filet. We need to see the cell phone records of our suspects."

* * * *

Big Daddy's log home rested halfway up the mountain. With cottages on both sides so close that the deck provided little privacy and the lake's public beach a long hike down the hill and across a busy road, Mac was unimpressed with the type of vacation home that Christine had nagged him about wanting for their family.

In comparing Big Daddy's lake house to Spencer Manor, Mac made a mental note to himself about how spoiled he was getting. Twelve short months before, the rustic lake house would have been far beyond his reach.

Don't be getting snooty, Mac, he chastised himself.

"Are you sure you want to do this?" David asked him before they got out of his cruiser. It was an older cruiser the department used for times when the regular vehicles were in repair, or totaled like his had been. It didn't even have a built-in laptop in the console.

For an instant, Mac considered taking him up on the offer to turn around and go home. Leave the dirty work to the professional. Then, he thought of his children and the questions they would ask. These were questions Mac needed to get answers to first hand.

"No, I need to do this." He threw open the door and stepped out into the driveway.

Sabrina answered the door. Her welcoming grin dropped when she saw David in his chief's uniform standing behind Mac. It then transformed into annoyed when she saw that David was carrying his valise.

"You do know that we're on our way back to the city for Christine's funeral," she told David while leading them into the living room where Roxanne was sweeping the floor with a broom. They were closing up the cottage for their return to the city. Their luggage was stacked next to the door. "Are you sure that you can't have us sign any papers you need later?"

"No, ma'am," David said. "This needs to be taken care of now."

Sabrina noticed that Mac was dressed in slacks and a sports jacket, well above his usual casual manner. "Christine would be pleased with how nicely you clean up now that she's dead."

Ignoring the backhanded compliment, Mac turned his attention to Roxanne. "My lawyer went through Christine's financial records, and he found where Stephen Maguire had done exactly as you said. Your mortgage company had made a transfer of one hundred and seventy-five thousand dollars into Christine's account, which she had in both Maguire's and her name. Then, fifteen minutes later, the money was transferred from that account into another account, which only had his name on it."

"See," Sabrina said, "Stephen Maguire was a scumbag."

Roxanne asked Mac, "Does this mean you're going to sign over the lake house?"

Wordlessly, Mac nodded his head.

Roxanne surprised him by hugging him. "You always do the right thing, Mac," she whispered into his ear. She squeezed his hands when she pulled away.

Sabrina was giddy with justification. "Maguire really did deserve to get killed. Taking advantage of Christine the way he did—a helpless woman."

"When you think about it, Christine set herself up to be taken advantage of," Mac said. "When we got married, she wanted nothing to do with taking care of business. The bank accounts. Paying bills and taxes. Certainly not living within a budget. So we had joint accounts and I did everything. I'd slip contracts under her nose with an X on the spot and she'd sign—no questions asked."

Sabrina said, "Christine simply didn't have a head for business."

"And she paid the price," he said. "Twice."

"Twice?"

"As soon as I was out of her life, she handed everything over to Stephen Maguire, who robbed her blind," Mac explained. "According to my lawyer, he did it legally because of her stupidity. He got his name on all of her accounts, except her IRA. That made her money his money. He used her money for their free spending and to support their rich lifestyle. Some he outright stole and put in his own accounts, like he did with the lake house transfer. After he'd sucked her dry, he left her."

"I had tried more than once to teach Christine how to manage money and protect herself," Roxanne said, "but she didn't want any of it."

"And then she put you in charge," Mac said.

Roxanne replied, "Like I said, I tried to teach her to protect herself."

"And when she refused, I imagine, as circumstances would have it, you couldn't help yourself."

Sabrina warned him, "Mac, you're treading on thin ice here."

Stepping in between Mac and Sabrina's glare, David fished a report from his valise. "When forensics examined Maguire's cell phone, they found that it contained a chip that would transmit everything—calls, texts, images—everything that happened on that cell phone was sent to a clone, which we found in Christine's suitcase at the penthouse. When Maguire got or made a call, whoever had possession of that clone was able to listen in." He showed the picture of the device to Sabrina. "That chip also had GPS capability."

"That was how whoever was tracking Maguire knew he was here in Deep Creek Lake," Mac said.

Lauren Carr

David went on, "Maguire's laptop had a similar type of spyware that allowed someone with a laptop to monitor what he was doing, including check his email and examine what he had on his hard drive or any flash drive he had plugged into it. Someone was keeping very close tabs on him." He said, "Christine's financial records showed that these devices, plus a laptop which we assume was used to receive this data, were all purchased on a credit line in her name."

"You have to give Christine credit," Sabrina said. "I never thought she was that imaginative. Did you, Roxanne?"

"No." When her voice squeaked, she swallowed.

"Christine wasn't that imaginative, nor was she that computer savvy," Mac said. "But you are, Roxanne." His eyes bore into hers as he stepped toward her. "Christine wasn't the only one that Stephen Maguire screwed over. He had been screwing you all summer in your competition for Deputy U.S. Attorney. Only he crossed the line by framing you for bribing a witness. Not only were you in danger of not getting the promotion, but you could be disbarred."

"I deserve that promotion," Roxanne said.

"Stop it, Mac." Sabrina reached around him to take her sister's hand and pull her close. As if to physically shelter her, she wrapped her arms around her. "Stephen Maguire wasn't half the attorney Roxanne is. The only—and I mean only—reason he was even in the running for deputy was because that ass Hunter thought he could help him to become attorney general. It isn't fair."

"Politics is never fair," Mac agreed.

Sabrina turned to David. "Those things that you found in Stephen's stuff proves nothing. They were all bought on Christine's accounts and in her name."

"But they were delivered to the U.S. Attorney's Office," Mac countered. "They were ordered while Maguire was out on sick leave after being poisoned, after he had a restraining order issued against Christine."

David said, "She would never have had them sent there because there was no way she could take delivery of them."

224

"Unless she asked Roxanne to pick them up for her," Sabrina argued.

"But she still would have needed access to his laptop and cell phone," David countered. "Roxanne had ordered them and had them delivered to the attorney's office where she had the means to set up the electronic surveillance on Maguire's cell phone and his laptop, which, since he wasn't planning to be poisoned, had been left in his office while he was at the hospital. Christine didn't have that access, especially with the restraining order."

Mac set up the sequence of events. "After Natasha Holmstead had tried unsuccessfully to kill Maguire, you took advantage of him being out of his office to break in to search for ammunition to use against him. As luck would have it, that was when Cameron Jones, posing as his long-lost daughter, called his office. Unaware of his lies about his lineage, she dropped a lovely bombshell when she mentioned that he had met her mother while attending Ohio State University, not the Ivy League Oxford that he had boasted about in his resume. That was when you determined to find out what else you could uncover. If he was to discover your spy devices, you didn't want them traced back to you, so you purchased them in Christine's name."

David said, "Since Christine already had a record of being unbalanced, they would be chalked up as another incident by a jealous ex-lover."

"That was the crux of everything in your frame," Mac said. "Christine was emotionally unbalanced. She was an alcoholic. She made bad choices in her actions and choosing who to trust. When you set out on this path, you laid the groundwork for Christine's psychological defense by filing a petition to have her declared emotionally incompetent. When Maguire came out to Deep Creek Lake, then your plan went into action."

"What plan?" In an effort to convince him, Sabrina turned to David. "Christine took off out of the blue and came out here on her own. Roxanne was home sick with the flu.

225

Sure, she wasn't in the office, but she was working at home. I brought her dinner on Saturday night. I'll testify to that in court."

"Roxanne brought Christine out here in her car," Mac said. "She wasn't home sick. I assume that she put valium in Christine's drinks to knock her out so that she could tail Maguire in her Nita disguise."

Sabrina said, "Christine was the one popping valium. No one had to slip it to her."

"Roxanne knows and regularly uses Spanish in working with defendants and their families in court." Mac turned back to Roxanne. "While you were here, you set up your alibi by working remotely. While monitoring Maguire's laptop, you used the laptop that you had purchased in Christine's name to connect to your laptop at home to make it look like you were working from your house in Washington."

David told her, "Our forensics unit examined your laptop. Of course, we have a warrant. They found where it had been remotely connected to a computer here in Deep Creek Lake during the days that you were supposedly home sick."

Sabrina challenged him, "But you don't have Christine's laptop."

"We'll find it," David said with certainty.

Mac told them, "I believe that on Friday, Roxanne, you believed you'd collected enough evidence against Maguire and went to Sully's where you knew he was meeting Cameron Jones based on a call that you had intercepted from his phone. After you thought she'd left, you confronted him with what you had and tried to force him to come clean with the truth about his real background and framing you for bribery. When he laughed in your face, you became enraged and went after him with a screwdriver, but he disarmed you." He concluded in a soft tone, "I think that was when you decided to kick it up a notch and kill him."

"You have no proof of any of this!" Sabrina charged at Mac. Stepping between them to block her attack, David backed her away.

"We do," Mac said.

David slipped another report from his valise to show the women. "Roxanne's cell phone records. At six-thirty-seven on Saturday night, the night of the murders, Roxanne called the Spencer Inn. At that same time, room service took an order from a woman identifying herself as Christine for two filet mignon dinners and a bottle of red wine. The cell phone tower that had been used for that call was here in Deep Creek Lake, which means your phone, Roxanne, wasn't in Washington at the time, but here."

Mac explained, "The manager who took that order re-members that the woman was drunk and identified herself as Christine. At that time on Saturday night, they would never notice if the call came from within the Inn or an outside line. If Christine had ordered it, she would have used her cell phone or the phone in the suite. Neither had been used to place that order."

David pointed at Roxanne. "You were probably already in the Inn, in your Nita disguise, when you placed that order. You waited at the service elevator to slip up to the penthouse floor since you didn't have a key card. Then, while the server delivered the food to Christine, you hid out in the room across the hall under the pretense of delivering extra towels. Once he was gone, you knocked on Christine's door and she let you in."

"Then, your plan for murder was in motion," Mac said. "You ate dinner with Christine. You drugged her and she passed out. Then you put all the dishes in the dishwasher and put on Christine's clothes because you didn't want any of Stephen Maguire's blood and DNA to get onto your clothes. You even kept your Nita wig on in order to protect your hair."

David jumped in to add, "You had a duplicate wig that you put in Christine's suitcase to make us think it was her pretending to be Nita. You made sure it was one you'd never worn so as to not inadvertently give us your DNA."

"After eight o'clock, when you had everything ready," Mac said, "you started calling Maguire on Christine's phone.

Lauren Carr
Lauren Carr

What you didn't plan was for him to refuse to come see you. So you started calling every few minutes until he finally came just to get rid of you. As soon as he walked in, you let loose on him with all your rage."

David said, "You stabbed him twenty-seven times."

"Then you put the steak knife in the dishwasher with the rest of the dinner dishes and turned it on," Mac resumed. "Now it was onto the next step in the plan. You took off Christine's clothes, planted the clone phone on which you had planted her fingerprints, and went into the bathroom to shower off all of your evidence and any proof of you being in the room. You even bleached the bathroom. As you had it planned, Christine would come to, find Maguire dead, and everyone would think she did it during a blackout. You'd convince her to plead insanity and she'd go to a hospital and get help." He sighed and said sadly, "But things didn't work out that way. Since Maguire took so long to come to the penthouse, it allowed time for the valium to wear off. Christine came to and attacked you. I want to think that you were defending yourself when you either pushed her or she slipped on the wet floor, and hit her head on the corner of the sink. Now your sister was dead."

Clutching her stomach, Roxanne broke down into deep sobs.

Blinking back tears coming to his eyes, Mac swallowed. When he tried to continue, he found that he had no voice. He cleared his throat.

David picked up the sequence of events. "That was when your whole plan went to hell in a handcart. You panicked. Not thinking about the shape of the wound, you put Christine in the tub to make it look like she'd hit her head on the towel rack while in the shower."

Mac found his voice. "You did think to soak her hands and wipe her down with bleach to destroy the DNA evidence from your skin under her fingernails."

"I want you both to leave." Sabrina grabbed her purse resting on top of the luggage. "Now! I'm calling our lawyer,

228

and you can forget about showing your face at Christine's funeral, Mac." Snatching her cell phone from her purse, she waved it in his direction. "You're not family anymore!"

David told Roxanne, "We have a picture of a VW Beetle registered in your name at the service station in McHenry the night that Christine and Maguire were killed."

Sabrina said, "Your picture means nothing. We told you the other day that Big Daddy's Bug was stolen."

"You said Roxanne sold it."

Smirking, Sabrina said, "No, we never said that. Did we, Roxanne?" She glared at her sister.

Checking a text message on his cell phone, David said, "We have a warrant to search a garage in Washington. My officers are there now. They're about to open the door. I believe we'll find Big Daddy's Bug inside. When we do, it'll prove that, after killing Stephen Maguire and your sister, you drove the VW Beetle that you kept here at the lake back to Washington in order to be there when the call came that your sister had been found dead. I also believe that we'll find the black wig you wore when you killed Stephen Maguire and, if we're lucky, the laptop that you used to keep him under surveillance."

"Keep your mouth shut, Roxanne," Sabrina hissed. "They aren't going to find a thing. Believe me."

Mac laid his hand on Roxanne's shoulder. "The pro-secutor will go much easier on you if you cooperate. Once they open the garage and find the Bug and the evidence, they won't need your confession."

"He's a manipulative bastard," Sabrina told her while pressing her phone to her ear. "I'm calling our lawyer. Don't let Mac get to you. You know how he works."

"They're about to open the garage," David announced. "This is your last chance, Roxanne."

Roxanne's voice was weaker than Mac had ever heard it. "I thought it was the perfect plan."

"Shut up!" Sabrina raged. "They're not going to find anything!" Into her phone, she asked a receptionist for their lawyer.

"I didn't send her to your place, I swear," she told Mac. "I was in the shower, and when I came out she was gone. I about went nuts. Then, when she called that she was at the Inn in your suite, it all came together. It was like God had planned it that way." She grinned nervously. "Stephen would never be able to hurt anyone else ever again. Once his lies came out, I'd be exonerated and get the promotion that I deserved. By pleading guilty to an insanity defense, Christine would get the help she needed at a hospital. She could be out in a few years and maybe even back to her old self." She sobbed into her hands. "I never expected her to come to so soon. When she saw the blood and Stephen's body, she went crazy. I thought she was going to rip my skin off. I shoved her off me and she fell." She let out a shuddering breath. "One minute she was alive and the next—her life was over."

Clutching the cell phone, David asked, "What did you do with the wig and the laptop?"

Sabrina ordered her, "Say nothing else. I have our lawyer on the phone now."

David told Roxanne, "You have the right to say nothing else to us."

"I know my rights," she replied. "I want this to be over." She looked up at Mac. "To tell you the truth, I had no idea how I was going to make it through Christine's funeral, knowing that I was the one who put her in that casket." She told David, "The wig and laptop are in the trunk of the car in my garage. They're in a backpack along with my underwear. I was wearing it when Christine hit her head. She was bleeding all over the place and her blood got on my underwear. That'll put me in the suite when she died."

While David ordered his officers to open the garage, Sabrina screamed at her sister. "You fool! I told you not to tell them anything. They aren't going to find anything."

Roxanne sighed. "Oh, Sabrina, shut up."

Sabrina pointed her red-tipped finger into Mac's face. "This is your fault. You have no sense of family. All this has been to you is another murder case to solve."

"It's good." David snapped shut his phone. "They found it. Everything was there as you said, Roxanne. The backpack in the trunk with the wig and what looks like blood, laptop, and underwear with blood on it as well. Everything is being taken into evidence."

"No!" Sabrina screamed. "That's not possible!"

"Why?" Mac asked her.

"Because..." Her bosom heaved up and down while she squinted at him with eyes angrier than he had ever seen them.

"Because your husband was supposed to get rid of the Bug," Mac told her. "He did."

David announced, "My officers were at a storage garage that we've discovered your husband had rented the day before yesterday."

"The day after Roxanne told you what had happened," Mac said. "You took it upon yourself to fix everything by ordering your husband to get rid of the Bug, and all the physical evidence in it."

"That makes you and your husband accessories after the fact," David told her. "We may also want to charge you with obstruction of justice and tampering with evidence."

Mac told her, "You didn't know about it the day you came out here with Roxanne, because you were upset about the Bug being gone. Roxanne told you that she'd sold it. But then, the next day, you told Archie to shoot Celia Tennyson because she'd killed your sister and stabbed Stephen Maguire with a steak knife."

David said, "We didn't release anything about the murder weapon being a steak knife. There was only one of two ways for you to know that. One, you were there."

"Two, the killer told you," Mac said. "That's what the two of you were fighting about in my kitchen. Roxanne wanted to tell me the truth. She wanted to confess, but you insisted that she keep her mouth shut."

He said to Roxanne, "You almost told me in the study, but changed your mind."

She nodded her head so hard that the tears on her face splashed onto his hand.

"After Roxanne told you about what had happened, Sabrina," he continued, "You were furious, especially when she told you about how Stephen Maguire got where he was by lying about his family connections."

"Yes, you were," Roxanne replied.

Sabrina backed up a step.

"Was it Roxanne who told you that she believed Sanders had accepted a bribe when he was working for Office of Personnel Management to let Maguire get in with his falsified background or did you put it together yourself?" Mac asked.

David said, "Your phone records show that you called Hamilton Sanders the evening he was killed. You talked a good seven minutes."

"Knowing you," Mac said, "you were raking him over the coals for everything that had happened to your family as a result of his accepting that bribe years ago."

"And that was all," Sabrina said. "I gave him hell, felt better for it, and we hung up."

David countered, "But we have a picture of your car in Sully's parking lot an hour later."

"Of course it was," Sabrina replied. "I was going into town and realized I'd forgotten my shopping list. I turned around in that parking lot and came back here."

Roxanne whimpered, "Oh, Sabrina."

"Shut up, you ninny. I did nothing wrong."

"You killed Hamilton Sanders," Mac told Sabrina.

"I did not!" she hissed at him. "You can't prove anything. You can't even prove I was ever there."

"We can," Mac said.

With a hand gesture not unlike that of a magician, she challenged him. "Prove it."

"Are you sure you've never been to Sully's?"

"Not even when it was open," she said. "They were always too pedestrian for my tastes with their pool tables and beer."

"Are you sure about that?" David asked.

"Positive."

Mac replied, "Then what are your fingerprints doing in the ladies' bathroom?"

Her mouth fell open.

"You wiped your fingerprints off the door handles and the screwdriver and tossed it into the lake," Mac explained. "But you must have forgotten that you'd used the ladies' room, probably while you were waiting for Hamilton to show up. That tells me that you weren't planning to kill him, but when he didn't give you a good enough explanation, or maybe show the proper remorse for what his actions years ago had done, you lost that famous temper of yours and killed him. After getting stabbed three times, he stumbled outside and off the dock. You tossed in the screwdriver, and wiped your fingerprints off the door and anything else you'd touched, except you forgot that before he got there, you'd used the restroom."

Roxanne sobbed. "Sabrina, what did you do?"

The two sisters hugged. When they pulled away, Sabrina clasped Roxanne's face in her hands. "Don't worry, sister. Once our lawyer puts Stephen Maguire on trial, no jury will ever convict us."

While David waited nearby with his handcuffs ready, Sabrina stood up tall to be led out to the cruiser with dignity.

Mac stepped over to them. "Sabrina, I'm very sorry."

She rejected the apology with a slap across his face.

EPILOGUE

One Week Later

Has there ever been a good funeral? Has anyone ever left a funeral proclaiming, "Hey, that was some funeral, wasn't it? Let's do it again next week."

Mac pondered this thought while lying on the sofa with his arm over his eyes trying to block out the last few days.

He could feel Gnarly staring at him from his love seat as if to ask, "Now that I've met *all* of Christine's family, what else are you going to subject me to?"

Under the circumstances, Mac wouldn't have gone to his ex-wife's funeral. He would have chosen to go to the cemetery alone to say his good-bye. It was for his son and daughter that he attended the viewing and funeral.

The Burtons had never been ones to keep their feelings under wraps. With no regard for appearances or respect in front of his children, they were openly hostile toward him. Attending the funeral to give support to Mac and his children, Archie was treated like a home wrecker, as if she'd broken up Christine's marriage to him.

When Jessica came to her father's defense at the reception following the funeral, Sabrina's daughter slapped her.

Jessica retaliated by dumping a filled punch bowl over her cousin's head.

Anxious to get on with their lives, Jessica returned to Williamsburg to catch up on her courses at William and Mary; Tristan returned to the Smithsonian to discover a new dinosaur; and Mac, Archie, and Gnarly raced back to Spencer Manor.

Claiming that she had a headache, Archie rushed off to her cottage before Mac could close the garage door. He didn't know if her headache was real or symbolic. Knowing his was real, he took two aspirin and reclined in front of the fireplace with a bottle of cognac. He was still trying to erase the memory of the past two weeks when David arrived to check on the manor as was his custom when they were gone.

When Gnarly refused to budge to allow room for him to sit on the love seat, David took the leather wing-backed chair next to the fireplace after pouring a drink.

"When did you get in?"

"Late this afternoon." Mac sat up and turned his attention to refilling his snifter from the bottle he had resting on the coffee table.

"I picked up my new cruiser today." David smiled like a child anxious to show off his new toy. "It has all the bells and whistles."

"A boy and his toys," Mac said. "You have that same expression on your face that Archie gets when she discovers a new gadget."

"And you get when you read about a new murder case in the area," David shot back. "While you've been gone, Ben and I have been working on our case against the Burton women. Roxanne is going to testify against Sabrina."

Mac uttered an involuntary groan. "Now I've turned sister against sister." He sipped his drink. The alcohol was failing to numb his nerves.

"You did what you had to do," David told him. "Ben and I have a question that maybe you can answer."

Mac said, "Shoot."

"When Roxanne took that call from Cameron, and she got her first lead that Maguire had lied about his past, why didn't she simply order a background check, which she was in the position to do, and then take her findings to the U.S. Attorney to blow the whistle on him? It would have achieved the same objective. Maguire would have been discredited and she would have been back in the running for deputy." David asked, "Why the spyware and surveillance? Why did she have to come out to Deep Creek Lake to confront him face to face?"

Mac replied, "Haven't you ever had a suspect that got under your skin so much that you had to see his face when you confronted him with the evidence that you'd collected against him?"

As much as he hated to admit it, David confessed that he had.

"If Roxanne had simply ordered a background check and taken the results to Hunter, then Christine would still be alive and none of this would have happened," Mac said. "But she had to see his face, and then...I can imagine that famous Burton temper flaring when he laughed at her. When you think about it, they'd probably both be alive if Maguire hadn't laughed at her."

"That's so often the case," David said. "If only the victim hadn't laughed. If only the victim hadn't been there at this time, or did that back then. That's what makes murder such a tragedy." His curiosity got the best of him. "I guess the funeral didn't go well."

"It was an eye-opening experience for me." Mac swallowed. "The pound of a judge's gavel isn't strong enough to break the bond of marriage. Maybe in some cases it is, but I wonder, in those cases when it does break it, I wonder if the bond was really that strong to begin with."

"I think you're right," David said. "It's all a matter of the level of commitment. Dad and Robin were never married. Their parents split them up before you were born. But even after years of being separated, when Robin came back, even though they never consummated their love affair because Dad was married to Mom, there was a bond there that no piece of paper or gavel could strengthen or break."

Mac took a sip of his drink. "Through this whole case, I kept correcting people. Christine was my *ex*-wife. She wasn't my wife. We were divorced. But then, when I saw her in that casket, all I could remember was the girl I married and all those years—good years." He sighed. "I never really got a chance to mourn our marriage. Things changed so suddenly. The day our divorce was final, I received all of this."

He gestured at the richness surrounding him. "One day I was a bitter divorced man. Literally, the next day, I was a millionaire playboy. The funeral made me realize the good things, the goodness in the life I had before that's now gone. My kids are grown and have their own lives. I'm not on the police force anymore. Everything has changed and I'll never get it back, no matter how much money I have."

Together, they drank in silence while staring into the flames.

David said. "You're not the same man you were when you and Christine were married. You're not even the same man you were when you drove onto the Point in that Viper six months ago. I haven't seen you wear a faded t-shirt in weeks. Your shoes don't have holes in them anymore."

"Only because Gnarly chewed the soles off them," Mac said. "I liked those shoes. They were broken in."

David held up the bottle from the coffee table. "You're drinking sixty-year-old cognac."

Mac admitted, "As much as I don't want to change, I can see that I have." He grinned at him. "I like that you don't give me speeding tickets."

"Don't press your luck." David drained his drink. "Now that I know you're all in safely, I should be getting home." He slapped Mac on the leg. "Do you know what you need?"

"What?"

In the reflection from the flames, Mac could see a wicked grin cross his face. "A nice back scratch." With a hearty laugh, David left.

Mac continued staring into the flames while he finished his drink.

Seeming to sense the lateness of the hour, Gnarly eased off the love seat with the gracefulness of a snake and stretched. He dug his snout down between the cushions. When it came back out, he had a teddy bear clutched between his teeth.

"Where did you get that?" Mac asked him as if he could answer.

The sound of his voice seeming to act like a gunshot starting a race, Gnarly galloped up the stairs to the bedroom. Before escaping, Mac saw a white price tag flapping from the bear's toe.

"Gnarly! I'm going to kill you, you thief!"

Mac's eyes rose up to the portrait over the fireplace. He didn't know if it was the headache or the cognac, but Mickey Forsythe seemed to be smirking at him.

What do you have to feel so down about? Yesterday is gone. Time to open the door to today and tomorrow. She's in the cottage at the end of the path.

Setting the bottle of cognac back on the bar, Mac looked out the window through the trees and saw the light on in the guest cottage. Sucking in his courage, he followed the path down through the rose garden until he came to her door.

Archie answered on the second knock. "Is Gnarly okay?" She was dressed for bed in her red nightgown and floor-length robe.

"He's fine. Why are you asking about Gnarly?"

"Because he's not with you," she replied. "And since you're standing here in one piece, I assume you're fine."

"I came to see how you were feeling." He asked, "How's your headache?"

"How's yours?"

"I asked you first."

"Well," she drawled, "I was going to have a snack before going to bed. Care to join me?"

"What kind of snack?"

She held out her hand to him. "Strawberries dipped in chocolate. I've been saving them for you."

"For me?"

"For us." She reached up to kiss his lips. "Care to come in?"

Before he could answer, an acorn flew out of the tree towering above the cottage to bounce off the top of Mac's head and strike Archie between the eyes.

Grabbing her face, she staggered backwards.

Squinting through the throbbing pain from the blow to his head, Mac called up into the tree, "Otis, I'm going to kill you!"

The End

About the Author

Lauren Carr fell in love with mysteries when her mother read Perry Mason to her at bedtime. She wrote her first book after giving up her writing career to be a stay-at-home mom. The first installment in the Joshua Thornton mysteries, *A Small Case of Murder*, was named a finalist for the Independent Publisher Book Award 2005. Her second full-length book, *A Reunion to Die For*, was released in June 2007.

Her new series, The Mac Faraday Mysteries, is set in Deep Creek Lake, Maryland, where she and her family often vacation. The first installment, *It's Murder, My Son*, was released in June 2010 to rave reviews.

Lauren is available for speaking appearances at schools, youth groups, and on author panels at conventions. She lives with her husband and son on a mountaintop in West Virginia.

Visit Lauren at her website http//laurencarr.webs.com for more information.